MW01250690

Home Free

Home Free

a novel by

Wayne Tefs

TURNSTONE PRESS

Copyright © 1997 Wayne Tefs

Turnstone Press
607–100 Arthur Street
Artspace Building
Winnipeg, Manitoba
Canada R3B 1H3

All rights reserved. No part of this book may be reproduced or transmitted in any form or by any means—graphic, electronic or mechanical—without prior written permission of the publisher. Any request to photocopy any part of this book shall be directed in writing to the Canadian Copyright Licensing Agency.

ACKNOWLEDGEMENTS

Thanks to David Arnason, Manuela Dias, and Marilyn Morton.

The information regarding grape and wine varieties is from Jancis Robinson's *Oxford Companion to Wine*.

Turnstone Press gratefully acknowledges the support of the Canada Council for the Arts and the Manitoba Arts Council for our publishing program.

Le Conseil des Arts du Canada DEPUIS 1957 | The Canada Council FOR THE ARTS SINCE 1957

Cover art: untitled watercolor, 1995, by Ewa Tarsia

This book was printed and bound in Canada by Friesens for Turnstone Press.

Canadian Cataloguing in Publication Data

Tefs, Wayne, 1947–

Home free

ISBN 0-88801-217-9

I. Title.

PS8589.E37H64 1997   C813'.54   C97-920151-9
PR9199.3.T4H64 1997

for the Willow Island Gang

I will arise and go, for always night and day
I hear lake water lapping with low sounds by the shore;
While I stand on the roadway, or on the pavements grey,
I hear it in the deep heart's core.

—W.B. Yeats, "The Lake Isle of Innisfree"

Part 1

Merlot Noir, the black grape variety associated with the great vines of St. Emilion and Pomerol, is Bordeaux's most planted black grape variety, and has been enjoying unaccustomed popularity elsewhere. Throughout south-west France and, increasingly, much of the rest of the world, Merlot plays the role of constant companion to the more austere, aristocratic, long-living Cabernet Sauvignon. Its early maturing, plump, lush fruitiness provides a complement to Cabernet Sauvignon's attributes. For the vine grower in anything cooler than a warm, hot climate Merlot is much easier to ripen than Cabernet Sauvignon, and has the further advantage of yielding a little higher to boot. The relatively early maturing, easy-to-appreciate Merlot is a wine with distinct advantages over Cabernet Sauvignon in times of inflation.

MICHAEL HAS JUST REACHED the top of the ladder and dipped the brush in the bucket of stain when the phone rings. This is what he hates. The cellular phone is supposed to be convenient for him, but what it really does is make him accessible to every jerk-off who can get his number. What is it this time—carpet cleaning, mutual funds, the *Free Press* offering a special deal on home delivery? He sighs. The fascia board will have to wait. He places the brush across the top of the can of stain and begins the descent. He eases down the rungs gingerly. This is another thing. At fifty-seven he has learned to move his body more slowly than his mind imagines it should be able to—but he has torn hip flexors and damaged cartilage in the knees to prove the mind wrong. At the last rung he pauses and reaches his foot down with care, pawing the grass with the tip of his sneaker before shifting his full weight off the ladder. The doughhead who designed this aluminum forty-footer had to have been the sub-normal brother-in-law of the manufacturer: the last rise is unaccountably two inches shorter than the others, and if Michael does not make a point of stepping off with that in mind he jars his entire skeleton. The last time he forgot, his pelvic bone and rib cage slammed together, sending a shiver of pain down his spine, a shiver not unlike the one he

5

experienced with the hernia a couple of years back. He isn't going through that again in this lifetime.

He crosses the grass at a quick shuffle and when he reaches the deck of the cottage snaps the bleating phone up with one hand and pulls out its antenna before punching the *send* button with the other. "Yes," he spits into the mouthpiece, much more petulant than he'd intended. There is silence on the other end of the line. "Hello," he says, "hello, hello." His voice is restrained but he's thinking *if I climbed down that damn ladder to get nothing more than the fucking buzz of a dead line, I'm going to be pissed right off.* What the hell is going on? This is three times in the past week he has picked up the phone to hear nothing more than the buzz of a dead line. He hates the thought that a former student with some imagined grievance is about to begin a campaign of harassment, as one did, he suspects, a decade ago, but what else could it be? He listens a moment longer, then punches *end*, shutting the phone off, before he replaces it on the edge of the deck.

Now he is upset. He can feel the bile churning in his guts and knows that in a few minutes he will get one of those burps that splashes stomach acids up the esophagus into the back of the throat. His doctor explained why this happens to men his age, something about a valve at the joint of the stomach and esophagus weakening over the years, *herniating,* nothing to worry about, but sleep on two pillows, torso slightly elevated. Michael swallows hard and tries not to think of how many signs he's had in the past few years that the old body is giving out. He glances at the sky: big prairie blue overhead. It's been an unbelievable summer, *magical,* Stephen called it the other day: the mid-afternoon temperatures hovering between twenty-five and thirty, the nights filled with soft caressing airs, little rain falling only toward the dawn, no mosquitoes. The lake, Michael sees, is nearly calm, a slate of glass reaching out from where he stands looking northward to where the horizon curves downwards, thirty miles or so away. He takes several deep breaths and returns to the foot of the ladder.

Before ascending he glances at the sky, a solid blue swatch above the roof of the cottage. He's always loved blue. He thinks of it as a peaceful color. In the trees to the side of the cottage warblers flit yellows and blacks through the green leaves and whistle. Otherwise it is quiet. Michael's hands tremble but he whispers to himself *think of Frost*, and he conjures up from memory some lines from the hoary New Englander: "My instep arch not only keeps the ache, it keeps the pressure of a ladder round." Good old Frost. The one poet whose verses Michael can remember. He repeats the lines to himself several times and then breathes until his heart rate is steady.

He climbs the rungs with practiced care, positions himself, picks up the brush, dips it into the orange-tinted stain and applies several brush strokes to the fascia board, enjoying the tug of the brush's bristles against the grain of the wood, but also feeling the sharpness of chemicals in his nostrils. This is what he'd been craving all week in the city: physical work, mindless labor. He lays on a few brush strokes, mindful of keeping the coat of stain thin, then pauses for a moment to admire his handiwork. He's good at this. He should have been a craftsman. But there's the burp. He coughs once and spits delicately between the rungs of the ladder onto the grass below, a small brown ring, not unlike a tobacco stain. Then the phone rings again. This is too much. He's considered canceling the service before and is determined by the time he reaches the bottom of the ladder that first thing Monday morning this infernal piece of technology goes. Gonzo Alonzo. He snatches the phone up, realizing that in his haste he's brought the dripping brush down with him and is holding it aloft in the air like a symphony conductor. "What?" he barks into the mouthpiece.

The voice on the other end of the line says, "Daddy?"

For a moment Michael sees Jane standing by the

roadside the way he'd finally located her one night twenty years ago, hair dripping rain, thin shoulders stooped inward, hands thrust into jacket pockets: she was hitchhiking that night, running away from home, one in a succession of such flights from his fumbling father's arms. But she's a mother of two now, with a home of her own and a herb garden in the backyard. "What is it?" he asks.

"Daddy, I wasn't sure it was you at first."

"Sorry," he says. "I was—I was up the ladder here at the cottage."

"You sounded angry."

"Out of breath."

"I hate it when you're angry with me."

Michael has placed the dripping brush on the edge of the deck and is watching globules of orange stain drop slowly from the bristles, forming a small pool, a gold coin on the green grass near his feet. "Well," he says, keeping his voice level, though his heart is racing, "I'm not—am I?"

"Good," she says.

He waits for a moment before realizing she expects him to begin the conversation. "How are the kids?" he asks, seeing in his mind's eye his two grandchildren, their nut-brown faces, their dancing eyes. "How are you and Brad?"

"The kids are okay," she says, though he can tell by the way she bites off the words that they're not, not really. "Ali's got some stomach thing which I'm sure will just go away, and Randy cut his hand last night on some paper, just a scratch, really."

"Good," Michael says. "Well then."

"Only it's not good," Jane says. She pauses dramatically, making sure, he thinks, that he is listening, and then says in a rush, "It's Brad, see, he hasn't been—he went out last night to the bar with some pals straight from work and—the thing of it is he usually comes in around one or so, so I was worried when I got up in the night to check on Ali's breathing and he wasn't there and then in the morning no sign of him either, which is really unusual, the morning and all, I mean, he's regular, he hates to miss work, I mean, so then I really started to worry, but then I thought—"

"Hold on. He'd done this before?"

"Not really. But I didn't want to panic or something, so I waited until past nine this morning and called in to the plant."

"And he wasn't there? Hadn't punched in?"

"They don't punch in, Daddy, it's the city."

"Right."

"I even talked to his best buddy, you know, the guy he plays ball with?"

"I don't," Michael says. "I can't say—"

"He was at the cottage that time, remember? Short and kind of bristly-faced but really nice? Red ball cap?"

"Oh yeah, the Jets fan."

"Spike, they call him. Anyways, he says Brad left the bar same time as him, got in the van and drove off as usual. Twelve thirty or so. Daddy, I'm worried."

"I can tell." Michael has placed one hand over his abdomen, the place he imagines his gall bladder to be, and is massaging the flesh gently in a circular motion: is that the beginning of an attack? Since she was a teenager Jane has always been in trouble and he has always paid for it in bodily pain. He has to steel himself against her voice: the kid could be in real shit this time, but then again it could be another tempest in a teapot. He used to be able to tell, but he can't any longer. Mary says that since his heart attack he's lost confidence, he's lost his judgment. He wonders if that's her polite way of telling him he's not the man he used to be. Does she suspect something? He thinks of her then, of Mary, leaning to kiss him this morning, her black skirt tight around her hips, her white blouse puckered over her breasts, sexy. But he is determined not to think of Mary today. He repeats, "I can tell that."

"Daddy," Jane asks, "can you, you know . . . ?"

He's lost for a second or two, dreaming other thoughts, but concentrates on the fear he hears in Jane's voice. "I can," he says, though he senses how reluctant he is in his voice and knows she can too. He takes one deep breath but this time he is not inhaling the wonders of Willow Island, a long afternoon staining fascia board in the summer sun. He is thinking *why me?* Finally he's got away from the college, from the stack of theses on his desk, he's finally in the sun with the birds. And now this. "I will," he states quickly, forcing his vocal cords to convey commitment.

"And Daddy . . ."

"But it could be an hour or so. Maybe longer," he adds. "There's all this stuff to clean up out here. I was staining and . . . oh hell, just hold on, honey, and I'll get there soon as I can."

Mary swipes at the sweat on her forehead with the white towel provided by the club but continues pumping her legs and watching the digital readout on the monitor in front of her. Calories Burned: 119; Heart Rate: 143. She has been on the bicycle for almost twenty minutes, the segmented red numbers dancing before her eyes inform her. Sweat on the palms. Lips cracking. She glances over to her left at Jilly. Green eyes, red hair, flushed cheeks. When Jilly smiles, twin dimples crease her peaches-and-cream complexion. Mary looks away, afraid she will be caught blushing.

Outside it is a bright August afternoon. Heat shimmers up from the asphalt of the parking lot. Reflected sunlight knifes off the windscreens of passing cars. Instead of sweating indoors she and Jilly should be running outdoors in the fresh air, she knows this; their friend Mark was extolling the virtues of hyper-oxidation the last time she spoke with him, but at forty-eight he still fancies himself an athlete. Men. Besides, Jilly has a weak ankle and is afraid of turning it on a patch of uneven ground. That's how she first injured her foot. "Stepped off a curb," she told Mary, "and *whamo*, down goes my ass like a sack of spuds."

Mary glances at Jilly out of the corner of her eye. Jilly's lips are set in a pout, and, unaware of being observed, she's narrowed her eyes in concentration as she strains at the pedals of the bicycle, willing away calories. Like Mary she is a few pounds overweight. Ten, maybe, to Mary's fifteen. Mary likes to think sometimes that the extra five pounds she's overweight can be attributed to the difference in their ages. Idiot. This is not the first time she's caught herself rationalizing the way Michael does. For a moment her mind skips to the half second they paused in the doorway this morning and pecked each other's lips, he on the way to the cottage, she to an early meeting with Freddo. Michael seemed sad, distracted, and she wanted to put her arms around him, feel his bulk. Couldn't, knowing she would be with Jilly in a few short hours. Does he know? Is she hurting him?

Mary swipes the towel at her brow once more, brushing away the beads of sweat from her eyebrows, and then she loops the damp towel over the hand rest between her clenched fists. After she's squeezed the glistening aluminum sensors again for a half minute she sees her heart rate has jumped to 154. She is past her aerobic zone and into the danger area. Slows the pace of her pedaling. Takes a couple of deep breaths and licks her dry lips. Tilts her head so Jilly is in her side vision again, one of the club's male instructors standing beside her machine now. Orange tank top, cup of water in one hand, toothy white smile. Making some kind of opening move, Mary guesses. If only he knew. The water he's sipping reminds Mary of her parched mouth and the cup of ice in the little wire basket attached to the handlebars, and she lifts it to her lips delicately, careful to maintain her balance and the tempo of her pedaling. Cold on her hot palate. She moves the chips of ice around with her tongue, recalling ice cream in a paper cup at the lake when she was a teenager and even before that, her mother in a red two-piece, her father in khaki shorts, *trunks*, he called them, and she and her—

"Hey," Jilly whispers into her ear, a hot wave Mary feels wash up her neck into her hair, "you off in dreamland again, babes?"

Mary gasps, "Thinking about being a kid." This time she is blushing but Jilly won't notice because both their faces are red with exertion. "Ice cream."

"Don't remind me," Jilly says. "Seventy-five calories per tablespoon."

Mary's pedaling has slowed to the point where the LED has blinked off. *Enough*, she thinks. *Twenty minutes.* "Seventy-five," she repeats. "Really?"

"You bet. Goodbye to that shit."

When Jilly says *shit*, Mary flinches and automatically glances around, afraid someone might have heard. This *can* be attributed to the difference in their ages: where Mary is reserved, and, she thinks, timid, Jilly is often loud and brassy, what Mary's mother would call *unladylike*. It goes with her red hair and the flashy bracelets Jilly wears on her arms, even when she's working out. It goes with her big laugh and the black cowboy boots. But Mary likes it, this loudness, this brashness; she wishes she had the chutzpah to try it on herself. Turquoise rings, mesh tights, pungent perfumes. She asks, tipping her head in the direction of the orange tank top, "So what did Mister Wonderbody want?"

Jilly laughs. "He's not so bad, really. They're having a half-marathon next month, four on a team kind of thing, and he wondered if I would join three guys looking for a girl to fill out their team."

"Fill out? He said that?" Mary sucks her teeth.

Jilly says, "His name is Tod, he tells me. They need a girl."

"A *girl*?"

"Don't start now. It's for a good cause. Heart association or whatever."

"I thought your ankle was hurting."

"I haven't agreed to do it."

"No. You just—"

"Jesus." Jilly stamps her foot.

"Sorry."

"Christ almighty!"

"Sorry. I didn't mean—"

"I know what you meant. What you're thinking."

Mary has finished the water, she realizes. She looks at the trash basket situated between her bicycle and the next, visualizing the arc the plastic cup will take when she throws it. "All right," she says, "just forget it."

Jilly says, "I won't." She stamps her foot again. "I will not forget it." Jilly looks directly into Mary's eyes and throws back her shoulders, bony limbs that give her the air of horsiness, Mary realizes. Then Jilly whispers between clenched teeth, "I am not one of your tight-assed Woodydell matrons, all smiles and forgiveness on the outside and stink-ass rage on the inside."

"Okay," Mary says.

"Don't you forget that."

"I couldn't," she says. "You wouldn't let me."

"You're right about that, babes."

Mary crumples the plastic cup in her hand and flings it at the trash basket. "Okay then," she hisses in a whisper, "fuck you. Just fuck you, Jilly Thomson."

Jilly snorts, but then she smiles at Mary, her pink tongue protruding between her big teeth. "That's more like it, babes," she says. She punches Mary in the shoulder and leans in close with hot, damp breath to whisper in her ear, "That's more like the Mary Mitchell we've grown to know and love."

Michael gears down but hits the accelerator as he wheels off the gravel road that runs out to Willow Point, spinning a cloud of dust and stones behind him. He points the truck across the highway, going south to the city. This is what he likes. The rubber tires hum on the asphalt, the engine growls under the hood. He drives a Mazda pickup these days, with a cap over the half-ton box. For a time he flirted with the idea of a utility vehicle, a 4X4 Cherokee, maybe, but the damn things are as expensive as Range Rovers and nearly as tony. Mary says he doesn't need anything more elaborate than a station wagon for his trips up to the cottage, the gravel strip is shorter than two kilometers in length and never difficult to negotiate, but he tells himself he needs a truck to haul building materials and whatnot. There is some validity to his contention: from time to time the lawn mower needs to be taken in for sharpening—and when he was redoing the bathroom he had to transport bundles of cedar laths from the lumberyard in the city. But the truth is Michael likes to drive a truck, to perch in the elevated cab, from where he can look down on the compacts and family cars with their cramped interiors and minimal ground clearance. In the city he can look over the rooftops of other vehicles and plot his lane moves, and on the highway he enjoys the panorama of the road ahead as it spreads out before him. In any case, station wagons and vans are for suburbanites.

He pushes the Tilley hat he wears at the cottage up on his brow and adjusts the sunglasses he uses for driving, nudging them up the bridge of his nose. Even though the Mazda is air-conditioned he rolls down the window to feel the hot summer air buffet his cheeks.

He tries not to think about Jane. There will be time enough for that. He flips on the radio but almost as soon as he's heard the violin strains on CBC stereo, he flips it off again. There was a time when he listened to the AM stations, following the news. But after his heart attack five years ago— no, seven, now he thinks about it—he no longer follows world events. It's the same old stories: political corruption, violence on the streets, right-wing politicians undercutting social programs. He doesn't want to read any more headlines about teen gangs, and the op-ed page just makes him sick to the stomach. Michael's slant on the world, a kind of small-*l* liberalism, leaning left, is out of favor these days. Besides, everywhere you look, things are whirling in a downward spiral: layoffs at the rail yards, farmers abandoning the land, teachers, nurses, and civil servants swallowing pay cuts and downsizing. Even the stock market is spinning into a vortex. Why listen to the radio when all it does is bring you down? He used to subscribe to the *Globe and Mail*, but in the past year he's let that lapse and has been buying the *Sun* every now and then to follow the sports scores, but since the Jets have left town he hasn't been doing that much either. A couple of years ago during the American elections he shocked his friend, Stephen, by not knowing who Ross Perot was, but he was half proud of the fact he was out of the information loop. He has been drifting inward, he realizes, and in the past year has started writing poetry, though he would never admit it to anyone: isn't that what all aging professors do— that and raise roses? Maybe Mary is right. He's not the man he used to be, though not in the sense she means.

He thinks for a moment of Mary's teasing blue eyes. In bed last night she had snuggled up tight behind him, *soup spoons*, she calls it, though there was no sex. She does that soup spoon thing sometimes, and last night she whispered something to him: *let's just move out to the cottage, the two of us.* Does she mean it? He's thought of that, too, especially after they've spent a couple of slow weeks at Willow Island in the summer: lazy mornings, warm afternoons, the lapping of the water at night. They could kick back quite easily, he thinks, get ready to grow old together. And it would be good for the body, too, maybe Mary would even feel that way about him again.

For some reason the opening lines of another poem pop into his head: "She is as in a field a silken tent." He smiles to himself, what he imagines to be a wicked smile, and on impulse picks up the cell phone he tossed onto the seat as he was leaving the cottage. As a matter of principle he makes a point of not talking on the phone while he's driving, but he makes an exception this time—for salacious Sandy.

Her line buzzes once, twice, and Michael is about to punch the *end* button before her message comes on, but she answers on the third ring.

"I'm in the middle of ironing," she blurts out, the words jumbled together in a blur, so Michael is not sure he's heard correctly. "So make it snappy."

He clears his throat, hoping to mollify her as well as set the conversation on a less trenchant path. "It's me," he says. "Michael."

"I was wondering when you'd get around to it. To me."

"It's been tricky," he says. "Running up to the cottage and back."

"Me too," she says. "I thought after the Coffee Cup we were on our way. We seemed to get on so good."

"Right." Michael liked the peach top she wore that afternoon, just snug enough. He also liked Sandy's matching coral lipstick. And the potent coffee. "Right," he repeats, "but then."

"So, anyways, you're saying later this afternoon?"

"Probably not. My daughter's just called and she's in some kind of tangle-up with her husband who's gone missing. I'm calling from the truck, actually, driving in to the city to see her." Michael's eyes have wandered as he's been driving, and he sees that he's massaging at that bothersome spot on his abdomen with the elbow of the arm he's using to manipulate the cell phone. God. This is what scares him. The organs are expiring. He had that heart attack about a decade ago when he was with Angela. Last year his brother Moe went in for gall bladder, the year before that Stephen for appendicitis. Michael feels twinges all the time: in the side, the gut, the groin. He knows his body is dying, that it is only a matter of time before they begin ripping out one organ after another, surgeons as lusty as pelicans with their sharp beaks. What will it be first—kidney stones, pancreas, gall bladder?

Sandy's brassy voice echoes abruptly in the cell phone. "So no dice, then? We're out of luck?"

"I'm not sure, actually, but I wanted to let you know. In case."

"Well, shit, I'm on my own then. Again." Sandy sighs audibly into the phone, making certain he hears her exasperation. "Of course, there's this stack of ironing. And there's these other guys who've left their numbers."

Michael swallows and says through dry lips, "Maybe you should leave a message for one of them," though what he's thinking is *bunch of fucking losers.*

"Yeah. Except it's such a hassle, you know, deciding which one to go for and calling back and setting up the preliminary meet and all. I was kind of counting on you and me, you know, after coffee the other day, seeing how it works before going through all that crap again. Men are so."

"I'm sorry," Michael says.

"Yeah. I can see."

"It's not much of a start, I admit." Michael is not used to being on the defensive and hates the tone he hears creeping into his voice: whining. He hardly knows this Sandy, this blowzy broad from a suburb in the north end, yet already he's groveling to her. Women.

"You got that right."

"Look," he says.

"No, you look. I've been thinking about things and let's let it drop."

"Just like that? I thought you and me . . . That seems—"

"Drop it, you know, for now. I'll give one of these other guys a dingle and when you get out from under your family shit, try me again."

Dingle? Michael thinks. When, he wonders, did this

thinking about things occur—in the past half minute? He moves the phone around so it isn't digging into his ear. "All right," he mutters. He hears weariness in his voice, and he realizes he is picturing his grandchildren again. He hasn't brought anything for them, not even candy.

"Yeah," Sandy says. "In the meantime, this ironing."

Michael stares out the window at the fields he's passing: wheat and barley nearly ripe. The whole phone thing was just an idea, he thinks, just a shot in the dark for a guy going without. He can try another number next week, he can try several. There's nothing exactly wonderful about Sandy. In fact, he can do without that attitude. Dingle! "All right," he repeats, forcing cheeriness into his voice.

"Okay then," she says. "Gotta run."

"Okay," he says. "Uh, good luck. With the other, the phone service."

"Yeah. You too."

He thinks of the list of numbers he has jotted down on a scrap of paper in his office. Then he imagines Sandy sitting at her kitchen table and calling the service after she's sorted through her messages and picked the most likely candidates to fulfill her carnal fantasies. "I'll call," he says. "You know?"

"Good," she says. "And, hey, Michael, thanks for the coffee, eh?"

Mary turns in the four-by-four-foot cubicle and lets the hot water strike the back of her skull and cascade down the vertebrae of her spine. She doesn't really like this, showering, she'd prefer a long inert soak in a hot tub filled with gently hissing bubbles, but this is what you get at the club: industrial-strength hair dryers, Vaseline lotion, Pert shampoo, raspy white towels. She shuts off the tap, pulls her shoulder-length hair into a tight ponytail and gives it a quick twist before stepping out of the shower.

Jilly is in the stall two down. Mary can see one bony elbow pumping up and down as she rinses her hair. She's making sounds, too, a low moan of satisfaction. Sexual, un-selfconscious, though not in the stagy way of Monica Seles hitting tennis balls. Jilly steps out of the shower. Big smile, but she's on the move the moment her toes, painted orange today, strike the floor tiles. She examines herself in the mirror. She examines herself in every mirror, checks her reflection in car windshields, even: do I look as good as I feel, does the world at large acknowledge it? Sometimes Mary thinks Jilly is nothing more than a poseur: so much effort to appear carefree and artless. But Mary envies Jilly's direct slant on life. In bed she cries out with pleasure, the whimpers of their first caresses leading to a gravelly, coarse grunt when they fuck, which is a word Jilly actually uses but Mary has trouble even thinking. *Fuck me*, Jilly says, *do me good and hard, babes.* Mary thought it would be all gentle and tender between women, *snuggling*, she would have said, the gnawing of soft mouths, a remote kind of excitation, concluding with a dull, cocooned sort of climax. And it's true, what they do does not involve the brutal gymnastics of penetration, but with Jilly things become quite energetic and violent most times. The orgasms long and powerful.

Mary rubs the calves of her legs and pats each ankle. When she looks up she sees Jilly's eyes on her, and when Jilly sees Mary looking at her, she smiles her big-toothed smile. Laughs. "You look great," Jilly calls out.

Once she said to Jilly, "You're a Degas dancer." And, blushing, Jilly responded, "Reubens, more like." Then she added, "And you, Mary Moo, are a glass of pink champagne. Ooo, yummy."

"Great," Jilly repeats. "You."

They are standing ten feet apart, naked except for their towels, pink bodies giving off heat. But even though they are the only two women in the locker area Mary senses a flush flash up her throat and into her cheeks as Jilly's voice echoes around the walls. This self-consciousness is something Mary has grown to dislike in herself since she's turned fifty. She hates her uptightness, but she's her mother's daughter, her mother who drove Mary to Sunday school until the day of her confirmation, who cluck-clucked Mary into suppressing bad words and bad thoughts, as well as anything resembling a strong emotion, who insisted men sweat and women perspire and ladies glisten. Mary steps closer to Jilly. "And you are gorgeous," she whispers. "You just take my—you glisten."

Jilly snaps her towel at Mary. "Get outta here," she says. "I mean it."

"I know." Jilly drops her eyes and lets the silence between them build as they breathe the heavy air of the changing rooms. After a few moments Jilly fans her bobbed hair out with her fingers, flicking away the last droplets of water, drying the ends. She tips her chin up and rolls her head from side to side, eyes closed, the shower of overhead lighting brightening her cheeks. She sighs. She wraps the towel around her breasts and glances at herself in the mirror one more time, evidently satisfied with what she sees there. "But," she says finally.

"But," Mary repeats. There are rules, she's learned, a code of conduct in Jilly's world, despite its surface cool, its brazenness. Some things are not said. A lot. This confuses Mary, who thinks the great virtue of women is that they talk, but she keeps her mouth shut, as she has learned to do.

Jilly is dabbing lotion on her arms and shoulders. Her face is a mask now, eyes narrowed, chin pointed straight at the mirror. This is a studied look, too. *Concentration*, her pose says, the focus of the athlete Jilly is so proud to have once been, but in Mary's mind the look in Jilly's face warns her *back off*. Over the months they have known each other she has learned to read not just the lines of Jilly's body; she has learned, too, the intricate code of the younger woman's emotional contours: when to offer a drink, when to bring a phone conversation to a quick close, how not to say *love* or touch fingertips, how to put away her VISA card. In Jilly's world there are brassy voices and grunted intimacies, but also there are stony looks and sudden silences that become echoing voids. There is something frightening in this girl that Mary cannot quite put a name to. She seems to swing on a pendulum between tenderness and violence—quite exciting, really —a roller coaster of emotions. Is she a paradox? Yes. But then, who is not?

Mary has moved to her locker and is fastening her watch to her wrist. 1:35. She should call Freddo about the condo conversion: something about the deal is off-center, some detail about the commission from the limited partners. It's not quite right. Freddo is in too much of a hurry these days. He's probably signed something he shouldn't have, and Mary will have to bail him out again. That should be foremost in her mind on a working day, a Friday afternoon, but her thoughts swing back to Jilly. It's because she was raised wealthy, Mary decides. That's what accounts for the web of paradoxes in Jilly's personality. Raised wealthy, with the luxury of rejecting it at eighteen but being able to re-embrace it at twenty-five. She's assertive—cocky—in a way Mary finds not wholly endearing. If she had met Jilly in an earlier period of her life Mary would have said *pushy, arrogant* and probably not liked her at all. Cocky like a man. Like Michael's friend, Ashton.

She should call Michael, too, go over some of the details of the party they're planning to celebrate his birthday, his fifty-eighth out at Willow Island, the following evening. Fifty-eight, it nearly takes your breath away to say it. Have they really been together that long, she thinks, blocking his birthday from her mind momentarily and counting back, has it really been twenty-two years? It seems barely a flip of the calendar ago when she was as wide-eyed as Meagan, a young woman starting out, eager, blood boiling with desires she wouldn't even have admitted were desires. The years whistle past. Mary should get in touch with Meagan, too, who's somewhere on the road between here and Baton Rouge behind the wheel of a truck. What a job for a young woman, rock-band roadie, but it's a peculiar generation, Meggy's nearly-thirties gang, and they have their own counter-cultural notions. Mary glances at her watch again, as if staring at its blinking numbers will gain her the time she needs to fit everything into her day. As usual she's over-booked and running behind. So much for an hour on Jilly's futon, the glass of golden Chardonnay she was promising herself for staying on that wretched stationary bicycle for the full twenty minutes.

Michael makes the turn off Henderson Highway onto Munroe Avenue and as the truck slows through the intersection he spits the gum he's been chewing out the window. He feels a guilty twinge for a moment, hearing the voices of Jane's children: *You're polluting, Grampa.* He had forgotten how self-righteous the young can be, and he smiles to himself as he glides through first one stop sign and then the second before pulling up in front of Jane's house.

This neighborhood isn't much better than the others Jane has lived in with Brad, but he has to hand it to them, their two-story house looks solid from the outside, and Brad does what he can inside to keep it up. As he closes the truck door and locks it Michael tries not to look at the houses across the street from Jane's—sagging, shabby two- and three-story affairs with peeling paint and cracked window glass, some the homes of several immigrant families stacked together, some boarding houses, though none yet condemned by the city. He shuffles down the sidewalk, glancing from time to time at the bay window in the front of the house.

No sign of Jane, who's probably in the kitchen or out in the backyard with the kids. The sidewalk is cracked and uneven in several places. Michael remembers he talked to Brad about levering up the heaved pieces and leveling them so the kids would not trip and hurt themselves. The front steps are sound but the verandah door sticks on the warped floorboards when it's about half open and Michael has to shift sideways to squeeze through. Three years ago when Jane and Brad moved into this place he'd made a mental note to hire someone to jack up and level the porch. But the money he's given Jane since then has gone for more pressing needs: car repairs, dental work for the kids, sometimes, he imagines, even food. A decade ago he had thought that when Jane had a place of her own, a man of her own, then he would no longer be reaching into his pocket for fifties and hundreds every few weeks, but things seem to have become worse rather than better in that regard. It's the burden of raising children—and their children—at the end of the century. His grandchildren, his precious progeny. Not so long ago he read somewhere it costs over a hundred grand to bring up a child these days, college not included. And what does Brad make working for the city waterworks department?

Michael rings the doorbell and while he waits to hear footsteps turns his back to the door and surveys the neighborhood: roofs in need of repair, kids' bikes and plastic toys scattered on lawns, rusted-out cars parked at the curb. Urban white trash, Michael thinks. Some years ago the city planted trees along the grassy verge between the curb and the sidewalk, *boulevards* the mayor calls them, but only a few of those saplings have survived: stunted little maples that even the sparrows avoid as they flit up from the grass to their perches on the power lines high above the dusty street. Michael's heart feels like a lead ball that's fallen into his stomach when he thinks about his daughter living here, his grandchildren growing up on a street where a teenager was swarmed by a gang a month ago and house fires are so common the insurance companies are threatening to refuse coverage. He rubs his abdomen reflexively and turns back to the door. He does what he can to buffer his grandchildren. *And it's her life*, he repeats silently to himself, echoing Mary. *The kid has to live her own life.*

When Jane opens the door he sees first the red splotches on her cheeks and the bags beneath her eyes, but also that she's brushed her hair to the point where its fiery ends spark the sunlight. She's always been proud of her frizzy mop of red hair. Michael hesitates a moment. He never knows which mood is uppermost in this child, his girl, but before he's formulated the wish that she would throw herself into his chest where he could wrap his big arms around her in a long fatherly hug, she wheels back into the hallway and says over her shoulder, "Youse took long enough."

There was a time when Patricia, Jane's mother and Michael's ex these twenty-five years, never tired of correcting the girl, but that seemed merely to harden her resolution to speak in the broken English that reminds Michael most of his immigrant grandparents. And embarrasses him, yes. Though in the past few years he's come to accept it in the same way he accepts his son Maurice's shaggy beard and ubiquitous work boots. There are worse things. "I take it," he says, avoiding her jab, "that you haven't heard anything."

"Duh," she says. They're in the kitchen now and Jane has glanced quickly out the window over the sink and muttered to herself "On the swings." As she entered the room she picked a mug off the stove top and now she asks him, "Coffee? It's a fresh pot."

"I—all right, sure." Michael swallows, anticipating the burning sensation in his stomach, the warning burp, but sensing it's going to be easier to deal with his own burning guts than the hurt look in Jane's eyes if he refuses. He keeps a roll of Tums in the glove compartment of the Mazda. Chomp down two and the old gut will settle.

She pours and says, "Milk, right?" She splashes some in.

Twenty years, Michael thinks to himself. "And one sugar. Please."

"Right," Jane says. "You know," she adds as she drops a lump in the mug and passes it to him without a spoon for stirring, "that there white sugar don't do no good for the stomach."

"I know."

"It, like, eats up the linings or something."

"I know," Michael says. He's thinking *so does this rot-gut coffee.* He has taken one sip of the brown liquid and is looking around for a place to put the mug down without drawing attention to it. He says, "About Brad."

"Huh," Jane says. She's glanced out the window again and has her back to him. He imagines the children out in the backyard, their dark hair being tugged to wisps by the breeze, their open nut-brown faces. He'll go out to the yard later. Wrap them up in his big arms.

"No word, I take it," he says to Jane.

"He's not the loser you think he is." Jane has turned to face him.

Michael looks up from the coffee mug, startled by this sudden attack. Did he say something? Instead of answering, he looks into Jane's eyes, such a bright green, so filled with anger. His mother had always told him never to trust a woman with green eyes—his mother, like his father, dead now these five years. He recalls phrases she used as if she had spoken them just minutes ago. *Green eyes.* Perhaps that's why she never really liked her granddaughter. "I don't think that," he says finally.

"He works really hard around here. He's a good provider."

"That's what I think. Precisely what I think." Michael takes another sip of coffee. "I don't know why you always say the opposite. I've told you."

"You *say.*"

"Yes. And—"

"But think? Really think?"

Michael sighs. This is ground they've trod over many times, a battlefield, actually. "He's a good man," he says, finally, his voice dropping. They are standing in the middle of the tiny kitchen, no more than two feet apart.

Jane takes a sip of coffee and wipes a dribble away from her lower lip. "Daddy. You don't like him."

"I do," he says. "That was a long time ago. Something I never should have said, something I've regretted ever since I opened my stupid mouth." He keeps his eyes fixed on hers, though it is not a stare-down he's after but the steady gaze of reassurance. "Look," he says after a few moments, "that doesn't matter. What matters is finding out where he is. Getting him back home."

Jane snorts. "Oh, right."

"He hasn't run . . . ?" Michael can't find the words though they're filling up his mouth like dentists' wool. "There isn't another . . . ?"

"No," Jane states. She laughs, more a grunt. "No, no, never."

"That's good."

"With him it's—well, it's a joke, you know, beer and his buddies, and the games on TV. That's our Brad. Never that."

"Good."

"Never women."

"Well, that's good," Michael repeats. He's taken three sips of coffee, a respectable show, he figures, and sets the mug down on the stove top exactly in the place where Jane's was when they entered the room. "Isn't it?"

"I guess."

"Of course it is."

Jane drops her head, and with the index finger and thumb of her free hand massages her closed eyeballs. "Only," she says.

Michael waits. "Only," he repeats.

"Only, there's this thing," Jane says, "that kinda runs in his family." She takes a deep breath and looks out the window in what Michael thinks of as a stagy pose. "I don't know why I haven't told you before, but his uncle and his cousin too, well, it's not exactly the same thing, they both have been in and out of those places where they send them when they—slashed wrists and phone calls in the middle of the night kinda thing, cursing, crying on the phone, accusing Brad of being against them, it's got a name, para, para something, and Brad's always been afraid that someday that would happen to him too, only I've always said that's crazy, he's so normal, I even used to tease him before he told me, I called him Normal Norman, but then he takes off on me, he takes off on me again." Jane looks at him. "I'm sorry," she says. "I should've told you."

"Paranoid," Michael says. "Paranoid delusions."

"Right," she says. "I'm really sorry, Daddy." She puts her mug down and this time she does throw herself into his arms, so quickly Michael is taken off guard for a moment, but he folds her in, his child, his little girl. He holds her tight, feeling her warm breath on his neck.

Tears want to start in his eyes but he chokes them back. "It's all right," he says. He places one hand on the back of her head and strokes her hair. *Again*, he thinks to himself, recalling something Jane just let slip, and senses the corners of his mouth tighten down in what Mary calls his *I told you so* look. After a minute he can feel that the sobs convulsing Jane's thin frame are subsiding and what he thinks is, *she'll move back in with us, except now she'll bring two kids with her, two beautiful grandkids, but still three more mouths to feed, I'll have to panel the basement and put up partitions for bedrooms, like the immigrant families across the street.* He almost laughs out loud but it hurts him too. "It's all right," he repeats. "It will be all right, honey."

Mary pulls into the traffic heading south on Pembina Highway with a brief squeal of tires. Pats the leather seat of the Cadillac. There was a time she scorned these cars, *boats* she once called them, *tubs*, preferring German engineering or British ergonomics, but now she loves the smell of brown leather and the swell of the ride the Cadillac gives her. She runs one hand back through her bobbed hair and sighs audibly. Feels the endorphins pulsing through her veins. Feels the swatch of prairie sun falling on her lap and, she likes to think, trim legs. Warm, the body, warm with desire. Mary sucks her teeth. Regrets again the Chardonnay she's missing, the velvet of Jilly's skin on hers, but what the hell, it's a good life whichever way you cut it.

She accelerates to make the light at Crazy Corner. This is what she loves, the lift of the car's engine beneath the hood in response to the pressure of her foot, the swish of tires on cement. Passes on her right the Garlite Grill where she and Michael met those ages ago over red-checked tablecloths and trembling knees. It will never be the same again. Love. She laughs aloud and says *love* into the air-conditioned silence of the car. With Jilly, for example, it's been so matter-of-fact, so adult and businesslike, it's a pity, really, losing the flush of excitement that lust brings. Even with Freddo a decade past. She cannot remember now the way it started between them, who first suggested it or where. Probably him. Mary was pretty submissive in those days. What she can remember: the thrust of Freddo's powerful thighs, his hot breath on her neck, the way he cupped her cheeks in his big hands and lifted upward as she pushed down. Mary feels herself blushing. Shifts about on the leather seat. She hates pantyhose. The sheer drive of men, the white heat of their energy. And Freddo had—has—beautiful hands. Tapered fingers, lovely blue veins above the wrists. Exactly what you would not expect from someone of his body type. Mesomorph.

When she was having that fling with Freddo a decade or so ago she used to consider sometimes what the consequences would be if Michael found out. It scared her a little then but her involvement with Jilly does not. It's not even in the category of "fling," is it? Is it? She certainly does not have any serious intentions. And Jilly seems—what?—cool? That seems to be the pose of her whole generation.

She picks up the cellular phone and beeps the office number. Hears at once Marika's sharp *hello, D and T Agencies, what can we do for you?* That's not what Mary wanted, and Freddo's—where?—in his car someplace, Marika says, Mary will try to track him down using her cell phone. But when she beeps him, no answer. Left the damn thing on the car seat while he wandered off. He does that, so what's the point, she's asked him, but she knows what the point is: he likes the fact that it bugs her. Probably stopped in at Grapes for a G and T, or, worse, at that awful bar at Picasso's where those Mediterranean lounge lizards hang out. Don't any of those guys work? What do they do to make money, push drugs? And how did Freddo ever get mixed up with them? No, she knows that. Ponies, the track. It wasn't enough that Freddo gambles away thousands a week on the damn nags, he has to go and buy a couple himself, partners with a Greek who owns a cafe and a Spanish cab driver with scruffy black hair. Where does a cab driver get the money to buy a horse—partners, even? It's all so seedy, Mary thinks. If she were to start out again in the real estate business, it would never be with Freddo, but she's in the partnership now, dollars for doughnuts.

She runs her hand over her brow and draws away moist fingers. Is she sweating from fear or is this the residue of her workout? Anxiety, she decides. Fear. It falls on her with the sunlight coming in the windshield, heating her and making her twitch on the car seat. She turns the air conditioner farther to the blue as the car pulls away from Stafford and begins the descent at Jubilee. She knows this: she has to keep an eye on Freddo now. His gambling is more than a pastime, and he does dangerous things at the office, things greed alone can cause: hastily drawn-up contracts, sloppy follow-up. She'll have to see a lawyer about the condo sale, for example. And while she's at it, find out about easing out of the partnership. Can she withdraw unilaterally? Jesus. Whoever said life's a bitch didn't know the half of it.

Mary takes a couple of deep breaths. What she would really like to do is drive home and repot the lemon basil plants so she can bring them into the house for winter. Touch of velvet. Scent of citrus. She loves those plants. Would like to spend her days puttering in the yard, growing good things. Has hinted to Michael that getting away from their jobs, their endless round of obligations, would free them to each other, something she would like, despite the club, the Jillys, the high of the Deal. *But not today*, she thinks, *not this day*. She sighs, picks up the phone again. She'll try Freddo one more time.

Before she can touch the keys, the instrument bleeps in her hand, and she nearly drops it. *Steady*, she whispers to herself. *Steady, now*. She half expects the voice to be Freddo's and is ready to leap to some questions that have been bouncing around in her brain about the condo sale, so she's startled to hear the sharper pitch of a woman and doesn't realize right away it's Meagan on the other end of the line—why would she, Meagan has never called her on the cell phone. "Maw?" she says. "Is that you, Maw?"

Mary sees her daughter's face: oval face, round brown eyes looking for reassurance. "It is, darling, what a surprise."

"You sound so—so far away."

"It's the phone, probably. I'm just coming out of the Jubilee underpass."

"There," Meagan says. "It's clearer now."

Mary changes lanes. She's a mile or so from the office, but she doesn't want to be negotiating lanes when she's talking to Meagan. "Where are you?"

"St. Louis." There's a catch in Meagan's voice. Mary's heart skips. Meagan on the cell phone reminds her of long-distance calls from her mother. Bad news.

"Are you okay?"

"No, Mom. No I'm not." Meagan hesitates before going on. Mary pictures the rig that she was driving for the rock band doing a slow-motion somersault into a ditch, the cab exploding. Screams. She must have seen a movie, the images resolve so fast in her mind's eye. Flames, the crunching of metal. Meagan says, "The thing of it is, I don't want you to get upset, Mom, I'm okay now and everything, but, Mom, I lost the vision in one eye while I was driving and then the other, it scared the hell out of me."

"Oh, darling," Mary says.

"But I pulled over, eh, as soon as it was safe. Nothing happened."

"Take it easy," Mary says. "Slow down."

"It's just that I was so damn scared, eh."

"But nothing happened?"

"No."

Mary is still picturing a roadside disaster, the blue and red lights of cop cars. She manages to say, "Thank God."

"And I radioed in for help and they came and took me to a hospital."

"Good," Mary says. Away from the rig. The farther the better. "Is that where you are now? The hospital?"

"They did these tests, eh, something-or-other oscopes."

Brain tumor, Mary is thinking. She asks, "A CAT scan?"

"And blood tests and my urine, eh."

"Good."

"The doctors think diabetes, maybe."

"Diabetes?"

"It's just one possibility. Sometimes people have an attack, which is the first sign, eh. They black out."

"That sounds odd to me, diabetes. Unlikely."

"Maw, are you a doctor now?"

"It's just that diabetes usually comes on slow."

"Well, they haven't told me anything for sure. It'll be hours."

"That's right," Mary says. "Don't worry. It'll be all right."

"That's what the doctors say. Only, Mom, I'm so scared, so worried, you know? I mean it was just like I'm winging down the turnpike, everything cool, the rig humming, less than a hundred miles to go before break and *pow*, I lose the sight in one eye. I blink, thinking it's like a contact or something, and then everything's back clear again and I go *whew*, but the next minute it's the same thing except in the other eye, like complete shutdown, and I'm like what the F is going on. The road in front of me is a blur of taillights and white lines, I can't see very far down the asphalt, eh? It's like the muscles in my eyes are just *dead*. What I'm thinking is *what if it's both next time?* Like shit scared."

"Relax, darling, you're okay. You're all right." Mary has pulled into the parking space behind their office building. Her hands are shaking on the wheel but she keeps her voice steady.

"It's just, Mom, do you think you could fly down here? I wouldn't ask, except I'm just so scared it might happen again. Or worse. Both, like."

"Sure," Mary says. She glances at her watch: 3:17. Even for her it will be a tight squeeze to get to St. Louis and back and still have everything ready for the party the following night, but what can you do, your only child? She'll have to phone Michael from the airport and ask him to take some things for the party in hand. Drinks, for example, he can handle that. Calling the caterer, picking up the last-minutes. He'll be excited about that. Not. His eyes had that look this morning, the whites dilated around the irises, as if he were waiting for her to call him back or say she loved him. Ruggles years ago. Slobber of need. She does. She does love him. Mary glances into the rearview mirror and puts the Caddy in reverse. "I'm on my way, darling," she says. "To the airport. I'll grab the first flight. Only you'll need to bring me up to speed on where you are, where you're going to be in the next few hours and so on."

"You mean," Michael says, "there's more you haven't told me?"

They're sitting at the dining-room table, Jane across from him, positioned to look out the bay window facing into the backyard to watch the kids. She's working on another mug of coffee, revolving it slowly in her hands, trying, he thinks, to impress upon him that she's a grown-up, that she can sit through this drama without histrionics. She says, "I don't really mean *violent*, not really, only sometimes I sit around here with the kids yelling at each other and the food burning on the stove and the phone ringing and crazy things jump in and out of my head. There's so much to do, so much shit pressing in on me. I start thinking crazy, like."

"Take it easy," Michael says. He reaches his hand across the table.

Jane's green eyes flash at him. "Daddy," she says, "you've got that look on your face, the look of Preston Manning. I hate it."

"Shit." He raises his hand to his cheek, as if he could feel the look there. "I only meant . . ."

"I know. You think I'm a basket case. Pity the poor kid."

"Well, I do. I feel sorry for you."

"Save it." She drops her eyes to the table and breathes noisily through her nose, and he waits, giving her time to compose herself, to compose her next statement. After a minute she says, "I'm sorry. I know you're just thinking of me. I'm all fucked up, see. I hardly slept last night and the kids were at me all morning."

"I know."

Jane looks at him and Michael expects her to ask, *do you, do you really know how it feels*, the start of another round of recriminations, but instead she studies him before saying, "Anyways . . ."

"Anyway. You were saying Brad might be violent? Has been before?"

"Yeah. There's this anger in him, this rage. Sometimes in the middle of eating dinner he just slams his fists on the table, rattling the dishes and so on, and then a few times he's gone into the basement at night and I've heard him smashing things around, tools and stuff, it sounds like the walls are going to come down or something."

Michael swallows hard, tasting the last of the bitter coffee on his tongue. He could use a drink now. "But he hasn't . . . ," he asks, "he doesn't touch you, or—"

"No." Jane's voice sounds hollow in the little room, which is silent except for the ticking of an appliance in the kitchen. "Or the kids."

"Well, good," Michael says. "There's that anyway."

"Nothing's happened, but it scares me. You know?"

"Maybe it's something at work. His boss or. These exasperations with jobs flare up. Then they suddenly pass." At the college he himself has gone through such vicissitudes: arrogant committee chairmen, irascible deans, pushy secretaries, a stream of increasingly demanding graduate students. Almost daily now he fantasizes about chucking the career thing entirely and retreating to Willow Island. He would like that: long slow days noting changes in the sky, birds and flowers, working with his hands. He likes to picture himself drinking beer with his buddy Stephen. Snuggling with Mary under the duvets and long mornings of squeaky bedsprings. He loves that. He loves that woman. He does.

"No," Jane says. It's not something at work." She's looking down at the mug she's turning slowly in her hands, preparing, Michael realizes suddenly, to tell him something she's been holding back a long time. He studies the part in her hair, the dapple of white scalp showing through. He glances at his watch: 3:55. He should call Mary. He's got his own complicated life to live, but Jane is going on, "When you asked earlier, see, about Brad and other women . . ."

Michael groans, "Oh, Jesus. Not that." He's placed both hands on the table, as if he meant to stand.

"No," Jane says. "I was telling you the truth. It's not him, see."

"Not," Michael says, a brief echo.

But before he can think what else it might be, Jane says, "Daddy, it was stupid, I promised myself never to tell you or Patricia, such a stupid thing for me to do, but then he didn't come home one night a month ago and the next day when he showed up he started yelling stuff at me, crazy mean things, things I never thought I'd hear from him and I was scared he might hit me."

"Oh, sweet Jesus," Michael repeats. He's thinking *the hens do come home to roost*, but what he says is, "Who was it? Someone he knew?"

"*Slut* and *pig* and that kind of stuff. Ugly stuff." Michael is standing at the window, watching Ali and Randy play on the swing set in the patch of green grass that constitutes the backyard. His heart goes out to them. He thinks, *grandchildren, they grant you the gift of unconditional love. They give you the luxury of being able to love without stint.* Jane comes and stands beside him, the smell of her hair in the air around them. "A guy that he worked with," she whispers after a moment. "It was stupid, Daddy, stupid. I never should have done nothing."

"Yes," Michael says. "I know, I know."

"It's just after Randy was born Brad was so far aways most of the time, like he didn't care about me no more. He didn't touch me for months there." Jane hesitates for a moment, glancing at him, her eyes searching for sympathy. "*Hello*, I felt like shouting, *I'm still here*. And then Phil came over one night and he was so nice to me, so . . ."

"It's okay." Michael puts his arm around Jane's shoulder. She's such a slight build, chicken bones, hardly more. He feels her crying again and pats her hair with his hand, thinking as he touches her of cotton candy at the circus, except he is not happy as he used to be at the circus. No.

"It's just bluster," Jane whispers. "I know he won't do anything to hurt me. Us. He loves us. He's always been a good father."

Michael says, "You never know."

"It's just bluster," she repeats. "He's a gentle man, really."

"No," Michael says. He tightens his grip on her shoulder to emphasize what he is saying. "You can't take the chance. If he's said things and smashed things to the point you're scared, that's the danger zone. That's it."

"I don't think so."

"You can't take the chance," Michael says. "The kids." Randy, he sees, swings higher than his sister even though she's two years older. But he swings with gritted teeth, a contestant in a competition, where she smiles while she waves at him. He waves back. *Grampa*, he hears her shout through the glass.

"I don't know what you mean," Jane says.

"I mean you should come and stay with us. Or the cottage."

"Oh, Daddy, no. That's so. The kids' friends are here. No."

"Just until he comes back." Michael has been running one hand over his chin. The smell of the stain he was using at the cottage irritates his nose and pinches his lips up as he says, "Until you see how things stand with him."

"No," Jane says. She's pulled herself free from his arm, though they are standing shoulder to shoulder, looking out the bay window. "Maybe after."

Michael sighs. He doesn't think this is the right course of

action; he knows she should be out of the firing range, but he's relieved to hear the resolution in Jane's voice, the determination. More relieved than he should be, he realizes. In his head he hears the words *not my problem*. He turns to face her and asks, "You sure? Absolutely?"

"Yes." Jane runs her hands back through her hair, sparking static along her fingers. "Maybe after things are settled a bit we'll feel we need to . . . Or we could come out to the cottage just to get away, have a change of scene kind of thing."

"Okay," Michael says. He watches the kids for a moment more, and then adds, "But in the meantime, my job is to contact the police and his boss at work and so on, and your job is to draw up a list of anyone who might know where he is— chums, relatives, friends, whatever—and call each and every one of them. We have to track him down. Right?"

"Right."

"And, honey." Michael pulls his hand out of his pocket. "Take this," he says. It's only three twenties, he should have stopped at the bank.

"No," Jane says, backing away. "We have money."

"Take it," Michael says. "Take the kids to McDonald's or somewhere better. Get out of the house for the night. Please."

"Okay." Jane puts out her hand. It trembles between them before she wraps her fingers round the bills.

"That's a good girl." Michael inhales and gives Jane his hang-in-there smile: tight-lipped but determined. "I'll just go out the back way," he says, nodding with his head, "and say hi to them." Hold them in his arms and smell their soft skin. "All right?"

"All right." Jane stuffs the bills into one front pocket of her jeans. She smiles back, imitating his grimace. "And thanks—thanks again, Daddy."

Mary pushes the key on the portable phone to the *off* position, relocates it in the seat back above her knees, and then punches the button that tilts her own seat backwards and slumps deep into it. *Krikey*, she thinks, *kids these days: you finally get them to leave home but before you can turn around, they're moving back in again. First Meggy and now Jane—with her two kids.* She stretches both legs to the maximum beneath the seat in front of her, wiggling her toes to promote circulation. She stands five six and the space in the Boeing seems cramped. How, at six foot three, does Michael stand it—or those bulky football players you see hanging around airports in suits made for gorillas? At least no one's in the seat next to her, but she hates feeling pinched up against the window. She glances at her watch: 5:43. She was lucky: there was an under-booked NorthWest flight leaving for Chicago at 5:30, and she'll probably be able to make a connection to St. Louis within an hour. Still she's been on the run since Meggy called and has only now spoken with Michael. It's cost her a fortune to use the in-flight telephone—but what the hell can you do? She glances at her watch again. Maybe Jilly will still be at home. Velvet touch of skin. Golden hair on arms.

The stewardess—no, the flight attendant—has brought her a rum and Coke and Mary sips from it and then leans deeper into the seat with her eyes closed, thinking, trying not to think, of Meagan, as she feels the rum seeping through her blood vessels. Her aunt Susan developed vision problems in her thirties, Mary recalls, so this could be a genetic thing, a weakness that flares up once in a generation. Unlike Meagan, though, who's never been in the hospital a day, Aunt Susan was sickly, she faded away in her late forties from one of those nineteenth-century women's ailments, Mary cannot remember the name. Still, you never know. On the other hand, Meagan's grandmother on her father's side had a brain tumor. Nasty business, that, though she survived the surgery and has outlived the grandfather some ten years or so. Mary sighs. Don't think about it. She takes another sip of rum and Coke. *Lime*, she thinks, *tart*. The flight attendants are beginning the meal service, so she could squeeze in a call to Jilly now. Peaches-and-cream skin. Mint on mouth.

It rings six times before Jilly answers. "Talk to me," she says.

Mary can tell she's happy. There are times when she's working on her computer at home when Jilly does not answer the phone, knowing she's abrupt with people, off-putting, but this is not one of them. "Hi," Mary says, keeping her voice upbeat, "it's me."

"Hi," Jilly says. "It's great to hear your voice."

"Me too." She usually pauses and lets Jilly spill out whatever is on her mind, but this time she asks, "Guess where I am?"

"On the way to the cottage?"

"No," she says. "That's tomorrow, the party."

Jilly suddenly sounds far away, distracted. "Oh yeah."

"I feel shitty about it too," she says. "You not being there."

"No sweat."

Mary hears her swallow and says quickly, "In a plane. I'm calling from the phone in the back of the seat, you know?"

"Huh. It's no different than the cell phone. Clearer, actually."

"Amazing, eh?"

"What's happened? Some urgent deal or something? The condos? Or are you and Freddo skipping the country?"

Mary laughs. "No," she says. She pauses before adding, "It's Meggy. She's in a hospital in St. Louis and I'm going down to get her. Something's happened to her eyesight. She had to pull the rig over on the highway but she's okay. No accident or anything."

"Jesus."

"She couldn't see out of one eye, she says."

"Jesus," Jilly repeats. "The risk those guys take every day."

"I know. All that momentum. The speeds they drive."

"Anyway, she's okay?"

"They've done some tests. I'm sure I'll be able to bring her back." Mary can see the flight attendant coming down the aisle with the hot meal service. Pungent aroma of steamed meat. Crackle of plastic.

"Right."

"It doesn't sound serious," Mary says, "but you never know. This may just be the first sign. In any case, it's a complete cock-up. She may be, you know, incapacitated. I thought she could move back in with us for a while."

"What?" Jilly asks.

"The bedroom in the basement kind of thing."

Jilly snorts. "Ugh. Really?"

"Yeah, I know. She just moved out. Was just getting started on her own life, in her own little apartment, but if she's blind or something . . ."

"Ugh," Jilly repeats. "The thought of it. Parents. Rules."

"Putting up with her rock music." Mary glances quickly to her left, the aisle seat occupied by the pin-striped suit with the aftershave. Businessman. Lost in the papers in his hands. Despite that, despite the fact she probably never will see him again, Mary feels uneasy talking to Jilly so openly with his ears barely two feet away. *Stupid*, she tells herself. *Guilt.*

"Maybe she'll be all right," Jilly is saying. "You said there were tests. Maybe it's just a false alarm or something innocuous."

"Yes. But even then. I'd want."

"Yeah. Of course."

The attendant has stopped in the aisle and is signaling for Mary to lower the tray on the seat back above her knees. Mary wrestles it loose with her free hand and takes the tray of food the attendant is offering before saying, "But that's just the half of it. Michael tells me on the phone just now that Jane's husband has walked out on her. *She* may have to move in with us. With her two kids!"

"Lord," Jilly says. "Walked out. The creep. The bastard."

"Well, it's not entirely clear."

"That's the absolute worst. The asshole."

"It's not completely clear. He just hasn't come home for a day or so."

"That routine," Jilly says. "Somebody should smack him around a bit. See how he likes it. Teach the bastard a lesson." Her voice comes down the line at Mary in bursts as blunt as punches. *Anger*, Mary thinks. *Rage*. Then Jilly says, "Your place isn't very big, is it?"

In the pause she leaves, Mary straightens the tray of food in front of her. Foil wrapper over chicken or lasagna. Chemical odor. Metal. "They hate each other," she says, "Jane and Meggy. I can't imagine them under one roof."

"God," Jilly says. "I'd forgotten that."

"Well, it may not come to that. There's the cottage."

"Yeah." Jilly's voice suddenly seems hollow down the line. Mary asks, "What's wrong?"

"I just realized something else, too."

"No," Mary says. "It won't mean that. It won't."

"It's already tough enough. Michael and Freddo and whatnot."

"I know. But."

"Jesus. All these demands on your time. It's only for an hour or two as it is—when you can fit me in."

"You behave sometimes as if that's more than you want."

"Get real," Jilly says. "Don't try to foist this off on me."

Mary feels her stomach tightening. *Don't fight.* She cuts a glance at the businessman. Forking in lasagna. "Okay," she says. "You're right."

There's a long pause and Mary listens to the crunching of plastic as the other passengers shift their trays around and begin to consume their meals. Finally Jilly says, "I guess we'll just have to see."

"Nothing will change," Mary says. "It's early days yet."

"We'll see." Jilly says this with a finality that is meant to let Mary know the conversation is over.

Mary hates these little bouts of pique, but she purses her lips and looks out the window. Below them the sky is clear, the greenish brown land of—is it Wisconsin?—stretches away to what might be a lake in the distance—Michigan? "That's right," she says. "It will be okay."

"We'll see," Jilly repeats. She sighs dramatically. "In any case," she adds, "this is costing you a fortune, babes."

"Right," Mary says. She puts her hand up to her forehead. When did this headache start? She clears her throat. "Call you Sunday?"

"Sure," Jilly says. "The morning's best, but I may be around anytime."

"No field hockey?"

"Not this weekend."

"Good," Mary says. "Well then, take care."

"You too," Jilly says.

Mary wants to add, *love you*, but the line is suddenly dead.

Michael is taking bottles of wine out of the box the clerk at the liquor store packed them in an hour earlier. He holds a bottle of Bordeaux up to the window and turns it slowly in his hand, watching the garnet colors of the wine wink sunlight. He loves this stuff, loves the bite on the tongue and the slight burn in the back of the mouth after the first swallow. *Tasting of something and the south*, he says aloud. Hmm, tasting of what? Other than Frost he can never remember lines of poetry. Other than Frost, whose lovely sense of rhyme he would like to imitate in his own poems. Well. He has bought two bottles of Santenay, too, because Mark spent some time last summer cycling in the Beaune region and they can talk about that again when Michael opens the wine. Years ago he thought Mark's enthusiastic blabber was too much, an affectation, but he's grown to love his younger friend's *oh wow* attitude to life, his big goofy laugh. Most of the people Michael knows have shrunk in spirit as they've aged: as if life were beating on their shells and they were turtling down. It's depressing. They're preparing for the grave without knowing it. But Mark has kept right on gushing about things and hooting at Michael's stories. He has what Michael's father fondly called *sand*, something Michael could cultivate in himself, he realizes. From the cardboard box he lifts champagne, Mumm's, for the toast to his birth. Can he really be fifty seven? He likes the off-apple taste of champagne and the tingle on the palate but sparkling wine gives him headaches, so he'll go easy tomorrow night. He also has some Chardonnay for Mary. She has a thing for it these days—German, Californian, but especially Australian. Michael has never developed a taste for whites and believes, snobbishly he realizes, that serious wine drinkers drink reds only. French, if possible, but a little experimentation can be useful. Last year he discovered a quite passable Chilean cabernet. At the end-of-term party he threw, his students loved it. So why is Mary onto this white wine thing? Maybe she's just grown tired of reds in the way she seems to have lost her desire for sex. Michael sighs. He lines the bottles up on the sideboard. He's bought nine, eight for the party and a treat for himself now: an Italian Merlot.

After he's opened the bottle and poured the Merlot in a glass, he takes the sandwich he bought at Grandma Lee's and stands at the kitchen window looking out into the backyard. In the spring he set tomato plants between the patches of borage and dill that Mary planted and they've been ripening for the past week or so. A good crop of beefsteaks. His father used to take a salt shaker out to the garden and eat a whole tomato fresh off the vine for lunch. Jane would say *Grampa's feasting* and run out to share with him. *Dead now*, he thinks, *how many years?*

The old man had a cyst at the base of his neck, too, about the same place Michael has one. *Calcium deposit*, Dr. Fayyaz said, but Michael isn't so sure. Maybe he should have a biopsy? It could be something they could nip in the bud. *As long as it isn't cancer*, Michael says to himself. Not that.

He looks at his watch: 7:15. He's expecting a call from Jane at any minute, though that could mean any hour with two small kids to put to bed. He remembers the way their small heads felt in the cup of his hands, the smell of their skin when he lifted them up for hugs in Jane's backyard. He chews down a bite of sandwich. After swallowing he lifts the glass of Merlot up to the light and then takes a tentative sip. *Strawberry*, he thinks. He sniffs the open glass, revolving it slowly, shrugs his shoulders and takes a larger mouthful. On the phone the cop he spoke to was perfunctory—but to his credit—reassuring, while the foreman where Brad works seemed distant and suspicious. The father-in-law calling? Neither had a scrap of information, though the cop ventured Brad was probably just blowing off steam and would be back home in twenty-four hours. *Happens all the time*, the cop said. Michael himself is not so sure. One of his uncles walked out of the house one morning thirty years ago and has never been heard from again. Another locked himself in a garage with the car motor running. Michael thinks, *The shit sticks sometimes. It isn't always just nothing.*

He's sauntered over to the refrigerator and found a hunk of cheese, and just as he starts to cut off a piece at the table he hears a *thunk* on the window behind him. *Bird*, he says aloud, *bird*, they're always crashing into the glass, breaking their fragile necks, dying with their beaks opening and closing in that pathetic way, but when he goes to the window and looks down at the flower beds below, he sees nothing. He's relieved. Another piece of bad news today would have been too much. He sips at the wine and, as he does, puts one hand on the wood frame of the window and runs his fingers along the grain. He installed this casement himself. In fact, he renovated the entire kitchen two summers ago, a job that gave him more pleasure than all the academic papers he's delivered in a long and distinguished career. Why is that? He wonders sometimes if he should have done more humble but more satisfying work in his lifetime, work like Maurice does, and when he thinks about it, he realizes the only time he has been happy at the college was when he filled in as the junior women's basketball coach that term when the regular coach was dismissed for sexual harassment. The college, he thinks: phone calls to answer, classes to prep, theses to read. It would be nice to retire. Write a book about pelicans, finish the volume of poems he's been scribbling away at. That's another thing which gives him satisfaction now, the words he forges into rhymes. Is there a pun there? He runs his fingers over the cedar laths running vertically up and down the kitchen walls, and then he brings his hand to his nose and smells his skin. He loves wood, he loves the place he's built for himself and Mary.

Just as he's pouring the second glass from the Merlot bottle, the phone rings, startling him. Even though the wall unit is within arm's reach, he crosses into the dining room and lifts the portable phone. He's expecting to hear Jane, but instead he hears a male voice: "Hello, Pop?"

"Maurice," he says. "This is a surprise."

"Pop," his son says, "I was just talking to JT."

Maurice is the only person other than Michael who's ever called Jane a nickname, and it pleases Michael to hear his daughter's initials used this way—T for Thekla, his mother's name. "She was going to call me," he says. "I half expected this to be her."

"I know," Maurice says. "She's in a state. Like bad."

"So we better not tie up the line."

"Crying and stuff," Maurice says. Michael can picture his shaggy-haired son standing in the kitchen of his downtown apartment, one hand holding the phone, the other nervously pushing black hair back over his ears. Once when the boy was a teenager Michael had called him a wolverine because of that hair. "They attack people," Maurice had asked, brown eyes dilated, "don't they?" Always he has been the one to feel Jane's pain the worst. As a teenager he used to wake Michael up in the night after he'd had nightmares about his sister. More than once Michael found the boy in his bedroom crying over something that had happened to her.

Maurice himself was a happy if somewhat broody teenager, though in the past few years life has dealt him a few blows below the belt and Michael has begun to fear he will never again see the cheerful boy Maurice was in his early twenties. The problem is he can't seem to find work he likes. Right now he's unemployed. Before that he was working in a lumberyard. He's good with his hands but hates working nine to five. There's a possibility he can catch on as a handyman at a hospital. A glimmer. But months of not working, of sitting in the apartment and brooding, have left him vacant and sullen much of the time. Patricia has told Michael that Maurice has talked to her about depression. She has reported drunken binges, an episode where Maurice smashed his fist through the window of his car. Michael wonders sometimes if Maurice's withdrawn and angry episodes might indicate a deeper problem than the usual travails of passing from the twenties to the thirties. He hopes not. *Flesh of my flesh*, he mutters to himself.

Michael says, "We're on the case. I've called the cops. And his boss."

"No, really," Maurice says. "You remember how she used to get?"

Hysterical, Michael thinks, *crazy*. But he says, "I was over there this afternoon and she seemed to be coping."

"An act," Maurice says. "A performance—for you."

"No," Michael says. "I don't think so."

"She could never let down in front of you, Pop. You know that."

"No. I offered her the bedrooms here. Or the cottage."

"Pop, you're not listening. I was just talking to her and she's bawling her face off to me. She's a wreck. Except she can't come out and say it to you or to Mom because she thinks you guys think she's weak."

"She wouldn't hear about it. Staying here."

Maurice groans. In the silence Michael can hear country music in the background of the downtown apartment Maurice has lived in with Victoria the past two years. She's older than Maurice by five years, the only woman named Victoria that Michael has known to be called that. Vicky, Tory, it usually ends up. Finally Maurice says, "I never really liked Brad, you know."

"You're kidding? I thought you were over there all the time?"

"I am. JT's dragged out with the kids. It was to see her."

"Working on car engines and so on." Michael runs his tongue around the inside of his mouth, tasting the tart berries of Merlot. Probably his teeth are staining.

"Not very often," Maurice says. "And just to show I wasn't, you know, aloof, or whatever. Thought myself better."

"Well, Jesus," Michael says. He leaves a silence and then adds, "I'll call her again. I will." He moves the phone from one ear to the other. He's noticed lately that he's been getting headaches after talking on the cellular, but he can't figure out whether it's something in the instrument or the kind of conversations he's been having. "Anyway," he says, "how are you, Son? You and Victoria?"

"That's the thing of it," Maurice says. "Not so good."

"The car?"

"No, we got that fixed. It was only fifty bucks for new

belts. No, Pop, Victoria found out today that she's been laid off."

Michael has been looking into the wine glass, considering taking a quick sip, but now he sets it on the side table in the dining room. "No," he says.

"Bingo. Like next week and neither of us is working again."

And the rent due, and the groceries to buy, and the car to fix, Michael thinks. Just minutes ago he'd been toying with the idea of early retirement, had pictured himself, stupidly, in the Tilley hat walking the beaches near the cottage, long afternoons of sunshine, writing and puttering around. He loves the birds out there: warblers, nuthatches, sparrows, wrens, gulls, blackbirds, pelicans. He'd imagined inviting Stephen out for coffee, his oldest pal, his colleague of some twenty years now, his friend, his confidant. He'd imagined quiet afternoons of subdued male chatter. The satisfaction of working with his hands. This is what he loves. But what he sees now is this: mouths to feed—three, four, six. All the kids flocking back. He feels weak in the legs suddenly and sits on a chair drawn up to the dining-room table. "Oh, man," he whispers into the mouthpiece. "Oh man."

"I know," Maurice says. "And we'd just made up our minds about the Mac. About setting up the business here and whatnot."

"I'll buy it," Michael says, "I'll get it for you, Son."

"No, Pop. Not this time."

"I will," Michael insists. "It will give you the start you need."

"Another one, you mean."

"Listen, everyone has trouble at first. You're no exception."

"I feel like . . . it's so . . ."

"No," Michael says. "I want to. I want to buy it for you."

"It gets me down some days, Pop. All the kids I went to school with are doctors and lawyers and whatnot and what am I?—nothing. A failure."

"You're not. Don't think that."

"I don't usually. It just gets on top of me some days."

"Listen," Michael says, "they've got their own problems. Working shitty hours, getting shit dumped on them by power-hungry assholes."

"I'm just bummed out by the whole job thing, is what."

"You come over tonight, we'll have a beer, maybe catch an inning of the ball game and we'll talk about it. Son?"

"All right," Maurice says. Michael can hear the relief in his voice, the way the words tremble on his lips when he says, "Okay, Pop, later."

"That's right," Michael says. He picks the wine glass up off the table and swirls the dark liquid around, tasting the piquant blend of berries before he's put the phone down. "See you in an hour or so."

Finally, Mary thinks when she hears the click on Freddo's phone line. She's been trying him steadily since the flight attendant picked up the snack trays over an hour ago.

"Hey, hey," he says, when he hears her voice. "My partner. My bud."

She liked surprising Jilly with it on the flight to Chicago so she asks, "Guess where I'm calling from?"

"A hot tub. Bubbling up those gorgeous boobies."

Drinking, Mary thinks. She pictures Freddo at his desk with the bottle of Crown Royal he keeps in a bottom drawer open at one elbow. She says, "Calling from a phone on a plane, you dope. I'm on my way to St. Louis to pick up Meagan, who's run into some trouble."

"Jesus, girl. Not an accident?"

"No, thank God. A vision problem of some kind." Mary looks out the window at the landscape below, wondering how much she should tell Freddo. Not much, she decides, and adds, "We've nearly begun the descent."

"You're clear as a bell," he says. "Amazing."

The Mississippi, it must be the Mississippi, winds below Mary, a blue squiggle on the green blotter pad that forms the American Midwest. "I've been trying you for hours," she says. "Were you in a bar? Picasso's?"

"No, Mom," he says in a fake chastened voice. "I was working, working at our business. Getting a check, if you must know, for the condos."

"Already?"

"I love getting checks."

"Christ, we agreed not to go too fast on the condo business."

"And now I'm celebrating," he says, "this fat little check for forty big bananas."

"It doesn't matter if it's a million if the deal goes bad."

Freddo sighs. "That little check goes a long way on my car payment, girl. It hasn't been a splendiferous month, if you recall."

"I do," Mary says. She can see the statement Marika drew up last week: their worst month in five years. "But I wanted to go over a couple of details," she says, "before we closed on that one. Remember? Legal details."

"Don't sweat it, girl. The check's in the bank."

"It's not the check," she insists, in the tone she remembers using with the teenage Meagan, a tone that makes her stomach tense up.

She expects Freddo to lash back at her but instead he leaves a pause and then asks, "What's up? You been drinking?"

"Sorry," she says. Fifteen years in business together, three in a raunchy but never-exposed affair, and they have developed highly refined signals for the danger zones: *back off, do not touch, listen.* Mary inhales deeply. Outside the sky stretching to the horizon is blue, but below them are dark streaky clouds, the kind filled with air currents that make the plane lose altitude suddenly. Mary begins to sweat just thinking about it. She clears her throat and says, "It's not a matter of money, it's a question of who becomes legally responsible if the deal falls through."

"I know that. I understand that."

"There's a wrinkle in this kind of deal, though. When you accept the check, you're saying you've checked things out."

"Some pun."

Mary burps slightly, tasting again the cheese of the lasagna. Awful. "I'm not laughing," she says, more petulant than she'd intended.

"I know," he insists. "Then you're holding the bag, legally speaking."

Mary pictures Freddo again, this time with his stocking feet on the desktop, the top button of his shirt unbuttoned, his tie pulled askew. He's taking in the words but what she's getting at hasn't sunk in yet. She says, "But there was something with the second mortgage, some hitch we had to look into. Remember?"

"No," he says. She can hear country music playing in the background. Country music and ponies. After a moment he adds, "Maybe I do remember."

She waits, listening to his heavy breathing over the line. He's thinking, working at recall. Never one of his strong points. He's the glad hands in their partnership, and she's the details person. She says in a studied voice, "You were going to read through it, remember? Something was defaulted if by a certain date . . . or was it in case insufficient notice was given? I remember because we'd touched on just that kind of clause in that legal course I took a couple of winters ago."

"I remember," he says.

"Good."

"The course, I mean."

"But not this contract?" She pauses, waiting for him to say it, and then she asks, "But you didn't go through it again, did you? After we talked?"

"I did. But I can't remember. Shit."

She can picture the sweat on his brow, his flushed fat face. *He's a heart attack looking for a place to happen.* Michael's quip. Michael of the solid back, the muscular thighs. She asks anyway, "And the check is in the bank? We're legally in possession?"

He says, "Jesus. What an idiot." She can hear the clink of his glass as he sets it on the desktop. He takes a deep breath and asks, "Could it be the down payment was defaulted if by sixty days following the offer the partners had not agreed to accept?"

"Yes. Exactly that. The down payment defaulted."

"But they have," he says triumphantly, "they have agreed."

"You talked to the general partner?"

"No, you were going to do that."

"Right. And yesterday she said there was some kind of minor hitch, two of the votes came in by proxy bearing the final date but were actually received on the day following. The general partner's lawyer said that just to be certain, to be a hundred percent, they should reschedule the close for two weeks later and call all the proxies in again. You remember now?"

"Oh, Jesus."

"And that date hasn't come yet. It's next Friday, right?"

Freddo says, "But surely if it falls through, it just falls through. So the deal's off, finito, but we're not out of pocket. Right?"

"Wrong," Mary says. "We've played our hand, buster. We have taken possession of the check. The partners can sue us for screwing up—for losing the deal. If they care to. If they're in a litigious mood."

"Which they might be."

"Which they definitely are."

"Oh, Jesus," Freddo repeats. "How much are we on the hook for?"

"Well, it may be nothing, it may come to nothing. Probably will." Mary pauses. The pilot is telling them they're about to begin the descent. There's a disturbance below. The landing may be a bit bumpy. Mary listens. She hears the whunk and crunch of the ailerons sliding into position. "But if it goes to court, who knows," she adds. "We could be on the hook for the whole down payment—five hundred grand—plus . . ."

"Plus the court costs."

And penalties. Mary swallows hard. In the aisle the flight attendant is signaling for her to bring the call to a close. "That's a lot of car payments."

"That's the Beamer, girl. Toast. That's the house. Toast with butter. The fucking cottage."

The trip to Japan, Mary thinks. *The Caddy. Early retirement.* She's been dreaming about that lately, growing dozens of different herbs in the plots of soil around the cottage, walking, fixing nutritious meals, and it is a dream, but a dream just about within reach. She has the phone pinched between her shoulder and ear and revolves the diamond ring on her wedding finger several times before saying, "Well, it could come to nothing. We'll just have to wait and see."

"So there you go then," Freddo says. "I guess we will."

JANE

The thing of it is, I'm totally pissed at my old man. He doesn't see it, of course, swaggering in here wearing hundred-dollar Birkenstocks and that goofy hat he bought to remind everyone he's been to Australia, and offering me whatever puny bit of cash he digs out of his pockets. Diamond Mike. *Take the kids to McDonald's, my treat.* Meanwhile he's heading out to La Vieille Gare for supper with Mary the Mouse, probably spend more than he's given me on those cute little after-dinner drinks with green and yellow umbrellas while my kids choke down mungy burgers and his daughter gets piles sitting on molded plastic seats at McCancer's. Gee, thanks Dad. He actually believes he can buy me off with a few twenties, always has, but when it comes to me asking for money for stuff that really counts, he gives me that pinched-up mouth that tells you right off how much generosity the man really has. Brad says he only gives us stuff so his own conscience is appeased—that's not a word Brad would use, *appeased*—though there's another reason I'm pissed, Brad bloody Fletcher.

See, I'm on the phone yesterday with this girl I met through the softball team Brad plays on, the Homers—boy, there's a bad pun for you, a double meaning not one of those jerks probably even recognizes—Brenda's her name, she's the wife of one of the guys, and she says to me, she says, *never trust a man, they think with their dicks, not their brains.* It's that simple, she says, all they want is one thing and when they've got it, see you later Sally. And I'm like *every guy?* But in my guts I know she's right and I was merely fooling myself a little there for a while with Brad.

Bradford William Fletcher is the father of my two kids, a guy I met on a dance floor at Belvu ten years ago now, going on a life sentence. Maybe that in itself isn't so awful, marrying a guy who picked you up at a dance, but I could tell the night he picked me up that he was only dancing with me to fill in the time while waiting for another girl, *chick*, he would have said, to show up. The girl he really wanted to be with. I should have known then. I did know then, but we were in lust, see, in those early months, after he'd ditched Bonnie or whoever, because he had such a sweet thing going with me. Those were totally wild times, smoking up, doing guys, dropping acid, it seems looking back now that's all we did for years on end there. I had a friend then, Sue Ann, who was even wilder than me, we were two witches on the loose, running like crazed horses, I can tell you that much, not the hag bag I've become, black pockets under the eyes, skin as patchy as a rash. I look in the mirror some mornings and I want to puke. I've developed these brown spots on my chin lately, probably cancer or whatever. Forget about that. But back then life was for the taking. So we took and took—sex, mostly, and mostly from guys just like ourselves, guys with nothing to lose, which we dignified with the word *dating*. *Rutting* is more like. I loved it, guys hanging over me, wanting me. I loved the screwing, too, I admit it, the long sweaty nights, the way my nipples ached after. It was an itch I couldn't help scratching. And Brad has these blue eyes and shoulders like one of those statues you see in art books, from Florence or somewhere. Sculpted. Beautifully developed from working out. He should have been a good one-night stand for a girl like me, but no, because my old man sees right away what's going on between us when I first introduce them, sex and sex only, something way down inside me says *I'll show you, you bastard* and I have to go and marry Brad Fletcher, like, to spite him.

He does that, my old man, makes you do things just out of spite. Me, anyways, though I know Maurice has crossed that line, too. Maurice the good son. Maurice the butt kisser. Like when I was just learning to drive and the old man is

55

going on at me all the time: *put the stick in neutral before braking at a corner, use the flashers, eject the tape before switching off the engine.* There's all these rules, his own private rules for every human act. He probably folds the toilet paper after he's wiped his ass. It's the same around the house: *switch on just one light in the basement if you're only going down for a minute, don't crank the taps shut or you'll ruin the settings, tear up the corn flakes box into flat pieces before putting it in the garbage.* Rules, rules, and rules. Living with him is being in a concentration camp or something. So one day I'm out in the car alone and when I come up to a corner—this was in the days he had that shitbox yellow Tercel thing he so kindly let me drive—I jam the stick into reverse. *Take that Pop,* I think to myself, Pop, which is what Maurice the Good calls him. The shitbox had a hernia on the spot. Blue smoke coming up from under the hood and black crap belching out from the rear end and a God-awful stink, after the initial whunka-whunka. The shitbox sounded like a hippo stuck in mud. *Take that Pop.*

Except it turns out he'd just had the transmission reconditioned and it was still under warranty so Speedo or whoever fixed it for free and threw in a yearly check-up on the house. Like, what gives with him? So then I had to drive the shitbox into the back wall of the garage to even the score. Thousands of dollars of damage. All those red and orange plastic light things smashed up. You see what I mean? He has a way of provoking spite, the old man. Ten years ago or so he pissed me off so much with his constant harping about drugs and sex that I started mailing boxes of dogshit to his office. I don't think he ever caught on. Maybe he doesn't see how much he provokes me.

The way I talk around him and Mary works the same. My poor English, I mean. I did actually finish high school and can actually speak correctly, but I know it drives the college professor in the old man nuts to hear it, so around him

I'm always going *anyways*, and *I done*, and *not nothing* just to
see him bite down on the corrections he's eager to offer, his
twitching mouth disappearing into disapproval. Velcro lips.
At times I hate him. He gave me so much shit about gram-
mar and stuff as a kid there's no way I could pay him back in
a whole lifetime—two.

The old man is so smart and so educated, see. Just ask
him and he'll tell you—on and on. Did I mention reasonable
and rational? Unlike me. When I was at home he was always
on about how my life would be so much better if only I could
act less unpredictable. *Perspective*, he says to me. If only I did-
n't have to push things to the limit all the time. Like when I
made a big deal about my best friend in high school, Lindy,
not getting a part in the Rainbow Stage production because
the mayor's niece got it and I made those phone calls, and
wrote letters with bad words in them, and camped out on the
mayor's lawn with a protest sign. He says to me, *it's not the
end of the world, calm down.* But I kept at them and eventual-
ly they gave Lindy a part, a small walk-on bit, and I says to
the old man, I says, *yeah, and Edmund Hillary lost perspective
too—but then he gained a lot more than any person ever had before
him*, and that shut him up, at least for a while.

See, he's never got over his guilt about dumping Patricia
for Mary when I was a kid, for hurting me by wrecking my
family, but instead of that making him more kind to me,
more gentle, it's hardened him toward me. He treats me like
I'm to blame or something. The thing of it is, Michael
Samuels, big-time college professor, cannot forgive himself,
so whenever he sees me, the victim of his playing around, his
lust, all his shame comes flooding back and he takes it out on
me. If he was really so damn smart he'd have figured this
stuff out for himself. I can tell you this, though, he's so
caught up in impressing people he hardly even knows anyone else exists. Another thing, you don't have to have a
Ph.D. in psychology to see when someone else is just passing

their shit on to you, the way he does with me, but then if you ask me that's what we're all doing here on planet earth, working through our pain and trying to pass it off on everyone else. It's sick is what it is.

The one thing I can say, he never tried anything with me when I was a kid. Touching and special snuggles or whatever it is fathers and uncles and so on think they're doing. It's shocking how many have. Mimi—she and Laura are my best friends, my only friends, *the three broads* we call ourselves— she tells me one night over beers that her old man climbed into her bed night after night, touched her breasts, lay on her, the whole fucking show, stuck it into her and everything. Ugly. Like what's with these assholes? She didn't know it was wrong at the time but even when she's telling me twenty years later Mimi is bawling her eyes out, and to top it off she suddenly bolts into my bathroom and pukes. It smelled like shit in there for weeks. I mean don't these jerks know their little bit of dick pleasure brings down a whole lifetime of crap on the girl? Their own daughters, for Christssake.

Though I saw a program on the Discovery Channel that really made me stop and think. In other places of the world, Africa I think it was, somewhere where they have brown skin anyways, it's like the regular thing for fathers to have sex with their daughters. Weird, eh? And nobody calls in the cops about it or has to go to psychiatrists and whatnot because that's just the way they do things in these tribes, same as some people cut off girls' clitorises and others circumcise newborn boys. It's a fucked-up world, I can tell you that.

Philip says *pain's the game*. He should know, being black and growing up in this end of town where kids are left to fend for themselves before they're out of diapers some of the time. Stabbings, rape, sniffing. His life, wow. I mean knocked about every day by *uncles* shagging his mom—his old man fled the scene like as soon as he was born, gonzo

Alonzo. His old lady drunk or spaced out on Lysol. Eating pork and beans cold from tins. No shoes, even in the winter. Everybody beating in everybody else's skull. Shit. It's a horror story. And when he tells it with those big brown eyes of his, like saucers they are, looking down at the floor or out the window, anywheres but in yours, it's enough to make you sick. Don't tell me about kids having it tough in India or somewheres halfway round the world, there's shit going down on this very street would break your heart.

That's why with Brad it seemed as if maybe there was a chance for me in this stink hole we call life. Maybe. He was there at first, and down deep he's not a bad guy, give or take a little irresponsibility. Mimi says *men, I haven't met one yet— they're all just little boys.* And Laura says there isn't a guy worth a woman troubling over until he's thirty. So why does Laura wake up so many mornings with a different guy in her bed? That's a cheap shot. The thing of it is, she needs men just like Mimi and just like me. She cracks me up, though. She says to me one time over beers, she says, *men, can't live with 'em, pass the doughnuts.* Like Mimi she was married right out of high school and then ditched by the bastard a couple of months later, pregnant of course.

I can say this for Brad, he's hung in there pretty good these five years and more—and I know how tough it can be with two snot-nosed kids cramped into a little house like this. The diapers, the puke, toys underfoot, screaming and crying in the night. He's said some crazy things. Done some too. He may not have come home a couple of times and he's probably had it off with some bimbo he picked up in the bar from time to time. I'm not stupid. He's still a good-looking guy and a lot of women go for that hangdog look he puts on after a few beers. He can turn a girl's insides to jelly. He can be charming.

Ages ago, before the kids, he bought me flowers all the time. Nothing fancy, no purple orchids in glass vases, but the kinds of things you pick up at the checkout at Safeway or from some girl outside the liquor store. That was when he was still buying me things. Calling me *honey*. I worked at the track, grooming horses then, and I was crazy about animals, so one day he brought home Montana, a beautiful golden retriever with that soft soft hair they have, dumb as two posts, of course, in the way of golden retrievers. I loved that dog. Walked her every day, brushed her coat once a week. She wasn't smart, but she sure was affectionate. That big pink tongue slobbering all over you. Brad didn't really like that. Some nights I would go down into the basement and curl up on the blankets with her, which Brad thought was a big joke, but he didn't mind, not really. Then she got run over by a car one day, chasing a squirrel or a cat, and when Brad came home I was sitting out on the stoop with her head in my lap, stroking her ears and crying quietly, the way you do when you can't change something bad that's happened. He didn't try to take her away from me, that's what I remember. He sat beside me. He just left me sit there with my dead dog and work through the pain, and after an hour or so he put his arms around me and that was the most comforted I've felt in my entire life, sitting on the stoop in the darkness with Brad's arms around me. Yeah, I wish he was here now. This morning I woke up and thought for a moment there he was snuggled down under the quilt beside me, I felt his warmth somehow, a kind of red glow, and knew in a minute he'd sigh, roll over, and put his arms around me and I'd feel my insides go squirmy the way they do, but he wasn't there beside me, of course, and after staring at the ceiling a while I got up and looked in on the kids sleeping their innocent lives away, and that red warmth ran up and down my spine an hour or more, and then Randy woke up and the three of us were into our little dance once again.

Part 2

Cabernet Sauvignon is the world's most renowned grape variety for the production of fine red wine. From its power base in Bordeaux, where it is almost invariably blended with other grapes, it has been taken up in other French wine regions and in much of the Old and New worlds, where it has been blended with traditional native varieties and often used to produce pure varietal wine. Perhaps the most extraordinary aspect of Cabernet Sauvignon is its ability to travel, to set down its roots in distant lands and still produce something that is recognizably Cabernet, whatever the circumstances. And what makes Cabernet Sauvignon remarkable to taste is not primarily its exact fruit flavor—blackcurrants—but its structure and its ability to provide the perfect vehicle for individual vintage characteristics. It is easily capable of producing deeply colored wines worthy of long maceration and wood ageing for the long term.

"TELEPERSONALS," MICHAEL REPEATS, insistent, though his voice is barely above a whisper, a harsh whisper.

"Like in the newspapers?" Stephen asks. "The back pages of the *New Yorker*?" They're standing on the deck, at the back of the cottage at Willow Island. Michael is hunched over the open gas barbecue, staring down at two large cohoe salmon wrapped in tin foil. The sun, setting behind them, reddens his hands as he manipulates the tines of a giant fork and expertly pries open the fold in one foil. *Ahhh*, he sighs, bringing his nose down to the steaming pink fish. In his free hand he has a lemon with the top sliced off, and he begins a sowing motion over the foil, slowly dribbling droplets of lemon juice onto the exposed flesh. When he is done, he uses the fork to open the second foil wrapper and dribbles juice on the other fish.

He looks up at Stephen for a moment. "Not exactly," he says. He tips his Tilley hat back on his head and adds, "You pay a fee and acquire a phone box, and you leave a message there, indicating who—*what* may be more to the point—you're interested in."

"And women call you up?"

"Yes," Michael says. "Leave you messages and phone numbers."

"Wow," Stephen says. He runs one hand through his black hair, a habit he's had for years, a habit Michael loves in his friend. He was hoping tonight to tell Stephen about the poems he's been writing. Stephen has led his own tangled life with two daughters in their twenties who have continued to live at home in the way kids do these days. But he's an upbeat guy, a kind person, and a friend. He will have good things to say about the poems, a word of encouragement, probably. His love never wavers.

"Except there's a couple of rules," Michael says, pausing for a moment to gauge Stephen's reaction. "Men cannot get women's phone numbers from the service—connections always have to be initiated by women."

"Right," Stephen says. "Sexual harassment."

"And women don't have to pay the fee."

Stephen wrinkles his eyebrows. Over the years his face has grown more fleshy, and his eyebrows, rarely trimmed, form one dark caterpillar across his brow. He asks, "How's that?"

"Supply and demand," Michael says. "For every woman on the system there must be ten—maybe twenty—men. So the women have their pick." As he speaks he reaches to the railing running around three sides of the deck and lifts a shaker marked Paprika from it and in a moment is dusting the fish with a light layer of the orange powder.

Stephen cuts his eyes toward the room behind the glass doors and drops his voice to a conspiratorial whisper. "And so then—what?—you meet them somewhere?"

"Yeah. Or talk sometimes, just talk on the phone."

"Just talk?" Stephen's lips have crinkled into a mocking but still jovial smile. He knows Michael. They love to tease each other.

"Well, erotic talk." Michael has put the paprika back on the deck railing and is carefully resealing the tin foil around the fish, making quick pinching motions—the foil is hot—with his thumb and index finger. "Quite erotic."

To his side Stephen is looking out past the deck to the west, where the sun is dropping to the horizon. "It's glorious," he says. "The color over there."

"Isn't it," Michael says. He has lowered the lid on the barbecue and has come to stand shoulder to shoulder with Stephen. They have both picked their drinks off the railing and are holding them idly in their hands, Stephen a mug of beer, and Michael a glass of wine. "The purples are a wonder."

Stephen says, "You have a great place here." He and his wife, Colleen, have a cottage ten miles to the south but it is not on the water. In the past few years Stephen seems to have preferred spending the summers in Europe. *Not this cowboy*, Michael thinks. *I need the space, the air.*

"Yeah," Michael says. He has, in fact, written a suite of poems about Willow Island, though he is afraid they might be too precious for Stephen's taste. If the occasion arises, he'll bring the manuscript out tonight.

"So mutual masturbation," Stephen says, returning to the subject of telepersonals. He pats his stomach with his free hand. He has not exercised much since he had the appendicitis attack a few summers ago. Now he is packing on pounds. "But sometimes," Stephen continues, "it's the other, too, real sex?"

"Sometimes," Michael says. "Sometimes sex." He sighs and lifts his glass to his mouth and takes a long swallow. This is what he loves. The taste of a well-aged Bordeaux, the caress of the summer breeze on his cheeks, the slow chatter of a man his age. These things are balm to the soul.

Stephen laughs. "I'll be damned," he says. He too takes a drink, foam from his beer catching in the hairs of his mustache, reminding Michael of the milk mustaches of childhood.

"Not very good sex," Michael adds. "I have to admit that."

"No?"

"But better than nothing." Michael laughs and Stephen

laughs too. In the distance they see a small flock of pelicans rise from the water and, after going south for a few moments, wheel to the east and head directly for them.

"They're not very attractive, then? These women who call?"

"Exactly." Michael takes another sip of wine. "Any attractive woman out there, any reasonably attractive one, does not need the telepersonals if she wants to have sex. You know?"

"I guess," Stephen says. He shakes his head of dark hair. Michael wonders sometimes what goes on in there. Stephen has been married to the same woman, an attractive woman, true, for nearly thirty years. Twenty-five, at any rate. Yet Michael has never known Stephen to be involved with anyone except Colleen, never even commit an indiscretion. What is going on? When they're sitting together on winter evenings playing canasta or listening to fifties rock music, the four of them growing comfortably old together, Michael thinks Stephen and Colleen must have given up sex in the past few years, just as they gave up playing tennis a decade or so ago—and jogging before that. He takes another sip of wine. *Better you than me*, he thinks.

"Whoa," Stephen says. The pelicans, twenty feet above them, throw a sudden shadow as they pass, the beat of their immense and powerful wings a blur of sound overhead. They seem, for an instant, to be right on top of the two men, about to knock them over.

Michael starts, too, but he thinks, *power, magical.* He watches the undersides of the giant birds as they sweep past and lifts his glass in a toast to them. To Stephen he says, "I guess we should go back in." He nods toward the cottage and glances into the dusk-darkened windows at the others, gathered in the candlelight for his birthday celebration, talking and drinking inside: their wives, Mark with girlfriend Alix, their friends, Ashton and Petra.

But Stephen doesn't move. "What about repercussions?" he asks.

Michael touches his fingers to his lips. "It's a fling," he says. "Sex plain and simple. Nothing. It wouldn't matter."

"You know," Stephen says, lifting his glass to his lips, "women don't think the same way as men about these things."

"This one does."

"Uh-huh," Stephen says.

"I mean it. It wouldn't matter to me if it were the other way around."

"Uh-huh," Stephen says. He takes another sip of beer before asking, "Have you considered the professional route?"

Michael pauses, considering. "A hooker?"

Stephen takes another swig of beer. "That's good," he says, holding it up to the sunlight. "Sharply tart. Hopsy."

"Kenyan," Michael says. "Tusker. I'm glad you enjoy it."

"I do," Stephen says. He laughs briefly. "But then I've never met a beer I did not like."

Michael laughs, too, and then says, "That's a difficult route for me to take. A hooker, I mean. For a romantic."

"Is that how you'd describe yourself?"

"I fall in love with women."

"Yes," Stephen says, "you fell in love with Mary."

"Right," Michael says. He takes a drink and looks to the west, where the sun is setting in glorious colors. "Does that seem ridiculous?" he asks. "In the light of what we've been talking about?"

"Hookers, you mean? Professional sex?"

"That I can profess to be in love with Mary and still . . ."

"Well," Stephen says, "I wasn't thinking of a hooker, exactly. I was thinking more along the lines of an escort service."

"Tiffany's?" Michael says. "Gloria's Gorgeous Gals?"

"Yeah," Stephen says. "Nice clean girls, I understand. College girls, some. No surprises. No nasty disappointments in the flesh aspect."

Michael sighs. "It's a lot of hassle."

Stephen looks at him. In the darkness their eyes meet, laughing eyes, the eyes of old friends. "Surely no more than you're going through with this telepersonal bit. Phone calls, secret meetings, disappointing partners."

"No, but."

Stephen laughs. His voice is bright and loud, it is suddenly all around them, the way the pelicans' wings were a few moments earlier. "Oh, no, old chum," he says. "Don't tell me it's the money. What you're saying is you can't stand the idea of paying for it. Right?"

"It's not that so much. Not that."

Stephen laughs again. "Old chum," he says. "Relax. It's a hundred bucks, for Christ's sake. And think about what you get."

Michael is looking at his empty wine glass. The taste of strawberries is on his palate, a taste he needs now. But there's the burp again. *Borborygmi*, the doctor calls it, this gurgling in his stomach. He wants to belch and fart at the same time, but neither brings lasting relief. There's so much can go awry in the gut: colitis, Barrett's esophagus, pancreatitis, herniated jejunum, cirrhosis. "I know," he says, returning to the subject of escort services. "I have thought of what you get. And of what you can contract."

"Me too. Of what you can get."

"You have?"

Stephen smiles over his mug. He drinks the last of the beer back and smacks his lips before saying, "Considered the idea, put it that way." He adds, "You know, variety is the spice of life and all that."

"But never actually acted?" Michael is standing with one hand on the sliding door. He is thinking of movies he's seen with call girls—*Klute*, *No Way Out*, a British mystery with a tall blonde. Maybe Stephen is right.

"Not acted yet." Stephen is smiling. "But life is short, old chum," he says. "You never know when the ride is going to end. So what's the diff?"

What is the diff? Michael asks himself. He looks at his watch: 8:15. In ten minutes he must take the salmon off the grill. "Exactly," he says in a voice he means to sound resolute, "you just never know."

Mary is standing over the stove. In her left hand she grips the handle of a wok, with her right she is spooning diced celery and water chestnuts out of a bowl into the wok and slowly turning them into a thickening mixture of wild and brown rice. Behind her she can hear the voices of happy people: Ashton expounding to Alix and Colleen about some retrospective at the MOMA, Mark and Petra laughing over something she's said about bicycling. This is what Mary loves. The sound of voices rising and falling, the clink of glasses, the warmth of bodies in a small room. An hour ago they had all walked out to the point at Willow Island to see the birds feeding, and when they came back to the cottage they brought with them the weedy smells of beach detritus and a pungent body heat that has permeated every corner of the room. *Seaweed*, Mary thinks. She inhales deeply. *No, gone.*

She checks her watch: 8:20. The salmon will be done soon. She has to take the Brussels sprouts out of the oven before she slices the mushrooms and adds them to the wok. Where is the paring knife? She turns to see if she has left it on the counter behind her, and when she does, she spots Michael and Stephen coming back into the room. Michael holds up five fingers and she nods. He looks good tonight, she thinks, *my man*, though she has to stifle a laugh, too, they've traveled so far from the innocence of that phrase.

He's wearing a faded denim shirt that she bought for him in Chicago last summer and the chinos that were her Father's Day gift to him a few months ago. They are younger than the clothes he prefers to wear. Younger and smarter. She thinks, *sky*. And tonight there is a ruddy glow to his cheeks, and his hands are in continual motion, a certain sign that he is enjoying himself.

Colleen has risen from the couch where she was seated between Mark and Alix and come over to the counter. "Can I help with anything?" she asks. Such brown eyes. Chocolate. At one time Mary thought brown eyes were as dull as brown suits. Now she sees the romance in them, the mystery of India and the East. Patty had brown eyes, Patty of the wicked tongue and crimson nails. Mary blinks her eyes and refocuses on Colleen.

"No," Mary says, cheery. "No, everything seems to be under—well, yes, you can pour me some of the white wine. The Chardonnay."

"This?" Colleen asks, holding up a Verde that Ashton claims is the best buy in the city. Something he came across in Italy, he would like them to believe.

"No," Mary says. "The other." And when Colleen puts down the Verde and lifts up the Chardonnay she thinks, *maybe tonight, maybe tonight we can be sexy in the old way, carnal and totally uninhibited—is that still possible?* She remembers a time twenty years ago when they made love in front of the fireplace on an old Hudson's Bay blanket, the room frigid except for the area immediately in front of the burning logs. The blanket chafed the back of both her legs, her ass was sore for a week, but it didn't matter in those days, nothing mattered then except being with Michael. And now she has to take a deep breath and try not to close her eyes as she counts to ten when he starts in on one of his pet peeves. Is this the way it is with all couples who have been together more than a decade? Mary glances up and down the counter.

When she reaches for the wine glass Colleen has filled to the top she thinks, *now what was I looking for?*

She takes a sip of the wine. Tastes Jilly. For a moment she lets her thoughts drift that way, the smoothness of Jilly's inner thigh, the mole on her cheek. Her skin is young and smooth, there are freckles between her breasts that Mary kisses, they smell of lemon. The taste of mint and basil. Such a sweet girl. Well, not entirely, not sweet entirely. She closes her eyes and thinks *light*. And when she opens them she discovers she has the paring knife in her hand and remembers then why it seemed important a moment ago not to lose it: white bone-handled, Meggy had bought it in a shop in Nevada and given it to her on Mother's Day.

At her elbow Michael says, "You're dreaming, love."

"Brooding," she says. She snorts. "Which is your domain."

"Not exclusive," he says.

She drops her eyes and says in a kinder tone, "No. Sorry."

"It's all right." Michael glances over his shoulder into the room and whispers, "That one dip isn't going over so great."

"The crab and Romano? I don't know why exactly."

"Maybe it's the bread."

"I love the bread."

"Yeah," Michael says. "But." He pauses and then adds, "I prefer the other one, the artichoke hearts with the Parmesan." He has refilled his wine glass and is standing beside her now. Scent of autumn leaves, of grill smoke. At least he's a manly man. He asks, "Brooding?"

"Meggy," she says. "Poor kid."

"She'll be all right." He takes a long swallow of wine and raises his voice to ask, into the room behind, "Anyone need something? A beer, wine?"

The chatter stops for a moment. Sounds of logs crackling on the fire, the hiss of the casserole in the oven. Heads turn, glasses rise but no one says anything. Ashton has one arm around Petra's shoulders and is whispering in her ear,

Mary notices, snuggling like young lovers. They are like that: gigglers, sharers of secrets. Mary pulls on the oven mitts and bends to the stove. Lifts out the casserole of Brussels sprouts. Hot. Her mother's recipe. Browned almonds on top. After she's placed it on the counter, she starts slicing the mushrooms. "The thing is," she whispers to Michael, "I am no good with the not knowing. Not knowing whether it's type one or type two. Not knowing which road Meggy is headed down."

"I know." He's looking into the room, shuffling from one foot to the other. In a moment he'll find an excuse to join Stephen and Mark, to talk baseball. "But," he continues, "she's home, she's with you, she's safe. That's what's important right now."

"I mean, they do the tests, why can't they tell?"

"They're technicians," he says. He places his hand on the middle of her back and slowly works his large fingers up her spine, circling and rubbing until he reaches her hairline. "Good technicians at that. But not gods."

"That's nice," she says. Ten hours of the last thirty in airplanes, rushing from airport to hospital to hotel. Hasty showers, fast-food meals. Mary is running on empty. On the drive up to the island this afternoon her head was swimming, she had to stop by the side of the road for a few minutes and rest her eyes. *Okay now*, she thinks, *back in control.*

At the base of her neck he probes with his thumb. "Knots," he says.

"Not too hard."

He lifts his hand away but in a moment resumes, more gently. "And in her case they cannot tell. Diabetes is tricky to diagnose. Especially when it comes on so fast."

"I know," Mary says. She cups her hands around the mushroom pieces, scoops them up, and adds them to the wok. Stirs. "But you'd think they could. You'd think they'd be able to at least ..."

He says, "It's a good sign this way. It probably means she's got the second kind, the not-so-bad type."

"I know," she says, "I know." She shuts off the gas and turns with the wok in hand to fill the serving bowl on the counter. Michael stands in front of her, the bulk of his body cutting off the room from view. He has put his wine glass down and his arms hang at his sides as if she had just scolded him. *Hold me*, she thinks, *for God's sake take me in your arms and tell me it will be all right.* But in his eyes she sees hesitation. So many rebuffs in the past year. Years. She looks up at him and cries, "Oh God, the fish!"

"No, no," Michael says. He looks down the table to make sure he has everyone's attention. "That is precisely the wrong time to buy in. When the market is heading up, that's when you sell. You get out." He jabs one finger in the air, emphasizing the point.

"But we were thinking about mutual funds," Petra says. She's sitting across from Ashton, and she glances at him before continuing. "Maybe one of those combination funds. For our RSPs. Mixed funds, is that it?"

"Yes, sweetie," Ashton says. He winks at her across the table and they both smile, the way they smiled when she discovered a pelican feather on the beach earlier and stuck it behind his ear.

"It doesn't matter," Michael says. "Bonds, equities, resources, mixed. The whole system is so interconnected now by multinationals and computer trading that everything—in fact, everywhere—goes up and down at once. Hong Kong, Frankfurt, London in lock step with the Dow. The TSE too. And we're at the peak now."

Mark has been staring into his wine glass but he says in the silence that follows, "But you just said the whole system was spiraling downward. *Fin de siècle* vertigo. So, up and down at the same time?"

Michael laughs. He should have guessed it would be Mark who would trip him up. The youngest of their crowd, open-faced and perennially youthful, Mark seems at first to be sim-ple-minded, but he's cunning, he sees the angles in things. Too often in the past Michael has underestimated his brown eyes, which could be mistaken for vacant. But there's that puckish smile playing at the corners of Mark's full mouth. He is more than amused. Michael laughs again, a chortle, and then takes a sip from his wine glass and runs his eyes along the length of the table. Stephen is looking out the window as he chews on a mouthful of cheese, Colleen is passing Alix the plate of melon slices, Petra and Ashton are nodding at him, her hennaed hair sparking points of light from the candles on the table. Mary is fingering her napkin, a prelude to sudden action. In a few moments she will interrupt him by rising from the table and beginning preparations for dessert. Michael follows Stephen's gaze out the window: a cool gray light hangs over the lake. He answers Mark by saying to Petra, "Don't think of the market as a straight line, think of it as a circle. When you're in the top left-hand quadrant you're at the apex, where we are now. Everything hunky-dory. But at any moment you might begin the descent, plummeting down the slippery slope of the right-hand quadrant to financial ruin. Finito Benito."

"So don't buy," Petra says. She glances again at Ashton, who's fingering his salt-and-pepper beard and nodding. Though she's ten years older than he is, her conversation is a series of deferential bobs in his direction.

"Not the market," Michael says.

"Ah," Stephen says around his mouthful. "What then?"

Michael takes another sip of wine and holds the glass up to light. "This is good," he says to Mark, who is sitting beside him on the right, "very good."

Mark says, "I had the '86, too, but even though it's an older vintage this is better. They're saying '89 is going to be the best year since '78."

Michael says, "The French. You can't beat them."

"I liked the Verde," Petra says.

"It was lovely," Mark says. "Crisp."

"Perfect for the fish," Mary says. She looks at Michael and smiles the way she used to smile all the time. That was when she couldn't tell him often enough how much she loved him.

Michael pictures them tangled in the sheets in the bedroom behind his back, his body on top of hers. Breasts, thighs. He likes the way she grunts near her climax. Whatever he might do with Sandy—with whomever—really would be a fling. This is what he wants, Mary. No—not wants, needs. He swallows hard and says, "Real estate."

"Get real," Ashton says. He's reached across for the bottle of Bordeaux that Michael and Mark have been hoarding down at their end of the table and is pouring his glass full. "All these condos, these MURB things, are going under. Pembina Highway is a picket fence of For Sale signs these days."

"Ah, yes," Michael says, "residential has pooped out, and commercial is right on its heels. But I'm not talking about that." He takes another sip of wine. "Cottage properties," he says. "That's the ticket." He waits for a silence to open and then adds, "The baby boomers, see, they're all finished buying up their city homes and now they're starting to acquire cottages. By the end of the decade, the century, you won't be able to buy a cottage. For one like this"—he waves his arm in an arc—"right on the lake and whatnot, you won't be able to touch it for less than a hundred grand—one fifty. Probably a lot more." He picks a piece of melon off his plate and pops it in his mouth. "That's the ticket," he repeats. "It's all in the demographics, see. The boomers are this inflated population bubble that passed first through the schools and college system—all those hirings in the late sixties and seventies, remember the golden years—and then through the housing market. Now they're poised to stampede cottage country."

He stops and then adds, "And they're loaded, they've got cash."

Stephen says, "Well, we've got our places, touch wood. We won't be adding fuel to that capitalist fire."

"Buy just property, if that's all you can afford," Michael says. He feels his cheeks warming. He smiles back at Mary. "Lakefront preferable."

"Um," Petra says. She's poured a little of the Bordeaux into her glass and is taking small sips. She asks Ashton, "What do you say, sweetie?"

"This Bordeaux is delicious," Ashton says. "What is it?"

"About buying," Petra insists. "About cottage property."

"Could be," Ashton says. His glance moves from Petra's face to Michael's, as if waiting for Michael to add more.

"I don't think so," Mark blurts out. "Demographics. Number crunchers. Anyone can predict anything, but they were all wrong about the baby boomers having babies, remember? It just did not happen."

"The baby bust," Alix says. She laughs and then adds with a sigh, "What a generation." She looks directly at Mark and says, sticking her chin out at him, "Couldn't even get it up."

"Hey," Mark says. His voice sounds like a slap in the face but the look he gives Alix across the table is pure caress. In her early twenties, she's half Mark's age, a slight blonde with a muscular body, and a gravelly voice that Michael finds irresistible. Along with her firm legs and buttocks. She cycles to work every day, runs on the weekends, plays field hockey. Her face is a perpetual grin. She must be great in bed.

"I don't know," Petra says. She wrinkles her brow, then reaches for the Verde and fills her glass.

"The properties out here," Michael says, "have all been gobbled up."

"Ah, yes," Mark says, "lakefront. Baby boomers are big on lakefront the same as they're big on Beamers. They love the high end. But take my word for it, you won't be able to sell a place at Winnipeg Beach—or any of those places—in a few years—unless it's lakefront."

Stephen says, "It's a spoiled generation, no doubt about that." Stephen has always said that, Michael realizes, though he likes the students he teaches at the college and has no fantasies of retiring early and scribbling poems. No, Stephen is that most rare of academics, the contented man.

"Take me, for instance," Mark is continuing, "I'm one of the two actual boomers here, right, and I don't own a cottage and have no intention of buying one." He sets his wine glass down sharply on the table and Michael sees his own face reflected there, flushed with intensity, leaning in to catch every word. This is what he likes, he realizes, bantering back and forth with friends over a good wine as the candlelight forms a cocoon around them. This is what he loves: a good meal, a great wine, and the chatter of friends.

"Yeah," Petra says. "But Ashton is the other baby boomer here and he does have a cottage." Her voice is brittle. She's the host of a national TV arts program, with two children from a previous marriage. An expert interviewer, she is used to being in control, and she does not expect contradiction, so her lips pinch in when Mark clears his throat and shakes his head.

"No," says Mark. "You own the cottage and that takes him out of the pool of buyers. Which is precisely my point."

Petra's mouth opens but before she can speak Michael says, "The real point is you two are hardly typical." He smirks at Ashton and then Mark. "You two with your bookend beauties." He pauses for a moment but no one takes him up, so he adds, "Check it out is what I'm saying. That's all. The market is going to crash any day now, so if you want something reliable, some *thing* that is going to be *there* when the Wall Street house of cards caves in, check out cottage property. Right, hon?"

Mary looks at him. "Right," she says. She stands suddenly,

smoothing her sweater down the front of her body, and Michael thinks *abdomen, belly button, breasts.* "But in the meantime," Mary says, "let's check out dessert."

Bullshit, bullshit, bullshit, Mary thinks. She is closing the cottage door behind her and looking carefully down, watching where she places her feet. In the darkness it is easy to slip on the decking. Evening dew, a transparent scum on the slick Varathane finish. Twist an ankle. She turns round the corner of the cottage and makes for the shed, set back in a lilac hedge, where there's an extra refrigerator and where she has stored the desserts for the evening meal. Tiramisu, pecan pie, and chocolate cheesecake, Michael's favorite. *Why?* Mary whispers under her breath. She knows why. Still, it bugs her. There's a real estate expert sitting at the table but *he* has to explain what's going on, *he* has to be the one in the know, the man with bestseller knowledge, second-hand and wrong. And he has it all topsy-turvy. As usual. Her fists are clenched, she realizes, tight as walnuts, when she reaches the step down to the lawn and has to grasp the railing around the deck to steady herself to the grass below. Stop here. Count ten. Breathe. Relax the muscles in the shoulders, the neck. His voice a tin flute, diminishing. Mary breathes in deeply. The scent of the lake. Leaves that have fallen already. Rot. Overhead the sky is a slab, obsidian. Half moon, angry. The air cool on her hot face, breath from the lake. Mary puts one hand over her breast. She inhales the air off the lake and half turns to face the breeze when she hears a rustle in the lilac bushes. *Mary?*

Her heart skips. *Rape*, she thinks. *Rapier in the guts.* This is the moment to flee, to cry out, but she turns and steps forward, her sandals unsure of the footing, and as she toes the ground a form emerges from behind the shed, a slight form, female. "Mary?"

"Who is it?" she says, though she knows the voice but is afraid to utter the name. Not here. Not on his turf.

"Come over here, out of the light, babes."

She takes two hesitant steps. "Jilly," she whispers. "Whatever . . ."

"Shh." Jilly puts out her arms, grasps Mary's shoulders with her fingers, then the full embrace. The scent of shampoo, Safari. Texture of linen on Mary's cheek.

Now Mary is breathing hard, heart pounding, wishing she were the one with her back to the lilacs, facing the cottage and the imminent disaster about to materialize through its screened door: Michael's silhouetted form. Oh God. And yet a warmth is spreading through her, too, as if a sore muscle were suddenly being released. She folds her arms around Jilly's back, closes her eyes to drink her in. They are silent for a moment, breathing. Then she pulls away and looks into Jilly's face. "You're crazy," she says. "Coming here."

"I don't know what happened exactly. One minute I'm drinking white wine and listening to the stereo and the next I'm in the car speeding here."

"Um," Mary says. "Chardonnay. Me too." She runs the tip of her tongue up between her front lip and teeth, sucking down the last of its taste.

"Something German, actually," Jilly says. "Burklin Wolff."

"What," Mary says, "what were you listening to?"

Jilly hesitates a moment. In the shadows her eyes are hidden but huge, black buttons in her moon face. "Natalie," she says, "Natalie Merchant."

"I thought so," Mary says. "You're always crazy then."

"I couldn't help it. I was moping and brooding. You out here with all your friends, drinking and laughing."

"Believe me," Mary says, "I would rather."

"No," Jilly says. "Jilly was watching you through the window. You're all so happy and relaxed. You too, babes."

They have moved back into the shadows of the shed,

hidden from the cottage, though Mary has taken a stance where she has a clear sight-line to the deck. Jilly's hand is in hers. Rings, longer fingers than you would expect. She played the harp in school, Mary has seen pictures in an album. Shoulder-length hair on a peaceful-looking girl, round eyes, freckles, dimples. Field hockey. Warm fingers. Strong. Mary says, "I have to go right back in."

"I know." Jilly's voice is hardly a whisper. Pleading.

"It's the dessert. I only came out for the dessert."

"I know," Jilly says. "I looked in the refrigerator. Cheesecake."

"You looked," Mary says. She shakes her head and squeezes Jilly's fingers. "You crazy, you."

"Marvelous texture. Yummy."

"You didn't."

"Look. Smell Jilly's fingers."

Mary wrenches Jilly's hand up to her nose. "Teasing," she whispers. She laughs, but her eyes keep the deck in sight. "Always teasing, you."

"I did," Jilly says. She squeezes Mary's fingers again. "Maybe it was the other. Yes," she sings, raising one arm in the air, "the other."

"You're just crazy."

"So I knew you would be coming out." Jilly pulls in close to Mary and tightens her arm against Mary's and whispers in her ear, "I knew you'd be coming out for the desserts, I just prayed that you would be alone."

"You're crazy," Mary repeats. Thinks of Jilly standing in the shadows, a sentinel over love. Thinks of when she and Michael used to meet in parking lots, at pizza places. The driving. The heart racing. Sex in the back seats of cars, under trees in parks. Thinks of Patty of the full breasts and insatiable tongue. It will be warm in Vancouver, warm and wet.

"I had to see you," Jilly insists. "Period." Breath warm in Mary's ear, the air around her head cool.

She twitches her neck, chills racing up and down her spine. "I have to go," she says, "really. But tomorrow."

"Yes," Jilly says. "The whole afternoon." She shivers. How long has she been standing on the wet grass? Jilly presses close again and whispers, "Forgive me?"

"Of course. It was just crazy."

"Jilly's young," Jilly whispers. "Isn't she supposed to be?"

"I guess."

"Wild and crazy?" Jilly tugs her arm, cackles.

Mary hesitates. From her vantage point she sees the bank of windows along the back of the cottage, the reflections of the people gathered around her table, distorted by the angle from which she's looking. Someone waving an arm. Someone standing and moving toward the back of the cottage. Voices. Laughter. She doesn't know how to tell Jilly, but begins, "It's just that you are always . . . you're the cool one." She pauses. "You."

"Me," Jilly says. "An act."

"You hang up the phone."

"A surface." Jilly presses her shoulder against Mary's. "I studied the movies," she says. "Surfaces. Gestures. Poses."

"You have rules about when we meet. Rules about—"

"They're for me. For Jilly."

Mary feels her cheeks flush. "No," she says.

"Don't you get it? Real estate lady?"

"Shh," Mary says. "Not too loud."

Jilly tugs her arm again, insistent. "I love you," she whispers. "Don't you understand anything?"

Mary looks at the ground. A moment ago she was hot but now she feels the skin of her legs is sprouting goose flesh. It is almost autumn. The breeze carries ice from the north in its teeth. Soon the geese. Mary clears her throat. "Right up until this moment I thought I understood everything," she whispers," but now I think maybe I'm just an old dodo bird."

Michael is sitting at the end of the sofa farthest from the counter which separates the kitchen appliances from the remainder of the one large room that comprises the main living area of the cottage, but closest to the fire, sipping from a snifter of Hennessey. Up to a moment ago Stephen was sitting on the chair next to him, but in the way of such gatherings, he has suddenly stepped across the room to speak with Petra and Ashton. Was it about his upcoming trip to Portugal? Michael has never been to Portugal, or Spain, either, though both interest him in a way. Maybe it's the tart wines, maybe it's an impression he has that the Iberian Peninsula is rocky and a tiny bit inhospitable, like the shield country a hundred miles east of where he sits looking out over Lake Winnipeg. It's a beautiful evening. The sun set over an hour ago but a few squiggles of purple and red float on the horizon, wisps of summer light. A breeze is blowing in at the window, which he left open a crack when he went out a few minutes ago to make certain the barbecue was correctly shut off. After he sips from the snifter, he cocks his head. If you strain your ears you can just hear the clatter of frogs over the chatter of conversation in the room. Michael leans back. It is a good life, despite Jane, despite Meagan, despite all their shit. Kids. Do what you will, they break your heart. He looks across the room and catches Mary's eye. She looks happy, flushed with the success of her party, he guesses. Maybe tonight when their guests have departed and they are alone in the silent cottage he will lift the satin top she wears to bed over her breasts. Maybe tonight she will run her cool fingers along his thighs. He has just begun to imagine the silk of her skin when Mark eases himself into the chair vacated by Stephen.

"You look happy," he says to Michael.

Michael laughs. "I gave up on *happy* a long time ago. Content, maybe."

Mark lifts his glass, soda water, in a toasting gesture, and says, "In any case, happy returns to you, big guy. And many more."

"Thanks," Michael says. He returns Mark's toasting gesture and sips from the snifter, sucking the oaky aroma into his palate and holding it there. "Yet another reminder that we're on the downward slope."

"Right," Mark says. He gazes over Michael's head out the window.

After Michael has run the brandy round his mouth a few times he lets it slide down his gullet. He enjoys the burnt wood taste almost as much as he enjoys good wine. "That was a fine Bordeaux," he says to Mark.

Mark smiles. "You're one of the few people I know who enjoys a good wine. Who it's really worth sharing one with."

"I know," Michael says. "I've been meaning to say that very thing to you for some time now." He laughs.

"Well, it's out in the open, then. Our snobbery."

"Exactly." Michael returns Mark's conspiratorial smile. "You know," he says, "I used to worry about what kind of wine people brought over for dinner. Thought I had to make up for their bad taste by always having good wine at the ready. Put whatever they brought aside and pour out the good stuff. Not any more. Now I figure, drink what you bring. If you bring bad wine that's what you must prefer, so drink it. You see?"

Mark laughs. "I do." He tips his glass in a gesture of toasting again and says, "So here's to snobbery. Our snobbery."

Michael laughs and Mark laughs too. There was a time they would have been mortified to admit they were snobs about anything, much less something as effete as wine. "So," Michael says, "are you two taking the bikes back to the Beaune this summer? Or is it the Dordogne this time?"

"England, in fact. The Cotswolds."

"Hills."

"And valleys," Mark says, smiling. "Give the old pins a workout." At the counter Stephen laughs suddenly, a sharp barking sound, and both Michael and Mark cut their eyes that way before looking back at each other. Alix, Michael notices, as his gaze shifts, is standing before the fireplace, studying the leaping flames. Mary and Colleen are sitting at the table with glasses of liqueur, talking quietly. Everyone seems content. He is content. This is the good life, the life he loves. Yes. If life were a game, he could on a night like this be tempted to cry out *home free*.

Michael says, "Britain is dead. It's all over. The Empire and whatnot."

"Britain, and England, too," Mark says, nodding. "But not the English countryside." He sips from his soda water and looks out the window again. After a moment he adds, "Or the English people, for that matter."

"Hated them," Michael says. "No warmth."

Mark says, "They're not the Italians. But then they're not the Greeks or the Turks either. Thankfully. They're hot but it cuts both ways. You can get stabbed in those places if you look at someone the wrong way. No, give me English reserve, if I have to choose. In any case, I have a soft spot for those Northern types. We're both from that stock, Alix and me."

Michael says, "You're right about the countryside, I'll grant you that."

He hadn't noticed but Alix has come over to join them. She seems about to say something when Mark puts his free hand out and places it on her hip. "Actually," he says, "there was something I wanted to tell you tonight, something I should have told you all before."

The conversation about the room, Michael notices, suddenly drops, as alert to the slight shift in Mark's tone as birds sitting on a telephone line about to take flight are alert to each flutter of wing. Michael turns in his chair to look Mark in the eye, but he does not say anything.

"The thing of it is," Mark says, "I have cancer."

For a moment Ashton and Stephen, elbows on the counter at the far end of the room, continue to chuckle about a joke they've just shared, but then the silence in the room becomes palpable. Their voices cease. As if on command, they shift their gazes to the far end of the room. "Oh my," says Petra, who, too, has materialized suddenly and is standing at Alix's side.

Not that, Michael thinks, *not cancer.* He blinks once at Mark and says, "But you look . . . you seem . . . "

"He is okay," Alix says.

"Well, maybe," Michael says, "that has nothing . . ."

"It doesn't," Mark says. He looks around. Mary and Colleen have risen from the table, Stephen and Ashton are staring down the length of the room, their faces pictures of puzzlement. "It's a tumor," Mark adds, "in the brain." He taps his skull behind his left ear. "Right there, actually."

Mary has crossed the room and is standing beside Michael. "It's so—so frightening," she says.

"Pushing away at the old gray matter," Mark says. He laughs, a small sound in the silent room.

"They came across it in a routine test," Alix is saying. "He was getting these headaches and the neurologist sent him for a scan."

Not that, Michael thinks. *Tumors, the brain.* "Oh God," he says.

"That's right," says Colleen, echoing Mary. "It's frightening."

"But there's this operation," Mark says. He's holding Alix's hand now, but still sitting, still cradling the glass of soda water in his other hand. "They go in, and in an hour they're out again. Just like that." He looks up at Alix, who's nodding at him, staring down, her blue eyes big, though whether with wonder, admiration, or fear it is impossible to tell. Mark's voice quavers when he adds, "If they get it all . . ."

"Let's hope," Mary says.

"Yes," Colleen says.

Michael thinks, *I need brandy.*

Petra is biting her lip. "I'm ... I don't know what to say."

"There is nothing to say," Ashton says from the far end of the room, flatly, though it sounds like a rebuke. "Christ."

Petra stares at him, and Stephen, too, who is nodding his head from side to side, lips pursed. He is patting his abdomen with his free hand and looks pale, as if he were about to faint. He lifts his glass of brandy to his lips.

"I wanted to tell you before," Mark says. "But it's hard to know when."

"It's all right," Mary says. She places her hand on Mark's shoulder, but in a moment withdraws it.

Michael is swallowing hard, trying to think of something to say. What he thinks is, *brandy, I need brandy.*

Ashton says, "There is no when."

He sits down suddenly on the nearest chair, and Petra goes over to him, kneels, and puts her hand on his brow. "Sweetie," she asks, "are you okay?"

Mark stands, nearly tipping over the chair he's been sitting on. "Look," he says, pointing, "there's a car pulling into the driveway. No, not a car, a truck, a van actually."

Mary is standing beside Michael, who is standing facing Jane and Brad in the beam of the van's headlights. Michael has his arms pressed to his sides. A moment ago they were holding hands, but when Michael put his free hand up to reposition his Tilley hat, he also released Mary's fingers from his grip. *Bark of elm*, she thinks. *Gnarled.* He is a big man who looks gigantic in the glare of the vehicle's lights, towering over stocky Brad, who has not shaven in days, it appears, and Jane, hunkered down in a dark windbreaker beside him. Waif. Urchin. The girl's body is so slight. Sticks for fingers,

Popsicle sticks. It has not rained but Jane's mass of red hair
has turned bird's-nest, after-rain frizzy. She is chewing her
lower lip, muttering monosyllables, trying not to tell them,
not to tell Michael, who is doing his best not to ask.

Mary shifts from one foot to the other. Rests her eyes on
the gravel patch between Michael and Brad. When they
came out on the deck, she and Michael, she glanced briefly
in the direction of the shed. Did she see a slight form there,
edging back into the shadows? Feather tugged by wind? She
tried not to look. Has been trying not to the whole time they
have been standing on the driveway, talking in subdued voices, her ears tuned for the sound of a distant motor starting,
perhaps behind the bushes to the west of the cottage.
Headlights flickering through the trees. Her breath is irreg-
ular. She gulps air, tries to steady herself, to take in the words
going back and forth, luckily not recriminations this time,
though her mind keeps jumping to the bushes behind them.
Love, she keeps hearing.

Mary shivers. It is cold now. Surely Jilly is not still standing behind the shed in her thin linen shirt. Teal, scent of yellow flowers and ambergris. Mary herself has come out without the Irish sweater she keeps by the door of the cottage.
They were running. *Jane?* She hugs her arms around her
breasts and tries to relax. She read somewhere that when
your muscles tense up, you feel colder. By now, she hopes,
Jilly is in her warm car, speeding back down the highway to
the city. Mary paws the gravel with the toe of one sandal. She
has been trying to follow the conversation but only phrases
have stuck with her. Brad said *it won't happen again*, and
Michael, *I'm trusting you with those kiddies*. Somewhere in
there Jane said *oh, Daddy*. Brad said, *pills, man, and then beer
on top*. And Michael, *drugs?* And Brad *just shit, pure shit*. And
then Jane said again *oh, for God's sake, Daddy*, and Michael, *it's
the kiddies I'm worried about*. Brad is wearing a hockey sweater
under a leather jacket, open. Logo of one of the new teams

in California. That mask from the teen screamer movies Meggy used to go to a decade or more ago. Both his hands are thrust in the pockets of his jeans, and like Jane's his shoulders are hunched forward. He looks diminished. On his feet he wears boots, Doc Martens. They both look repentant and scared. Defeated. Such a scrawny pair, kids, at any moment they could put out their thumbs and set about hitchhiking home. And yet they have two kids of their own. The kids have Brad's dark skin. He's from east European stock. Hungarian? He is saying *flipped out, just total shit, won't happen again*. And Michael is nodding, tongue protruding between his lips. He shifts from one foot to the other.

There is a pause in the conversation. The motor of the van is running and Mary watches the exhaust rise past the red taillights and into the air above the roof. She shifts her feet. Gravel in the open toe of her sandal. One time Meggy came home from a school field trip with tiny round stones she found on a beach. Pink, streaks of pearl white. Rough to the touch, tongue of kittens. Mary has them in a box in the basement. Stones, photos, locks of hair. Her child in a cardboard box. And Tuesday it's more tests, a new scan, a different neurologist. Meggy is adamant about keeping her apartment, *toughing it out*, she says, brave kid, but if she has to stop working, who will pay the rent, the phone bill, groceries? She was just barely on her feet, just getting it together. Mary can see what's coming. So can Michael.

Maybe, Mary thinks, that's why he's been so testy lately. For a few days she feared he had discovered something. Tossing in bed. A log rolling down a roiling river. But maybe it's only these crises with the kids. He's a worrier, a brooder. Sits in his chair and looks out the window. He keeps it all in, silent as stone, but then drinks half a bottle of Scotch to knock himself out before bed, and then comes an attack of the hives. Arms dotted with knots of white flesh. Scratching. Daubing on the cortisone cream. Mary looks at his face, looking at Jane's. She's saying, *both great, just sleeping under an old army blanket in the back.* She tips her head in the direction of the van. Even in the blue dark of the August night Mary can see the rust spots on the van's body, plates actually, around the wheel wells and beneath the door panels. The radio antenna is a bent piece of clothes hanger fastened onto the stump where the aerial was snapped off. One tire is soft. Probably the sleeping tots are not wearing seat belts.

Mary sucks the autumn air into her lungs. Smell of something burning. Not firewood. And it's too late for the farmers to be burning stubble. She inhales again and sighs aloud. Jane looks at her. When the eyes of the two women meet, Jane drops hers but not before Mary has seen the knives of light thrown her way. Jane has never forgiven them, her, for what happened more than twenty years ago. This is what she hates. The iron hardness of the young, their refusal to forgive. She will carry Jane's hatred with her to the grave, whatever Michael says about forgive and forget, whatever her mother said about time healing all wounds. She decides, standing there on the gravel, that she's had it with Jane. After all the years of trying to please the girl, she's out of that game. It's not her problem, it's Michael's. She has her own kid to worry about. Besides, she's never really liked Jane, though she's bent over backward to win her over. *So fuck you, too.* Mary takes a deep breath. She can hardly believe she thought that. Fears for a moment she may have said it aloud. But no, Jane and Michael continue to talk in quiet voices, their heads bent forward, ghosts of breath escaping from their mouths. Behind her in the cottage Mary hears the clatter of plates. Her guests are clearing up. In a few minutes they will be pulling on sweaters, starting motors. Goodbyes, hugs in the driveway. She glances at her watch: 11:45. She's exhausted. Grit in the tear ducts.

Michael is saying *at least come in for a beer,* but Jane has one hand up and Brad mutters something about *enough for a while*. He tries to laugh but it comes out a sputtering snort. He drops his eyes to the ground.

Michael asks Jane, "You're okay?"

Jane is starting to turn toward the van, anxious to be on the road back to the city, but she pauses and says quietly, "Yes."

"It's late," Michael says. "A long drive in the dark."

"We're okay," Jane insists.

Brad is standing beside the van, one hand gripping the door handle. "We wanted you to see," he says. "Right away like."

"To see you," Jane says.

"That was good of you," Mary says.

"It was," Michael says. He has reached down and located Mary's hand, squeezes her fingers. His palm is hot. He says, "I'll call you tomorrow."

"Mañana," Brad says.

"We're okay," Jane calls. She is opening the door on her side of the van, stepping in and holding one hand up in a gesture of farewell. "We are," she repeats, "really." And then the headlights are receding down the driveway.

Michael's face is in the pillow. He shifts his hips so his mouth is free of the pillowcase and he can breathe easier. Bright red dots dance on his closed eyelids, expanding and contracting with the insistent pounding of his heart. He breathes through his nose. Beside him he can hear Mary panting, though he can no longer smell the Chardonnay of her mouth, their breaths have mixed so thoroughly. He feels numbness creeping up from his abdomen to his chest and knows in a few seconds he will lose consciousness. This is what he loves. Fucking. Animal pleasure. Brute but not brutal. If only it weren't for the burning sensation in his groin he would drop into oblivion and remain there for hours, perhaps until morning. But they went at it hard, too hard, and he feels a burning sensation from his belly button to the tip of his penis. Maybe something got strained, muscles in the abdomen or lower. He will probably hurt for weeks. Still, it was a wonderful piece of tail, though he knows he is not supposed to call it that, *piece of tail*, too fifties for the end-of-the-century man, insensitive. That screwing was the perfect antidote to their long discussion of Mark's cancer, Michael's queasy stomach, his fear of death. Michael sighs. *Lovemaking*, then, a pallid word to describe what they were just doing, but right for the times, right for Mary. He opens his eyes. She is studying his face, as he guessed, her blue eyes glassy, cheeks flushed. He loves the way her perfectly coiffed hair tangles and mats during sex. She cried out at her climax and tightened the grip of her ankles on the backs of his thighs. He puts his hand out and touches her cheek, traces the line of her cheekbone in the contour of her face.

"You all right?" he asks.

"Uh-huh."

"I didn't hurt you?"

"No," she says. She shifts her weight and he thinks she is going to turn her back to him, as she has several times recently, but instead she reaches out her hand and touches his face. "You were talking earlier like somebody who believed what they were saying." Her voice is soft, almost inaudible.

"Red wine, you mean?"

"No, the market. Buying cottages and lake property."

"Oh," he says. "That." It seems like days ago. His mind is blurred by alcohol and drowsy with sex. He cannot remember clearly what he said. "You don't agree," he tries, hoping to draw her out.

"I do, actually. Though Mark has a point. We haven't seen an upswing in sales in cottage country, as you might have predicted. They."

"Yeah," he says. He closes his eyes. Sleep is moments away.

Mary asks, "Is that what you intend to do? Buy up the remaining lots on Willow Island?"

He inhales and exhales twice before answering, counting to himself: *one, two*. When Jane was a baby, colicky, he had to do that forty-three times after she first snored before he could be certain she'd fallen asleep. "Funny, that," he says. He senses his voice is drifting away with his consciousness. "That is precisely what I have not done."

"With the money from your father's estate?"

"Uh-huh."

"You put it in GICs, in bonds?"

"No," he says. He opens one eye. "I did something a little crazy," he says. He's been dreading this moment, but in the stupor of post-coital slumber the revelation does not seem as momentous as he had imagined it would be in the light of day. In any case, he's done with the idea of retirement. He studies Mary's face for a few seconds and then adds, "A limited partnership."

"A condo?" Mary's voice has rung up sharp, like the bell at the circus that clangs when you get the hammer down just right.

"No," he says, happy to have dodged her reproach, if only for a moment. He pauses while he listens to his thumping heart and says, "Bees, actually."

"Beans?"

"*Bees.*"

Mary has pulled herself up on one elbow. "Honey bees?"

"Yes," he says. "The honey industry is exploding on the prairies. It's the right climate for the strain of bees which has evolved. More important, there are few diseases in the wild plants hereabouts." He too has elevated his torso. "Kroft says it's going to be as big as jojoba beans were a decade ago. They made millions. Shampoos and all that."

Mary says, "Honey," incredulous.

"No threat of killer bees up here in the Great White North."

"Hives, honeycombs, pollen. That stuff?"

"It's a real science, apparently. The retrieving and production end of it. Breeding, brood cells, the storage of pollen." He looks into Mary's eyes. They are glazed, and not with alcohol only. She is frightened—and angry.

She shakes her head and snorts through her nose. "You're one crazy cowboy," she says. "You just went ahead and bought into it."

"Yup."

"You didn't want to talk about it first? Hear my opinion?"

"I didn't want to risk your disapproval. The thunderstorm I see on the horizon of your eyes this very minute." He puffs his cheeks out with a blow of air. He shouldn't have said that. He can taste the residue of wines and liqueurs on his gums. He has forgotten to brush his teeth. They will be stained purple.

She closes her eyes, shutting him out, and when she reopens them says, "The whole fifty thousand, then?"

"Yes. In for a penny etcetera."

"Wow." Mary shakes her head again.

Michael sinks down into the pillow. "It's a solid thing," he says in a weary voice. "Pretty solid. As solid as it gets. Last year they hit twenty-five percent net return, Kroft says, and over the past five, eighteen average."

"Honey bees," Mary says again. They are silent for a minute. Michael listens to the calls of night birds in the bushes outside the window. Something rustles in the grass and underbrush. Michael thinks again of Mark, of cancer cells multiplying in a tumor and pressing against his skull. Absent-mindedly he places his hand on his abdomen. The burp is coming, he knows it. Mary says, "It's a seasonal thing, right?"

"Strictly seasonal."

"So what happens to the bees in winter? They die?"

"Heavens, no." Michael blinks his eyes, eager to explain. "You'd lose everything you'd built up that way. Have to start over each spring. That would be a risky investment." He pauses for a moment. "But that's the beauty of the beekeeping industry today. The advances they've made. Now they put the hives away in the autumn. Winter storage."

"And the bees?"

"Well, some die, the natural cycle etcetera, but the queen of every hive and a select number of workers, they put them to sleep in the hives in barns, huge specially adapted barns."

"What, they gas them?" She's looking into his face. Her eyes are no longer glassy, though there is still a residue of anger there.

"Precisely. A mild dose of a mild gas. Just enough to keep them under until springtime rolls around. Then they're all primed up for another summer. Up and at 'em, get that honey rolling in."

"Jesus," Mary says. She is silent for a minute. "What if they wake up too soon? Start intermingling—wouldn't that mess things up?"

"A guy goes around every week or so in the spring to make sure that doesn't happen. It's all under control."

"Or what if they give them too much gas? The wrong gas?"

Michael had felt himself on the verge of oblivion a few moments earlier but he realizes his eyes are wide open now. The gray cells have started to re-align themselves. "Not to worry," he says. "Those things don't happen. Never have. Besides, it's a limited partnership, remember?"

"Exactly," Mary says. "That does not mean what people think it does. That their liability is limited merely to what they've invested. No way. When a limited partnership goes down, it takes its investors with it. You've read about all those doctors and lawyers in the States screaming blue murder about condos in Florida that are falling apart faster than wet cardboard? Well, they're not just pissed off about losing what they initially invested. No. Now they find out it's not just the hundred grand or whatever they first put in that's at risk. Legally, it turns out, they're on the hook for the entire project."

"I hadn't," Michael says. He swallows once. "I had not read that." Though he is not thinking of that but of Mark lying on an operating table in a hospital. He will be gassed too.

"Well, maybe you should have," Mary says. She sinks down into the pillows with a sigh. "Or taken the time to ask someone who had. Jesus."

"Don't worry, honey."

"You will let me see the prospectus? Figure out how much we're on the hook for if the whole thing goes down the spout?"

Michael closes his eyes. Once you've missed the drift of post-coital slumber you can lie for hours staring at the ceiling. And he feels a headache coming on: wine, brandy, rich food. Fretting about death. "Don't worry, *honey*," he says in what he hopes is an arch tone. He reaches out for Mary's hand and squeezes her cold fingers in his. "Everything will *be* all right."

Mary wakes with a start. She does not know for a moment where she is and experiences the sensation that she is falling backwards into darkness, arms flailing out at her sides, a sensation she has occasionally in dreams and dreads. The abyss. One hand claws the air reflexively. Her neck snaps to the side and she sees in front of her, much closer than she's used to, the red numbers of a digital clock radio: 3:18. The cottage. That's why the room is so black, curtain of night. Mary sinks back in the pillow with a sigh. Pulse racing. She lifts one hand to her forehead. A headache is building there, a big one. *Should have drunk water*, she thinks to herself, *should get up right now and down two large tumblers of ice-cold water.* Hangover is merely a matter of dehydration, Jilly claims, and the few times Mary has had the discipline to drink water, lots of water, after alcohol, she has, in fact, not experienced headache. So Jilly is right. How does she know things like that? She also knows which muscles hurt in Mary's body after they've been working out. Their peculiar names. How to relax the muscles with finger massage. Mary closes her eyes and feels the throbbing in her temples ease. *Love*, she thinks. Beside her she hears Michael snoring and snuffling. Up until the time of his heart attack he was a light sleeper, started at the sound of a motor in the neighborhood, but in the period after he came out of the hospital and was doing the cardiac refit routine he was taking a mild sedative along with the nitroglycerin pills, out like a pig every night, and even when he quit the sedative he kept on sleeping as if he'd been hit on the head with a brick. She glances over at him. He sleeps on his back. White hair matted on the pillow, muscles in his cheeks twitching. Her man.

The sex was good—great—she has to admit that. Men's mouths hunger for breasts. Then there's penetration. That pounding of bone on bone at the pubis. Powerful arms crushing her torso. The weight of chest on chest. And Michael had had just the perfect amount to drink. Lasted her into a second and nearly third orgasm. How long has it been since that? She thinks to herself, *relax*, and tries to relax the muscles round her eyes. Temples. Tracks dots in the vague shape of digital numbers across the inside of her eyelids before they fade away. Retinal comets. Her mouth is incredibly dry. She needs water.

It's a good thing Michael does sleep so soundly these days because in the past year or so Mary has been getting up and prowling the house in the dead of night. Why does she wake up? She falls asleep well but then wakes somewhere past 3:00 AM and cannot coax herself back to sleep until 5:00 or so. She hates taking pills, so at first when she started waking up this way she got up and drank warm milk, her mother did that years ago, but all that did was give Mary gas. Then she took to watching late-night TV. Unbelievably stupid stuff. She tried reading. Her eyes burned. Writing. Had nothing to say. She considered doing something useful, ironing, but that seemed too purposeful. She feared she would become involved in the task and stay awake into the day, altering the rhythms of her life. Become an insomniac. So now she sits in a comfortable chair and plays a game she calls mental solitaire, a game she imagines herself playing someday in an old folks' home, though they don't call them that these days. Golden-age centers or some such thing.

She rises from the bed, being careful not to disturb the duvet. Crosses the bedroom on tiptoe and goes directly to the bathroom, where she hangs her robe. In one pocket there is a pair of wool socks, which she slips on before returning to the big room of the cottage. Pours a tumbler of water at the sink and downs it. Mineral taste. Iron, maybe limestone. Mary sucks her teeth. Pours a second tumbler to the brim and brings it with her into the semi gloom of the sitting room. She glides over to the wing-backed chair and settles down, feet propped on the coffee table. It is still extremely dark outside. The stars are tiny diamonds the gods have sprinkled on the heavens. She sips from the tumbler of water. Thinks, *I hate this stuff, it's no wonder people don't drink enough of it.*

Tonight the card she has decided to flip for mental solitaire is their trip to Munich a decade ago. That's the game: recall a wonderful time from the past, a magic time, the kind that defines the value of living, and drag from the vaults of memory every detail, hold them in the mind's eye and say, *yes, yes, this is why we go on, this is what makes a life.* The beer they drank in the market square beneath the glockenspiel, for instance, green beer with tiny buds of unfermented stuff floating up in it, *weissbier* the Germans called it, and there was a name for the little buds of stuff, too, *phafel*-something, or *poppel*, something Mary cannot recollect, though Michael would, he drank three glasses of it. He was wearing a blue tweed jacket over a white shirt. She wore a dress, a crepe material, blue, and a sweater. No, a linen jacket. Mary takes another sip of water. Tonight mental solitaire is not going so well. Details are slipping Mary's mind. Whenever she begins to fix on something from that Munich afternoon she hears Jilly saying *love*.

What does love mean? Mary no longer knows. She knew when she was twenty. Guesses now that it's a term the young use to flatter themselves that lust is more than animal desire. That's too cruel. *Want* she understands. *Hold*. Whatever love means, Mary no longer has much truck with it. Fidelity she understands. But she doesn't mean something as simple-minded as not sleeping with someone other than your mate. Sleeping? Fucking. She means hanging in there over the long haul, being there through thick and thin. Years and years of it. Watching someone you care about grow old. And not getting sick to the stomach when they get fat around the middle or start to lose teeth. Mary sighs. The odors of burnt wood and of ashes tickle her nostrils. She shakes her head. Maybe there's more to that marriage blather about sickness and health than she once thought. She runs one hand over her forehead. The headache seems to be subsiding already. Incredible. She gulps the remainder of the water down in one swallow.

The way she's been there for Meggy, she thinks. And her mother was for her. Only will she be able to do anything for the kid this time? The doctors say not to worry, it's probably the slow-deterioration type of the disease, the occasional little bout of sickness and maybe the diminishment of certain body functions in twenty years or so. Almost a normal life-time. But what do they know? The kid might die before she does. Mary gets up to pour another tumbler of water. When she passes the window she hears the water lapping up the beach. Shh, shh. It's telling her to go to sleep. She thinks of her father in his casket. Face of wax. She kept saying *it's not him, it's not him, that is not my father.* Now she realizes her words probably upset her mother more than the death of her husband. Well, not more. No. And now Mark tells them he has cancer. She expects any day to pick up the phone and have Jilly tell her something dreadful has happened to *her.* That would be about the limit.

Mary eases into the wing-back chair. *Love.* Is that what she feels for Jilly? She likes being with her. There's an inti-macy you can develop with a woman that you cannot with a man. She'll have to think about that. And she's flattered by the fact Jilly is younger than she is. No denying that. Mary takes a swallow of water. That's not all there is to it, though, Jilly's young body. They laugh about the same things. Jilly has the poise and ease about her that kids who went to pri-vate schools seem to acquire behind those ivy-covered walls. Plays the flute. Rides a horse. Maybe Mary should take that up again. She knows people who have stables just outside the city limits. She loved riding. Horses. The pong of oats in the barn, horse dung. The way horses fidget from foot to foot, slobber on your fingers with their rubbery tongues. The way their muscles ripple under their skin. She had sex the first time in a barn. Hayloft. Stable boy—stable man, actually. She can smell the hay still. Hot that spring, the spring she graduated from high school, so she would have been what, seventeen? They did it without using anything for protec-tion. Crazy. But she loved it. Always has. She was told it would be awful, a thing women must endure, and has never understood what those women who said that to her were going on about.

But that wasn't love either, she knows that, too. Mary takes a long drink of water. If you don't think about it, the stuff doesn't taste so terrible, though the metals have oddly combined with the alcohol residues in her saliva, making her think *galvanized*. Does Jilly love her? She saw need in her eyes tonight, though she did not see it earlier. Thought that flicker was caution. Fear. Mary sighs and repositions her feet on the coffee table. She hasn't learnt to read Jilly well yet. She knows she has a fiery temper. Has witnessed that. Jilly broke a bottle of hand lotion on a counter of a department store in front of a startled salesgirl who had refused to let her sample it. *Try this on, bitch.* Would she be enraged if Mary said they had to stop seeing each other? Create a scene at the house in front of Michael? Their friends? She does have a violent streak.

Mary's eyes are tired. She looks out the window. Gray is beginning to come into the horizon. But around the door of the cottage there is a bluish gold hue, a pulsing ring of color. Mary blinks her eyes, expecting—she does not know why—to see her mother standing before her, but she sees instead a frog sitting on the table next to the door, a green spotted frog about the size of a beach ball. *Monstrous*, she thinks. It has huge bulging eyes which are staring at her, yellow eyes as big as softballs. The skin of its body is puffing in and out with each breath it takes; she is fascinated and repulsed by the way the frog's skeleton protrudes beneath the rubbery folds. She wants to cry out *go away!* but instead she finds herself asking, *who are you?* The frog blinks. *I am mud*, it says. Mary thinks *you're a frog, not mud, and what's more I don't like frogs, so go away*, and she intends to ask *what do you want?* but instead she says *what should I do?* The frog is silent for a moment, blinking its huge yellow eyes. *Go down in the mud*, the frog says. *Go down in the mud*, Mary repeats, and then she is not sure the frog said the words at all. She thinks maybe the words were merely her own thoughts echoing in her skull. She shakes her head. She remembers once when she was washing the dishes in the house in the city she distinctly heard her mother speak her name, *Mary*, softly but clearly; Mary jumped at the sound and looked about, expecting to see her mother, but she was alone in the kitchen, alone with her thudding heart. But that's how clear the frog's voice seemed, yet now the frog itself is fading, resolving into the golden bluish hues around the door frame. *Wait*, Mary cries out. She blinks and the frog is gone. *Mud?* she thinks. She stands. Touches one hand to her head. *Gotta stop drinking*, she thinks.

JILLY

Sunday, 26 August

It was crazy of me to drive out there. Irrational. Crazy to skulk in the shadows and wait for her to come out to me. My heart was beating, my palms were sweating. Teenagers do this, but not grown women. But that is what I am, irrational, and the thing which reasonable people do not quite grasp about those of us who are irrational is that we are completely that: beyond the scope of reason. Quite literally. To put it another way, I do not understand myself some times—I do not understand why I do certain things and say certain things. *Why.* There was a cat once who kept climbing onto the hood of my car at night, leaving its muddy paw prints tracked from the grille up the windshield and across the roof. I hated that cat. I swore at it every morning. Black bitch. Then one day I was doing some painting in the garage and the cat happened to poke its stupid head in and I dumped an entire can of enamel on it. Yellow, fluorescent yellow enamel. It must have choked to death, that black cat, died horribly under a bush somewhere trying to lick the paint away with its sticky pink tongue, but I was not sorry then and I am not sorry now. You see what I mean? Irrational. I recognize it, but recognizing you have reached the edge, recognizing you are twisted in some fundamental way does not necessarily change your behavior—does it Doctor Jung, whatever you may have said about the Zider Zee.

The phone calls, see, I cannot help myself. I punch in the numbers, I listen for his voice, I hold my breath, a thrill runs down my spine when I hear that plaintive second "hello," that tiny hitch of terror coming down the line. He swallows. He starts to sweat. He knows someone is messing with his head. My heart races. Will he stay on the line—*hello? hello?* I toy with him, then, breathing just enough so he knows someone is there. But who is it? I am bad and I know it. And love it. I love hurting people. Yes. There was a girl once in the days after Saint Hils, Nancy, I made her eat my shit. She was fucking some guy, see, Nancy Dearden, and that I cannot abide, being two-timed. I am not unathletic. I grabbed her by the hair. I wrestled her down, got my knees on her arms, pinioned, I believe is the word, and crammed a handful of shit in between her clenched teeth, her head was sawing from side to side, she had blonde hair, long blonde hair. Bitch. You do not fuck with me when I am fucking you.

So I don't know what I am capable of or what I might do next. I know my mind goes blank sometimes. I fantasize, though. I want to write something in blood, in my own sticky red menstrual blood, where he will find it. On his bathroom mirror. That appeals to the bitch in me. Or the windshield of his car. I have not formulated the words yet, though I'm looking for something to shock him. The lines of a poem, maybe. Something he recognizes, or half recognizes. Something that reverberates in the skull like a nightmare. Suck on this, Lord Wonderful. But then I am afraid she will stumble across my bloody message, not him, and what shall I do then? My lovely little Mary Moo. I cannot deliver the blow.

But then tonight I said *love*. Three hours ago. A mere two bottles of Chardonnay past. Ridiculous. And she is standing there in the semi-gloom with her mouth gawping like a guppy fish. Do not ask me if I meant it, I do not know myself. I must have in some way, yet I hold with the theorists here—it is not love we seek but passion. Thwarted love. Lay the sword between Tristan and Isolde and watch the words of yearning fly, the pining, the groaning. Yes. We do not want satisfaction or fulfillment, not really; we want to wallow in our failures, in unrequited love. But throw in the occasional orgasm, yes. That is the story. That is our only story.

Oh God, it is 3:30 AM and I make no sense. I hold the pencil, I scratch black words on the white paper. Slug back more Chardonnay while watching the hands of my watch creep inexorably round. I seem to be wishing my life away these days. And I am not even trying to understand what is happening to me, merely forcing the time to pass by spinning out words. I may as well be masturbating. I am masturbating.

Monday, 27 August
Someday I shall write about it, write my opus on the subject of women and women, if it hasn't already been done. Of course it has. What hasn't? In Gotham's new Barnes and Noble at Christmas while I was visiting Kare I was overwhelmed, *overwhelmed*, at the lesbian section, pornography. It isn't only Mapplethorpe, is it? Tits, penises, assholes, mouths. But I would take as my subject nothing so chic, but the far more pedestrian issue of body shape. The hows and whys of our mutual attractions. Visceral reactions. I read in a book years ago that sexual attraction lies not in how we respond to facial beauty or the smile and whatnot, much less that most ridiculous notion let loose by the late Romantics, *personality*—God help us!—but the curve of the ass as seen from behind as it moves away in the field of vision.

Rabbits, I seem to recall, a virtual phalanx of white smocks performed these experiments on captive rabbits, or squirrels, some rodent in any case—fittingly—and discovered both male and female, *female*, grew aroused (grew horny!) in the presence of a certain asinal contour only. At first the smocks used live specimens to conduct their research but then they moved on to dead ones—same results—and then upped the ante with cardboard cut-outs, masses of paper I recall, leading to the same conclusion. Arousal is a function of the profile of the buttock as seen *a tergo*. Throw the old ass in front of the male—tumescence:

he erects. In front of the female—secretion: that baby leaks. Yes! Though some huge percentage (ninety-seven, was it?) of human subjects, when they were interviewed later, asserted their chief interest lay, lay, in facial beauty, the smile, and all that. Good God, the lies we feed ourselves in the interests of appearing civilized. Displacement, Freud called that particular human foible. The ass urge explains why so many men have to take women from behind, though, doesn't it? Bum fuckers, the lot. Doctor Freud, I offer you a name for those of us hung up in this phase of human development: the asinal complex.

But no one, to my knowledge, has written about the human ass divine, the peach, let us say, which calls woman to woman. The tucked peach I love. The twinned fuzzed globes, split by that intriguing crack which hides what it at the same moment offers up. The slit, the clit. The dimpled crease I have to touch. Have to have touched.

I've never pretended it was anything else with me. (I've pretended much, though!) The fat ass, that's what attracts me. Well, let's not say fat, let's say rather, *buxom*. Corpulent. Plump. Those two solid cheeks, that delicious pucker at the junction with the thigh. You can run your hand—*hand?*—over the conformation of a plump rump, feel the baby softness, drink in the carnation odor, sweet pink of petals. (The smocks were right, I grow aroused with every word!) Directly from the days—nights!—of my first love, Deb, who shared my locker in grade ten at Badmorals Hall, Deb Williams, my bed in grades eleven and twelve, it was the ass I had to have. Of cheeks and the girl, I sing. And Deb was not like me, whose sinewy calves, flat gut, square shoulders Mary calls *athletic*, and I pronounce *horsy*, no, my Deb was round and soft, a regular Mary herself. Giving, if not necessarily forgiving.

I've just read over all the shit I've written and it makes me sound sadder than I usually believe myself to be. Not sadder and wiser, as the poet said, but pompous and garrulous at the same time, the thing I detested most about the dons at Saint Hils that terrible year I had the misfortune to spend there. Ugh, the British. So afraid of life. Life! Afraid to fart! But always maintaining with their pursed lips and their famous averted gaze that their shit doesn't stink—only the Swiss are worse. And yet here am I sounding like the worst of them. Let's blame it on the bottle of Chardonnay—empty, alas!—on the table beside my elbow. Let's blame it, too, on the color photo of Mary I look at when I pause for a moment, pencil to my lips. "Lips, hands, and arms": who wrote that? Some man, no doubt. I must look it up tomorrow.

Come on, Time, hasten me into the dawning! Into tomorrow when she returns to me. I can't bear to look at the clock on the wall—at its slender black second hand plinking off the particles of duration until we meet again. Plink, plink. I wait. Scribble in this stupid book, all the while becoming pissed on wine that puckers my lips and fuzzes my teeth. Headache come the morning. I could amuse myself with Clarisse or Tanis but the artful flirtation scene seems pointless now. Well, not pointless, entirely. But it's gone 2:00 AM and my pretty maids are all abed. And not a one with me, oh.

(Later.) Watched a bit of *Personal Best* on the tube. Nice ass, Margot Hemingway. Bad actor, though. She keeps saying—well, not saying but telling us with her downcast eyes and whatnot—that she can't help herself, can't help wanting the other one, but that's exactly the point—she can. It's not biological, the urges she feels. Shit on that! She wants it. Wants the other girl's ass—or tits, whatever—that biological crap is just that, a crock to make desire seem something we cannot manage, a thing out of our control. What we humans want is a way to shift the responsibility. It's like the comedian said about Liz Taylor's weight being the fault of her glands: she doesn't want that dozen éclairs, see, it's her *glands* that want them, gobble, gobble. Come clean, Liz! Come straight, Margot! You want to suck what's-her-name's little boobies. Kiss her nape. Whatever. It's not your glands, babe! At least let's be clear about that.

Tuesday, 29 August

Walt Whitman: "Do I contradict myself? Yes, I contradict myself."

I have not been bad for a long time now. I have been good. All right, there is the dildo, wretched toy, but a girl needs a little vibration every now and then. I was reading recently about a two-pronged instrument, one for the vagina, the other for the rectum. You place the base where the two prongs join together on the floor, it seems, and plump yourself down on the prongs, one up each orifice, flick the switch and undulate away. Sounds delicious, no? And right, Herr Doctor, there's your asinal complex again.

And the movies, yes, I admit I drop in at the X-rated shop from time to time. Women aren't supposed to do this. It's all men in there, men whose furtive little eyes strip you bare while they pretend to examine the videos. I flash my tits at them. Make a to-do of bending to the bottom shelves, my ass in their grubby little mugs. Grab a good eyeful of what you'll never get your paws on, sucker. Men.

During her spring break Kare and I traveled to Florence for two weeks. It was supposed to be a romantic tryst, but we met up with two women from Boston doing the same trip. The Uffizi, Michelangelo's *David*, all that. We had drinks together, many. The Happy Cunts, we called ourselves: Octavia and Mimi held hands on the Ponte Vecchio, Kare linked her arm through mine as we toured through the Duomo. We flaunted. It drove the men mad. *Mad.* Italian men, see, they define the word *macho*. We could hear them muttering under their breath as we passed. "Puta, puta." We

109

laughed louder, we threw our arms around each other in the piazzas and gave each other big wet kisses. We were brassy as broads. We threw it in their faces. At every opportunity we took photographs, and we insisted, if we could possibly orchestrate it, that an obliging wife snap the four of us happy broads together, arms around each other's shoulders, the husband gnashing his teeth off to one side. "No daughter of mine," you could almost hear him saying. We were bad. But the bastards deserve it.

Some of those photos turned out real nice. I have one of the four of us with our butts perched on the stones of the Ponte Vecchio, a golden Florentine sun setting along the sparkling dark blue Arno behind our heads. We are all smiling. Oh, those were jolly times for the Happy Cunts. It is not always fear and desperation, though it helps to be in a foreign country. We are always in a foreign country, in one way. We *are* a foreign country.

(Later). Three entries in succession, quite a record for me. M tells me that tonight Lord Wonderful goes away to some conference next week, New Orleans, and just when I get my hopes up, also that another battery of tests is required for her daughter, she may have to travel to the Mayo Clinic, gone to Minnesota for the same week. Shit and double shit. Not even the wine helps tonight.

Sunday, 8 September

I was doing pretty good there, three entries in a row, but lately I haven't been able to get my ass on the chair to write a line—keep my ass on the chair, as Dorothy Parker once said. I don't know how authors do that, any artist for that matter, push on through whatever mood is upon them. I wallow. I drink wine. But I am going to bring a halt to my weaknesses tomorrow.

Flying back from Toronto this evening I sat beside a gay

man. He was wearing a beautiful white cotton shirt, buttoned to the neck, but did not have a tie on. He smelled so good. His black hair was combed just so. Out of the corner of my eye I studied him as he ate his in-flight lasagna: meticulous bird-like movements over the tray. Soda water with lemon. He seemed so relaxed, so comfortable with himself. I thought *that can be you, Jilly, if you learn to relax into who you are and live your life minute by minute.* Yeah, right.

In the *Glob and Shlob* I read about a man who had a basement full of cats he had tortured to death. Hundreds. Some he caged and then burnt with hot pokers—he had a fireplace—others he starved to death in a wooden barrel he'd fitted out with breathing holes. Some he just strangled with his hands. It was gruesome. He'd been doing it for years, a well-groomed accountant in his mid-forties who took the subway into the city every day and mowed his green lawn on Saturday afternoon the same as everyone else. The neighbors noticed an odd smell coming from his basement and asked the police to investigate, otherwise it might have gone on forever. And I thought of myself, the horrible things I've done (and fantasized doing), and decided *Jilly, you better start up again with Doctor Jackman, pompous ass that she is.*

She says I cannot make up my mind about things. She says that despite my loud talk, my assertive demeanor (*pushiness* is what she means), I am a basically passive personality. Passive aggressive, I take her to be saying. She says I let other things make decisions for me—other people. Let a conflict build to the point where action must be taken—where it becomes a crisis. She says I have to assume responsibility for my own fate. She says I should either force Mary to a commitment (*force* is not a word Doctor Jackman would use) or bring the thing to an end. Yeah, right. Real estate lady is going to take a chance on a mercurial dyke of twenty-seven when her own life is a complete tangle. Especially now that her kid has taken up residence in the basement again. Now her idiotic business partner has them teetering on the precipice of a lawsuit which may plunge the lot of them into ruin. Never mind what Lord Wonderful is cooking up. I don't like him. Sometimes I don't like M, though I love her always. But Doctor J says I must learn to love myself and then I can love others, learn to forgive myself and then I can forgive others. I look into her hazel eyes across her oak desk when she says these things and I want to laugh aloud. Do they actually teach that stuff in psychiatry courses!

It is past midnight again. Again I have downed a bottle of Sauvignon Blanc (headache beginning). Tomorrow we meet at the club and work out, maybe after come back here and undress each other. *Maybe*. A stolen hour, no more. On Thursday I return to T.O. and make an offer for the Dennis Burton on behalf of the gallery—an offer his family will not accept, though I can tell they are embarrassed by the painting and would prefer to be shut of it as well as his reputation. On the weekend M is having the gang out to Willow Island to celebrate the release of Lord W's new book, dyke lovers cordially NOT invited. Fuck that. Fuck them.

I grow tired of it all.

Part 3

Chardonnay, a white grape variety, and the one vine variety that has successfully escaped the confines of botanical nomenclature to become a brand, a wine name as familiar and popular as any to which consumers have been exposed for more than a century. In the late 20th century it was transplanted to most of the world's wine regions with such a high degree of success that Chardonnay was by the 1990s a name known to far more wine consumers than Meursault or Montrachet, two of Burgundy's greatest white wines. It can suffer from coulure and occasionally millerandage and the grapes' relatively thin skin can encourage rot if there is rain at harvest time. Basic Chardonnay may be vaguely fruity but at its best Chardonnay is merely a vehicle for the character of the vineyard in which it is grown. In many other ambitious wines fashioned in the image of top white burgundy, its flavor is actually that of the oak in which it was matured. Chardonnay cuttings are sought after the world over and in many countries this is the white variety for which nurserymen found the greatest demand in the late 1980s.

THE WIND IS BLOWING steadily on an October afternoon that finds Michael rounding the point at Willow Island. Earlier in the day the lake was calm. But as the hours since have come and gone, the gentle westerly breeze of midday has become a north wind, and now the waves out in the bay are choppy. Foam is being flung onto the shore. When he stops at the furthermost most reach of the point Michael takes off his Tilley hat, shakes his long white hair for a moment, and then readjusts the hat on his head. He leans for a moment on his walking stick, a diamond willow branch some five feet in length that Maurice gave him for Father's Day last spring to compensate for the loss of Ruggles, the golden retriever who used to walk these beaches with him. It is a beautiful piece of wood. Michael lifts it in his hand and holds it out at arm's length, pointing to the north and enjoying one more time its heft in his hand. He has always liked diamond willow, and his son has sanded this piece to perfection. It is magical. He sighs, thinking of Maurice, but he has resolved to put negative thoughts from his mind on this walk, so he focuses on the foam-flecked eddies near his feet and wills his mind to go blank for a moment.

He looks at the sky. Far in the distance, hovering over the water, he sees what appears to be a golden ball, its outer edges fringed with blue spear-points. He blinks and it is gone. Is this a sign? Michael wonders. And if so, what does it mean? Ten years ago he ignored just such a sign. He kept seeing a man in a knit woolen cap, the kind dock workers wear, a menacing but silent figure who disappeared almost before Michael could be sure he had seen him—in the city, on walks at Willow Island, around the college campus. And then Michael had the heart attack while making love to Angela. In the years that have elapsed since, he has convinced himself that the man in the black cap was warning him to stop seeing Angela, to go back to Mary. And he ignored it. He has sworn not to make that mistake again.

When he resumes walking he has turned back to the west, retracing his steps to the cottage. The wind seems less intense now, which surprises him, he thought it would be more in his face on the return journey, though it's true the spit of land called Willow Point does not project directly east-west, and the wind has been shifting throughout the day. Perhaps it will be northeast by nightfall. He hopes not. That usually means unsettled conditions, that usually means blasts of northern air, and with the gang coming out for Thanksgiving dinner on Sunday afternoon, he would prefer the weather to be pleasant. He thinks, despite his earlier resolve, of Mark. What can Michael do to help his friend? He has a cousin who works for a major drug company. Maybe he could help. Michael resolves to call his cousin on Monday. But for now he stops for a moment and studies the sky, which is a solid mass of gray cloud, typical for this time of year. He senses there are no clues up there, though there are a couple of gulls riding the air currents just above him.

He points his walking stick at them: *bang bang*. It is duck- and goose-hunting season, and if this were a typical year, he would be out with some of his cousins—with Maurice—in the marshes to the south, bagging a goose for the dinner tomorrow. But this isn't a typical year. He has wrenched his back again and cannot sit for more than twenty minutes at a time before his sciatic nerve begins to cause paralysis in his legs. He certainly could not crouch in a duck blind in the damp, waiting for geese to fly over. And Maurice is in the hospital and cannot be released, Dr. Stone says, until the cuts scab over, and even then it may be the psych ward. Michael lowers the walking stick. The gulls have wheeled to the west, and his thoughts, despite his best intentions, have dipped into the black pool he was barely able to drag them from this morning. Kids, he thinks. You are supposed to delight in their infancy, treasure their childhood, suffer through teenagerage, and then put them behind you after that, aren't you? He left home at eighteen to attend college in the city and never gave his parents a spot of grief again, as far as he knows. But things are different in the dubious nineties: unstable, ambiguous, unpredictable. There are no jobs and yet the entire generation seems driven by the need for money. He's happy he isn't a youngster trying to start out these days. He sees the harried looks on their faces at the college every term. But it's not a comforting feeling—not with two children—three, including Meagan—being buffeted in circles by the uncertain winds of the imminent millennium.

Michael has resumed walking again. With each step he sets the end of the diamond willow branch down in the sand of the beach and shifts his bulk forward. There was a time—was it merely a decade ago?—when he used to jog up and down this shoreline, but now walking can be difficult on some days. His left knee seems always on the point of collapsing. His back hurts. He gazes ahead along the stretch of sand, looking for the circular impressions left by the walking stick on his journey out. The rings are larger than he expects, and the indentations deeper. For some reason he cannot explain, these details comfort him. He thinks momentarily of E.J. Pratt and mouths the words of a poem he learned in school: "it took the sea a thousand years." He remembers, too, that an English poet wrote about leaving marks in the sand. Shelley? His memory for these things has never been good. Except for old Frost, who wrote about how people look out at the sea but never can quite grasp the meaning of the signs that nature sends them.

He is almost back to the cottage now. He stops again, not because he is tired, but because he likes the feel of the wind on his cheeks. There will come a day soon when he will not be here to feel it, he thinks sadly, a day Mark feels more near than he does. Michael swallows hard. This thought is not comforting to him. He rotates his whole body to catch the full brunt of the air on his face. It's carrying the scent of rotting fish and is colder than he expects. Grains of sand swirl up into his eyes. He brushes at his cheeks. Earlier in the day he was painting the little shed beside the cottage where they keep the extra refrigerator and store lawn chairs and the garden hose, and his hands are dotted with brown stains. His father's hands were always healing from cuts, knuckles scraped, nails blackened from hammer blows. His own are tan from the sun, soft and unblemished except for these paint stains, though they are bigger than the old man's, even if not as muscular. Maurice has Patricia's stubby fingers and freckled forearms. Maurice: Dr. Stone says not to worry, the crisis period has passed, but Michael cannot turn his thoughts away from the boy—*man*, he says to himself, *man*—no matter what mental tricks he tries to divert himself. Maybe part of the problem is he's always thought of Maurice as *the boy*. Maybe Mary's right about that—about that, too.

He draws a line in the sand with his toe. His father would have said *it's all in your head*. He would have sat Maurice down and told him a man does not do certain things, like slice your own arm with shards of glass because things have got you down. The old man had a way of making you want to do your best, of making you do the right thing. Yes, he would have straightened the kid out. Maurice would not have drifted into a vortex of self-pity. The old man would have helped him. And he would have gone to the police about the phone calls after the first week. But then the old man would not have had to answer questions about the women he'd associated with in the past—questions about Angela, whom Michael hasn't been in contact with for years, but whose face comes back to him often. How long ago it seems now: blow jobs in his office, screwing on this very beach. He was a different man then, though he still answers to the same name. He was a man who took risks, a man who could run two miles before breakfast, who could say *what the hell*. There was Rebecca something-or-other before Angela. Why can't he remember Rebecca's last name? Maybe the cops already know all about the telepersonals. No. He cannot face the embarrassing questions and the smirks exchanged between the cops. Better to leave well enough alone.

But then does he run the risk of violence? Bernard Goetz went to trial a few weeks ago for blowing away that black kid in the New York subway. The Davidians are rumored to be running a restaurant in the core of the city. One of Michael's colleagues started a fire in his office and then leapt out the third-story window, killing himself. *The shit does stick.* And there are kooks everywhere these days, kooks who do not hesitate to cross the lines of sanity which used to be so clear. If he is right, the person calling him is an ex-student with a grudge—someone who didn't get into medical college or was turned down by some grad school—who wants him to suffer the way she or he is suffering. It's standard stuff these days around colleges, a kind of stalking, more common than the sexual harassment receiving all the publicity. Most of the time it blows over in a few days, weeks at most, but occasionally it turns into something nasty. Two years ago a woman came at Stephen with a butcher knife. A professor in the States had his car Molotov-cocktailed.

Michael has reached the deck of the cottage. He clumps up the wooden steps and rests the walking stick against the door frame. He wasn't supposed to think black thoughts today. Mark, who has taken up meditation, says you have to free the mind not to think. *Let thoughts be the birds that flicker across the sky of your mind*, he says. This is not easy for Michael, though he likes the metaphor. He likes, too, the Zen peacefulness which has come over his friend since he found out about his tumor. *Why can't I be that way?* Michael thinks.

He turns to look at the lake one more time. In the gray sky about twenty feet above the surface and a hundred feet from shore a golden ball is hovering over the water. *UFO*, Michael thinks, almost laughing aloud. But it is not a UFO, he sees after blinking his eyes, it is a bird, a giant pelican. It floats in the air, moving slowly toward him without moving its wings and in less than a minute stops only a few yards from the deck of the cottage. The pelican is monstrous, its heavy downy body almost as large as Michael's, its wingspan that of a small airplane, thirty feet, maybe forty. Michael's mouth has gone dry. He swallows. The pelican is looking directly into his eyes, its huge head bobbing slowly. It is so close Michael can feel its breath on his face. It fixes him with one gigantic yellow eye. The eye does not blink but it rotates slowly, studying him. He has never realized how like dinosaurs pelicans look. The beak on this one resembles the beaks on the pterosaurs in the books he bought Maurice twenty years ago, gigantic and frightening. The beak is opening and closing slowly as the pelican breathes in and out. He imagines it suddenly pecking him, ripping into his flesh. That beak would tear Michael's heart out of his chest, rip his guts into bloody shreds. He looks for signs of intelligence in the bird's eye. He half expects the pelican to speak to him, to communicate some crazy environmental message: *No More Hunting.* But the pelican makes no sound. All Michael hears is the pounding of blood in his throat. He is taking short breaths and he hears himself thinking *don't hurt me, please don't hurt me.* He knows a young pelican will rip the heart out of its parent's breast to feed. *Don't hurt me*, he thinks. But he does not say anything, and after studying him for a few more minutes the pelican begins to float away, disappearing in the same way as it appeared, receding over the water until its form dissolves into a golden ball in the sky. Michael blinks. He puts his hand over his heart, which is beating the way it does when he wakes from a dream, as if it were enclosed in too small a space. Michael studies the sky but it is empty now, empty and gray. He clears his throat. *I need a Scotch*, he thinks.

The point is, women understand women. Mary seals her glossy red lips on this thought as she brakes coming out of the Jubilee underpass, slowing for a fat man in the crosswalk between the Cambridge and Pembina Hotels. The Cadillac's nose dips but otherwise you'd never know it had suddenly decelerated. Mary watches the fat man. The point is, a woman intuitively knows when another woman needs comforting, when she is about to break down or cry. No, not intuitively, that makes it sound mystical, mysterious, which is just what men want to believe. That it's something spiritual and other-worldly they can never get a handle on. Feathers, dandelion seeds buffeted by the wind. No, what she's talking about, the simpatico between women, this thing is learned, it's part of the business of growing up feminine. Female. A woman understands when another woman needs flowers, a shoulder to cry on, tender and loving caresses. Men have no idea what flowers are all about. Bring them when *they* feel good, not when a woman feels bad. Or needs propping up. And men always think caressing has to lead to sex, so when a woman is most vulnerable, unsure of herself, when she reaches out to be held and comforted, with a man it always spirals into exactly what she does not want, cannot handle, right at that delicate moment—penetration. This another woman knows.

Besides, women laugh about the same things. Cry. They both—all—had nagging mothers to endure, they suffered through junior high with the Sarahs and the Heathers. Bras, boys, pimples. Somehow there's no pressure when women are together. No, not none, but a different kind than with men, de-fused, de-sexualized.

The man in the crosswalk, Mary sees, thirtyish, overalls and work boots, is giving her the finger. *You too, dickbrain.* Stumbling from one pub to the other. *Go soak your fat proletarian ass in more hops and yeast.* She reaches into the console for a fresh stick of gum. Guns the engine when the flashing lights go off and the cars beside her start to move forward again. *Eat my dust.*

Mary licks her lower lip. Lunch is still there. Salt. Egg. Slate taste of wine.

And the subjects that are important to talk about: respect for the other person, communication, that sort of stuff. This also a woman knows. Mary pops the stick of gum into her mouth and crumples the foil wrapper into a tiny ball which she drops between her knees onto the floor mat beneath her. Could it be that women would be better off living with other women, in pairs, maybe, or a big group-home arrangement, kids running all over the place, bunk beds in crowded bedrooms, communal shopping trips? Men with men? She can see there would be certain harmonies in the set-up—food, for one. Though maybe, too, certain discords. The girls at Miss Emily's went after each other like cats. Linda Lawson clawed Mary's nose with her nails and Mary still has to powder over the tiny seam left on one nostril to disguise the reddened welt. She was not without her own streak of viciousness. But was that because they disliked each other or because they were rivals for the attentions of boys—of men? Bottles of face cream thrown across the dormitory, buttons ripped off blouses. But also holding hands on walks around the quad, singing rounds in the dorm after lights out. Playing "thumper." If she had to do it all over again, living with women, with one woman, might be the route to take. Let men have their sports on TV, softball games, their *Playboys*, beer, their endless juvenile talk about dumps and farting.

She has wheeled into the driveway almost without noticing it. The lawn needs one last mowing before winter settles in. Michael should have cut the peony stalks months ago and put them in the trash bin. The narrow strip of blue trim beneath the bay window is blistering. Didn't Michael paint it just last summer? Mary runs one finger over the smudges around the door handle as she inserts and turns the key with the other hand. Inside she has not closed the door before she smells it: cigarette smoke.

"Meggy," she calls out. "You here?"

"Yeah," she hears from the basement, muffled. "Gimme a minute."

She puts her briefcase on the bench in the foyer with her bag and crosses the living room into the kitchen. Pours a tumbler of cold water. Last night she and Jilly stopped at Grapes after working out and she had one glass too many of white wine. It was good stuff, though she cannot remember the name. Was it Italian? Meursault, maybe, that sounds French. Meggy has clumped up the stairs from the basement, bringing with her the putrid reek of tobacco smoke. She is wearing a black T-shirt whose white lettering reads: Haulers Pull Out In Time.

Mary asks, "You okay?"

"Yeah. Just having a nap." She looks it. Hair frumped up in back. It appears she's just pulled on the sweat pants. Fumbling with the draw cord. Maybe, Mary thinks, she was masturbating. Meggy will be twenty-seven come February but has never had a steady boyfriend. Overweight. Loud.

Caustic to the point of mean on occasion. Not often. She scares men away.

"Darling," Mary says, "you know how Michael hates cigarette smoke."

"Maw."

"Me too, actually."

"Yeah, since you quit, eh?"

"That was ages ago," Mary says, massaging her palate with the tip of her tongue. The water tastes off today. Tincup. Galvanized. She adds, "Before you were born." She is trying valiantly to keep her voice even. The kid needs comforting, she keeps telling herself, the kid's sick. So much more reason not to be smoking.

Meggy has opened the fridge and brought out a carton of juice. Pours until the tumbler is half filled and leans back against the counter. "But you were a bunch older than me," she says. "You got in a good twenty years puffing the weed—and God knows what else—but now you're lecturing me."

Mary had forgotten the defiance in the girl. No, not forgotten. "That is hardly the point," she says. "The mistakes I made in my twenties."

"Oh, right."

"I was hoping you'd learn from them."

Meggy sniffs and swallows some juice. "The point being?"

"You're sick," Mary says. She has finished drinking her water and has positioned herself over the sink, where she's washing out the tumbler. "You should be taking better care of yourself."

"The point being it's your house. Your rules, eh?"

"Come on," Mary says. "We've had this fight."

"Duh."

"The point, darling, is your immune system is weak."

"Bullshit." Meggy sets the tumbler of juice down on the counter with a crack, sloshing liquid down her fingers and over the Formica.

Mary grits her teeth. Finally she says, "It's such an awful stench." She turns and looks Meggy in the eyes but the girl refuses to meet her gaze and stares out the window. Gray sky. The leaves off the elms and maples and oaks are thick in the yard. She did the lawn last week, and Michael should have raked under the dogwoods and honeysuckles where the leaves are matting and beginning to rot already. Another year. She asks in a softer voice, "Can't you smell it?"

"The point is you have to have your own way."

"That's not true."

"The point is you don't give a damn about me." Meggy has raised the tumbler to her lips again, and drops of the spilled juice that collected around the bottom are dribbling down her chin onto the T-shirt. "Right?"

"Wrong," Mary says.

"Sure, you invite me here, toss a bed into the basement, but it's the same old story, we have to play by your rules."

"There's three of us living in a small space. That's the point. There's no room for . . . the smoke gets into everything. We have to breathe it."

"So? Other people manage."

"Other people get heart disease and lung cancer."

"Oh, so now you're saying I'm poisoning you. You're blaming me." Meagan's cheeks have flushed, as if she'd been working out. Her lips are scrunched together in a pout. "And I suppose you think I brought diabetes on myself too?"

Mary sighs. Her watch reads 3:20. She wonders why she came home, why she didn't stay at the office and finish up the paperwork. The lawyer tells her they either have to reach a settlement by early next week or prepare to go to court. Two hundred thousand, the other side insists, for their—for Freddo's—mishandling of the condo deal, but they'll settle for half of that, Mary's lawyer tells her. Why did she come home to fight with Meggy when she could have stayed at the office and fought with Freddo? If he were there. If he weren't out with his irresponsible pony partners, getting sloshed on rye and seven. She stoops and opens the cupboard beneath the sink. Brings out a bottle of Vouvray Blanc. "You know full well," she says to Meggy, "I think no such thing."

"But drinking is okay."

"Darling, it's not the same thing at all."

"Alcohol's a drug, Maw, the same as tobacco."

"Drinking white wine does not invade the personal space of others."

"Christalmighty. Do you ever listen to yourself?"

"Those you profess to love."

"Do you ever listen to the words coming out of your mouth?" Meggy has finished drinking. She sets the tumbler on the counter, leaving a second orange ring for Mary to wipe up, and stomps across the room to the doorway and the steps leading to the basement. "If anyone calls," she shouts over her shoulder, "I'm napping."

Mary studies her retreating form. Listens to her feet thumping down the wooden stairway. Mary purses her lips. Six months ago it seemed the fighting was over. The cat spitting. They talked a couple of times late into the night, the hanging shade over the kitchen table cocooning them in diffused golden light. They laughed together. She drove around the Wolseley area with Meggy, helping her pick out an apartment. She and Michael spent a day packing boxes and shifting bits of furniture to Ethelbert Street, a nice two-bedroom on the second floor of a grand old Tudor house, air-conditioning, newly renovated bathroom. Air and light. Mary pries the cork out of the wine bottle. Pours a glass, watching the golden bubbles wink to the surface and then vaporize. In a moment the thump of rock music starts to vibrate the floorboards under her feet. She glances at her watch again: 3:28. Will Jilly be home from work yet?

Ordinarily on the Friday night of the Thanksgiving weekend Michael is at Willow Island, preparing for the dinner he and Mary host for their friends at the end of the season. But this Friday finds him in the bar at the Westin, where he has been sipping a large Scotch and observing the other patrons, businessmen mostly, pinstriped suits, clean-shaven faces. There are a few women, too, wives, he guesses, perfectly coiffed hair, diamonds. He has been sitting at the bar, despite his father's advice that a man should always occupy a corner seat in a bar. What sort of experiences must the old man have had to lead him to that piece of hard-won wisdom? Michael checks his watch: 7:54. Early, as he planned. This is not something the old man told him, but Michael makes a point of arriving early to appointments. He likes to give himself enough time to appraise the room, to grow accustomed to the lighting and noise level, and to study whomever he is meeting as they enter. This dimly lit room is not much: bar stools, Formica tables, a gray and red carpet imitating—poorly—the Persian style. Some light muzak is trickling through speakers hanging from the high ceiling. The patrons chatter in subdued voices. Thankfully, he does not recognize anyone. Or they him.

On his drive in from the cottage that was the one thing that worried him. He does not need the hammy hand of a college colleague on his shoulder when he's already on edge about how the evening will develop—though much worse would be the x-ray eyes of one of his colleagues' wives. Michael takes a sip of Scotch and feels its amber warmth spread through his stomach. This he likes. He says to himself, *relax*. The real reason he's sitting at the bar is to make an easy exit if she doesn't show up—or if she doesn't look the way he hopes. He's paid merely a fifty-dollar deposit. That and the ride into town are all he's lost if things do not turn out—which is what he half suspects will happen. Although

"Tiffany" seemed very confident she'd find the right girl. He takes another sip of Scotch. Writers are as well known for drinking Scotch as academics for swilling beer. Stephen, for example, who thinks Mark is doing great, who loved the handful of poems Michael showed him the other day. *Like Frost*, Stephen had said, wrinkling his bushy eyebrows. And Michael's heart had swelled. Since then he's written two more poems.

Then he spots her coming through the door. He hadn't expected her to be tall or slim, but then he hadn't expected high heels and a strapless black dress cut just above the knees, or the utter composure she shows in running her eyes cursorily about the room before strolling up to the bar stool next to him.

She glances at the folded newspaper he's placed on the bar beside his drink and smiles. "Hi," she says, "I'm Ethena."

"Michael," he says, smiling. He isn't sure offering his hand is the correct protocol, but he does.

"I've kept you waiting."

"No. I was early." Her eyes are gray. Her face is lined, harder than he expected, though she probably has not seen a thirtieth birthday. It's what she does for a living, he thinks, that has worn her face, but he has warned himself against becoming sentimental, so he suppresses his pity.

"I love your beard," she says. She puts one hand up and touches his face just where the skin of his cheek shows. This close he can smell her perfume, one of the spicier scents, it tickles his nose for a moment. She smiles and adds, "Reminds me of Kenny Rogers."

He laughs. "People are always saying that."

"Except you're more healthy looking. More handsome."

"Ha," he says. "We won't tell Kenny."

When she laughs she makes a more hearty sound than the tightness in her cheeks and mouth led him to think she would. Her gray eyes dance. She is pretty, really, and her legs are well shaped. Probably her best feature. "Well," she says. She is still standing at his elbow. "Should I have a drink or not?"

"Have a drink," he says. "What do you want?"

"The other option," she says, "is I've booked a room upstairs. We could have a drink there while we get to know each other a little better."

This is smooth, Michael thinks, *very nice*. A room upstairs has already been booked. He wondered how that detail was going to be handled. "If that's the case," he says, rising from the bar stool, and making a sweeping gesture with one arm. He leaves a ten-dollar bill on the bar and gently places one hand on Ethena's elbow, guiding her out of the room to the elevators in the foyer.

Once inside the room Michael stands awkwardly at the end of the bed for a moment, wondering if he should pour them each a drink, but before he has time to make up his mind, she is in front of him, those gray eyes staring up into his. There is something that could be dangerous in her look, volatile, but he ignores it. "You haven't done this before," she says, "have you?"

"Not this. No."

"Okay," she says. "That's okay." She has placed both her hands on his hips. "There's just one rule," she states. "No sucking my tits. Okay?"

"Okay," he says. Her lips are thin, he sees. He does not like thin lips. He puts his hands on her shoulders, then lifts her short blonde hair between his fingers, exposing her neck. The skin has a fine fuzz on it. The smell rising from it tickles his nose. He stoops and kisses the tanned skin of her shoulder and throat, and then runs his tongue into the hollow above her collarbone.

She has been stroking the backs of his legs, running her fingers over his behind, and now she moves her hands around to the front of his thighs, gently squeezing the muscles between his knees and his groin. Her hands work fast, the tools of an expert, and she leans into his shoulder, rubbing against him like a cat as her fingers stroke and then seize him through his pants. His reaction is instant. He doesn't know if he has ever been so stiff, so large, certainly not for many years. Probably never this fast. And her hands are so practiced, they grip and squeeze with subtle but great pressure. He moans aloud when he feels her fingers undo his pants and free him from his underwear. She pulls both items of clothing down with efficiency, bending quickly to slip out of her dress and underwear so they stand torso to torso. Then she loosens the buttons of his shirt and pulls it off too. She tosses it on top of her dress. Her hands are on his chest, the ends of both fingers making circles on the curled hair there. His bare toes are dug into the pile carpeting. Behind her head there is a framed painting of dolphins leaping out of blue water. He moves his hands down her shoulders, encircles her firm, small breasts. The aureoles are large, the nipples brown and extended, the texture of erasers that he pinches gently between his forefingers and thumbs. He wants to suck, but she whispers *no* and presses against him again, rubbing her breasts on his chest and her thighs into his. "Come into me," she whispers, hot breath in his ear, "take me now." He has closed his eyes, drinking in the feel of flesh on flesh, the knot of her mound against him, and when he opens them, he sees she has closed hers, too, though now her fingers are caressing him again. His flesh is rigid and swollen with blood. It hurts so wondrously he wants to cry out when she runs her hands up and down it until he begins to pant and then feel weak in the knees. His legs buckle. He wants to shout *stop stop*, he does not want to ejaculate at this point, two erections are rare these days, he wants not to waste this, he wants to be inside her, on top and pounding, but then he's spurting onto the floor, against her thigh, and she is down on her knees taking the final two or three spurts into her mouth, something she not only does by habit, it appears, or out of tidiness, but because she likes it.

He stands trembling for a few minutes after, her face buried against his thighs, her hands clasped around his buttocks. He can feel her coarse hair on his skin. She is breathing deeply. On the drive in he had imagined lifting her skirts and taking her against the door, the way Sonny does in that scene in *The Godfather*, lifting her so she can slither onto him. Or bending her over the end of the bed, face forward, his toes pressing against the insides of her feet. He imagined taking her until his lust was spent.

Instead, she has taken him, but he does not feel diminished.

When she stands she kisses his cheek and looks him in the eye. She does not laugh but there's a crinkle of a smile on her mouth when she says, "You needed that, didn't you?" And when he nods and smiles at her, she smiles again and says, "Now we can get down to the real thing."

Mary is sitting at the dining-room table under the cocoon of light shed by an overhead lamp. There are open files spread about the surface of the table, a calculator, pencils, and a bottle of white wine. Mary is holding a wine glass to her lips and studying the figures on a sheet of paper in front of her. It's a mess. Even if she allows no salary to either her or Freddo for six months, even if she projects gross sales of a couple of million—and who knows about that?—even if they scale back the office and lay off Marika, they each will have to put capital into the company to keep it afloat. And where will that come from? Thanks to the fact Michael draws a salary from the college, she can forgo earnings, and she has maybe forty grand in savings she can contribute to the pot (she will not touch the RSPs), but what about Freddo? He has a wife who stays at home, he has payments: cars, a cottage, God knows what else. Those damn ponies. Mary takes another sip of wine and breathes out slowly. The numbers on the sheets in front of her are beginning to swim. Rorschach test. And Freddo has no savings, it's a foreign concept to him and his wife. He will have to sell something—his Beamer, his wife's Jeep, the cottage—just to stay afloat on the day-to-day stuff. Mary studies the numbers again. If Freddo sold both the cottage and one of the cars, they might manage it. Struggle through six months while paying out the hundred grand to the limited partners—don't forget the lawyers' fees—and re-open the office on a full-time basis early in the new year. January and February are slow anyway.

Mary stands and goes to the bay window, looking into the backyard. A wind has come up from the northeast, swirling, gusting. Treetops sway, a tin sign is rattling in the back lane. It will be cold tonight on Willow Island. Frost maybe. Michael will have a fire. She has tried to reach him on the cellular a couple of times since supper, but he seems to be out. Walking the beach, in all likelihood. He does that more and more now. Solitary black figure in a barren land-scape. He's brooding about something. Maybe he knows. He has never had a woman go away from him, it's always been the other way around, and he does not know what to do about it. He's needy. Despite his appearance on the surface, independent, cool, standoffish, Michael has to have a woman who loves him at his side. He needs constant comfort and support. Adoration. A voice to greet him when he comes home, a warm hand in his at the end of the day. A back to soup-spoon against in bed. Mary knows that if she were to die suddenly, he would be one of those men who remarry within the year. And yet he prefers to walk the beach at Willow Island alone, returns with that dazed look in his blue eyes. Trance. Smell of sand in hair. Algae stuck to his boots. Could she actually leave him?

In the basement she hears Meggy moving around. She

has a microwave oven down there as well as a TV. Watching rock videos and eating popcorn. Guzzling beer. Mary thought the girl had made a few friends in the months she worked for the rock band, but so far no one has come round. Maybe they meet at bars. Those truck stops on the edge of town. Fries, coffee, burgers. It's no wonder Meagan has put on weight. Absent-mindedly, Mary runs one finger up and down the window glass. As soon as she's done the calculations, she'll call down to the girl. They can have a chat, maybe laugh together the way they did when Meggy was in school. It hurts her that Meggy thinks she does not care, that she's too busy for her. The one thing Mary wants is to be a good mother. She is a good mother, dammit.

The sound of someone moving around on the front steps startles Mary. It's past ten o'clock. Michael would have phoned if he were driving back from Willow Island. She crosses the living room cautiously. The neighborhood has been plagued with break-ins recently. On the other side of the city a pensioner was beaten and robbed in her own house last month. Mary swallows hard and feels her heart racing. Whoever it is has no hesitation about banging with their fist. Mary looks through the slit of glass in the wooden front door. Her heart freezes, but she opens the door quickly.

"You shouldn't come here," she says. "Can't come here."

"Get real," Jilly says. Her voice is loud, even in the wind. Her hair has been tossed about her head and her face is flushed. She is wearing a heavy Irish sweater and baggy jeans. Unaccountably, Mary thinks, sandals.

"Meggy is downstairs," Mary whispers. "She'll hear."

"So?" Mary has been standing in such a way as to block the doorway in case Meagan comes up from the basement suddenly. Jilly puts one hand on Mary's chest and pushes her backwards, forcing her way into the foyer. "Tell her we're pals," she says.

135

"No," Mary says, stumbling but regaining her balance. "This is crazy."

"I warned you," Jilly says. "So am I." She has barged past Mary into the living room and is standing with her back to the light coming from the kitchen, her face in the shadow. With her hair puffed up around the crown of her skull, she looks like the devil in nineteenth-century woodcuts. Mary can smell her breath, and she sees that in her other hand Jilly is holding a wine bottle by the neck. Jilly says in a singsong voice, "One crazy cat. That's me."

"You're drunk," Mary says.

"I *need* a drink," Jilly says. She holds the wine bottle up to the light for Mary to see. "Empty," she says. "Dead soldier."

Mary takes the bottle from Jilly. Her hands are sweaty. Only moments ago at the bay window she was feeling chilly. "You should go," she whispers.

"One drink. One itsy-bitsy." Jilly holds the forefinger and thumb of one hand up, leaving a tiny space between them. "Just one."

Mary swallows hard. Of course she can tell Meagan that Jilly is a pal from the club who just dropped over for a drink. She can tell her that or any number of things. People do just stop by. But her stomach is in a knot. *This is not right*, she's thinking. *His turf.* She has been telling herself all along that she can keep the two domains apart, separate lives. "It's a bad idea," she says.

"One damn drink!" Jilly screams. She stamps her foot on the floor.

"Jilly," Mary hisses back.

"Hey Mom," Meagan calls from the basement, her voice barely audible over the thump of rock music. "You okay?"

"Yes," Mary calls back down, much louder than she means to. "It's just a—just a friend dropped by." She cuts her eyes at Jilly, indicating she should follow her into the kitchen and keep silent. Listens, but does not hear any response from the basement. Apparently Meagan is satisfied.

Jilly has picked the wine bottle off the table. She drinks directly from it, smacking her lips when she sets it down. "Yummy," she says. Her sandals are wet, Mary sees. She has tracked sand across the carpets. And now Mary can smell something too, the stench of decaying matter—ditch water?

"This is crazy," Mary says. "Really crazy."

"Hey relax, babes," Jilly says. "You look a mess." She steps forward and puts out her arms as if to embrace Mary but Mary backs away.

"Not funny crazy," Mary says. "Scary crazy."

After she withdraws her arms, Jilly closes her eyes. She holds them shut for the count of five, the fingers of both hands knotting and unknotting. Mary hears the refrigerator start up. Cars going by outside. When Jilly opens her eyes she whispers, "Jilly does not want you saying that."

"You frighten me."

"You or anyone." Jilly has picked up the wine bottle again. She takes a deep breath and then a long pull from the bottle. "Jilly is not crazy. Not."

Mary has leaned back against the counter with her hands extended along its sharp edge. She is trying to appear relaxed and in control, though what she hears in Jilly's voice is making her knees tremble. "You should go now," she says. "Please."

"Jilly," repeats Jilly, "is not crazy. Not."

"Right," Mary says, "but she should leave and not upset her friend."

Instead of answering, Jilly looks about the room. "This is nice," she says. "Cedar paneling and track lighting. Jilly digs track lighting."

"Please go," Mary says.

Jilly runs her eyes around the room again, as if trying to cement details in her mind. "All right," she says, finally. "Jilly shall split."

"Yes," Mary says. "Okay. Go then."

"Jilly's a good girl."

"I know."

"Jilly was just out for a walk, see, in the area, like, stomping about and enjoying the wind in her ears, sipping back a little of the blanco al fresco, and she decided to pop in and check out how you've been keeping. Thought you'd be pleased to see her. But you're busy. All right. Jilly can see that, babes. Didn't mean to scare you." Jilly takes a deep breath and closes her eyes again. "So she'll split," she mutters. "That's cool." She hums something to herself, a tune Mary does not recognize. When she opens her eyes they appear to have cleared. She smiles in a tight-lipped way and starts to cross the living room to the front door. "Splitsville," she says. "Outta here."

"Take—please take the bottle," Mary says.

Jilly pauses halfway across the living room. "What?"

"If you want. The wine." Mary has the bottle in one hand, offering it.

"Good," Jilly says, reaching for the bottle. "Jilly thinks good idea."

"Cheers," Mary says. She swings the wooden door open and stands on the concrete landing as Jilly makes her way down the sidewalk. Her sandals click over the concrete. She seems happy, and Mary half expects her to do a skip step. But she does not.

When she is almost to the street Jilly turns and waves the bottle in the air. "Sleep tight, babes," she calls out. Her words are just distinguishable above the sound of the wind.

"Ram it into me," she cries, "now." Her ass is two globes of mottled white flesh, quivering before Michael's eyes. He is rigid again and throbbing, and he is amazed, hardly a half hour has passed since he first ejaculated, yet here he is, swollen with desire again. "Ram me," she cries, "ram me now."

He is standing at the end of the bed, naked except for his black socks, his wristwatch, and his wedding ring, and she is kneeling in front of him, her face lost in the two pillows, her voice muffled despite the fact she is almost screaming the words back at him. He moves toward her. There are identical blue veins running vertically down the twin globes of her ass into her thighs, a map he wants to grasp in his hands. Michael shifts his legs and groin into position behind her. He guides himself with one hand and lifts on his toes slightly to drive himself home.

"No," she screams, her head turning toward him suddenly, so their eyes meet for a brief moment. "The other, the other." She lifts her mouth clear of the pillow and cries, "Fuck me up the ass, you bastard! The ass!"

Michael trembles for a few seconds, withdraws, and elevates on his toes again. The room is swimming. Muscles in the small of his back and along the insides of both his thighs twinge as he shifts his weight forward again. In the morning he is going to be sore through his entire abdomen.

"Right," she cries. "Harder, harder. Fuck my ass right off."

He grunts and rams his weight into her. Sweat is beginning to run down his brow and into his eyes. His fingers grip the soft pouches of flesh above her hips. The muscles on the backs of his hands pop. For a moment he thinks of the heart attack he experienced years ago while making love to Angela, and his torso tenses, a hot wave of fear runs through his gut, but he knows the doctors were right: the coronary had nothing to do with sex as such. It was just the occasion. It could have been lifting a box that brought the spasm on. Besides, the stress tests show he is normal again. He is no more likely to be a victim of heart attack than any other man his age. So live life to the fullest. "All right," he says, feeling himself slide in.

"Ram me," she cries out. "Now, now."

He cups the rounded top of her pelvic bones in his hands and jerks back on her as he thrusts forward. He says between dry lips, "Like this, bitch?"

"Harder, you bastard, faster. Drive it right up into me. Pound me."

He thrusts forward. The pleasure he feels throughout his groin is almost equally counterbalanced by the pains spreading through the backs of his legs and into his gut, but he is resolved to go through with it. To be a ram. "Bitch," he says between gritted teeth.

"Bastard."

And then he comes. Fast and hard. "Christ," he says, surprised.

"Yes," she says. "Got ya." She rocks her haunches forward quickly, so he slides out, a wrenching, burning moment in which Michael reflexively curls forward to protect himself, and she collapses sideways on the bed, curling into a fetal position, a position he imitates when he topples forward onto the bed beside her, one hand on his burning groin.

"Christ all mighty," he whispers. He reaches out for a pillow to cradle his head. That's when she hits him in the back.

"Bastard," she screams. The blow lands between his shoulders, sharp and cutting, a punch in the middle of his spine, and he winces, despite the fog of post-coital slumber just beginning to roll over him.

"That's my vertebrae," he moans weakly.

She strikes him again, harder than before. "You fucking bastard," she screams. "You sodomized me!" Her voice is much louder than before. For the first time Michael thinks someone in an adjoining room might hear.

"What?" He rolls toward her. "You asked me—"

"Sodomized me! Fucking creep!"

He is up on one elbow now, revolving his torso toward her. "You—"

She strikes him in the face with her fist, a blow that lands on the cheek but instantly brings tears to his eyes. "Bastard!" she screams. "Bastard!"

"Christ all mighty!" Michael is struggling to come out of the daze which their sex and the drinks he downed after the blow job she gave him have eased him into, trying to shift his legs and thighs so he can use the full strength of his arms to ward off the blows she's throwing at him.

A second punch lands on his face, almost in the exact same spot as the first. Pain sears his cheekbone. "I'll kill you, you bastard," she says. "You raped me. Forced me."

Michael's eyes are tearing, but he has come out of the murky trance that his body had longed to slide into for the remainder of the evening just moments earlier. "You're crazy," he says between gritted teeth. He has one hand up in front of his face as he tries to maneuver around on the bed, trying to gain time. His eyes meet hers and he sees now clearly what he only glimpsed before: the anger in her eyes, the rage. A moment earlier he was confused but now he realizes he could die in this hotel room and the thought creates instant lucidity in his mind. He will not die, he will not succumb. And he realizes in a flash what Mark has been going through these past weeks. *God.* He realizes too that this woman, this Ethena or whatever, is dangerous: mad.

She is sitting on her knees above him. One hand is a tight fist, the other is holding the bottle from which she was drinking beer minutes ago. Heineken. The air is dense with her cloying perfume. "I've killed a man before," she says. "And loved it."

Psychotic, he thinks. "Please don't," he says.

"You raped me, you bastard. Stuck your filthy cock up my ass." She has raised the beer bottle into the position to strike. Michael can see he will not be able to prevent the blow, merely deflect it with his free hand.

"Don't," he pleads. This is not the way to die. He tries to position his hand between the upraised bottle and his eyes.

"You think you can stick your filthy cock wherever you want. Right?"

"No," he says weakly. "I do not."

"Right," she insists. She shakes the bottle in a menacing way.

"Right," he says, "all right."

"You're a piece of shit," she screams between clenched teeth. She drops the bottle to the floor and swings her arm at him again, all in one motion. The punch she lands on his nose throws her forward on the bed and across his body, but before he can clear his sight enough to grab her, she has rolled clear and is moving quickly across the floor toward the bathroom.

Michael rolls on his back. Blood is coursing over his lips and into his mouth. His teeth hurt. There is a dull pain above his left eye and another in the center of his back. He groans. In his mind's eye he imagines leaping up from the bed and pounding her face into a bloody mass. But instead he sinks back on the pillows. His hands grip the sheet and pull it up over his legs and then his chest. "Oh, mother," he whispers to himself.

His heart is hammering in his chest and the ache in his side seems more pronounced than usual. *The body is dying*, he thinks. Most of the men he knows over sixty have prostate trouble, or kidney stones, or gall bladder problems. It's just a matter of time. He closes his eyes. *Spare me*, he whispers.

Then he hears her moving quickly back into the room, and when he opens his eyes he sees she is fully dressed, her hair straightened, the bag into which she slipped the three hundred bucks earlier grasped in both hands across her waist, almost primly. Though she is moving quickly, she seems completely relaxed, completely in control. "Hey," she says, taking one step toward the bed on her way to the door. "Just kidding, big guy." She laughs, not the tinkling sound her voice made in the bar, but a guttural snort. "Just kidding," she repeats as she opens and then closes the door behind her.

Mary is dusting. This is what she does when her nerves get the better of her. It is past eleven o'clock, the national news is over, she should be pulling on her nightie and getting into bed with a good book, but instead she is bent over the bookshelves in the living room, fluffing dust off the tops of the first-edition hardcover novels Michael has collected over the years and is so proud of. She has pulled a thin sweatshirt over the blouse she wore to work earlier in the day. Lime green is in this year and she loves it. Mango, coral, citrus. The soft hues of temperate climes. Motes of dust float across her line of vision. She pauses at her labor and reaches out to catch some in her hand. They dance away from her fingers. Dandelion seed. Feathers. She read somewhere that dust bunnies under the bed are inhabited by millions of dirt-ingesting bugs which are imperceptible to the eye. Chomp, chomp. That human skin is covered with millions of micro-insects which consume skin cells as they expire on the surface of the body. All this eating going on. Chomping. Teeth. Stomachs. Micro-biotic defecation. It is Mary's job to hold it in check—at least within the four walls of her own home. She wipes the back of one hand across her brow, feeling the grit of the dust she's been stirring mixed with the warm sweat of her flesh. She thinks of her mother: sweat, perspire, glisten. She laughs aloud.

Listens afterward to the thump of rock music coming from the basement and recalls she had intended to sit quietly with Meagan over a drink, but, in the confusion Jilly caused, forgot. Is it too late now? She places her duster on a shelf and goes into the kitchen where she pours a glass of cold water. Leans back against the counter and wonders again what to make of Jilly. They have only known each other four or five months—she counts mentally backwards, six, actually—but she thought she had a pretty good handle on her. Thinks, truth be told, that she is a good judge of character, and that with Jilly what you get is more or less what you see. Though her behavior tonight has changed all that. She is unstable, Mary decides, she talks about herself in the third person, she becomes so angry her eyes glaze over. Maybe Jilly is dangerous. Mary finishes the water and places the glass in the sink. Thinks that a glass of wine would make a nice nightcap, and is just drawing the cork on a bottle of Chardonnay when she hears a knock on the front door. One sharp rap. She stops, cork in hand, and waits to make certain her excited imagination has not leapt into overdrive.

This time she does not reach the door before it is flung open and Jilly steps in, carrying not the wine bottle she left with but a wooden field hockey stick, its striking end wrapped in white tape. Jilly's hair is more disheveled than earlier and her jeans and sandals are dripping mud. The wool sweater has leaves and bits of bark stuck to it. Has she been rolling on the ground? Fallen into a ditch? One thing for sure: she has not been playing field hockey.

Reflexively Mary says, "Don't come in here like that!"

Jilly stares at her blankly. "I'm not through with you," she shouts. She has left the door open behind her and her words are partly swept away by the wind. She is brandishing the hockey stick in the air.

"Close the door," Mary commands.

She moves forward, arm outstretched for the handle, but Jilly steps back suddenly and slams the door shut, causing a vacuum of silence to settle momentarily over the room. "Ha," Jilly says.

"You're a mess," Mary says. She has been backing up and is again on the opposite side of the room from Jilly.

"And you're drinking again."

Mary looks at the wine bottle she's brought from the kitchen with her, for a moment abashed that Jilly has caught her out. Drinking alone, isn't that one of the first signs of alcoholism? "Your jeans," Mary says. "Your feet. Just look at you. Krikey. Where have you been, girl?"

Jilly looks down at her sandals and legs, as if only now aware that there is anything amiss with them. Then she looks up at Mary. Her eyes seem cold. Gaze empty. "What have *you* been doing, babes?" she asks. "There's a black streak across your forehead."

Mary touches her brow. "Dusting," she says, lamely.

"Exorcising demons," Jilly says.

"You."

"Ha."

Mary says, "As a matter of fact, I was just about to pour some wine. As you noticed." She tilts her head in the direction of the kitchen. "Join me?"

"All right," Jilly says.

"Kick those off," Mary says. "You're a mess."

Jilly looks down at her feet again, then takes a step forward, as if to follow Mary into the kitchen, but then she stops abruptly. "No," she says.

Mary turns. "No?" She has no intention of debating the issue, but she jerks back on instinct when she sees the stick in Jilly's hand fly up suddenly.

With her left arm Jilly swings the stick, slamming it into the floor lamp which sits beside Michael's favorite chair, the chair he chooses to sit in to read his novels while sipping Scotch. The glass fixture and light bulbs explode on impact. Shards of colored glass. Mary sees them float up off the end of the stick, then settle in a shower on the carpet. The metal lamp stand teeters for a moment on its base before crashing to the floor. Bits of glass shower Mary's feet. She must have screamed because Jilly shouts, "Shut up! Shut the fuck up, you bitch!"

Mary's knees tremble. She reaches out for the back of the

sofa to steady herself. Her heart is pounding. She feels the thud of blood in her throat. The music from the basement suddenly stops. She hears Meagan shout, "Mom?"

She looks into Jilly's eyes. Feels Jilly's boring into her. They seem to be waiting for each other to move, they seem to be counting to ten. "Mom?"

An hour ago Mary was thanking her lucky stars Meagan had not ascended the stairs but now she is thinking *Get up here, get up here now.*

"Shut up, you cow!" Jilly swings the stick to the right this time, toward Mary's head, but it misses and hits at the end of its arc a picture hanging on the wall above the sideboard. The glass cracks. The frame tilts, wavering on the hanger fastening it to the plaster, and then crashes to the floor.

"Stop!" Mary shouts.

But Jilly is not listening. She takes a step toward the picture and strikes it again with the stick, the way she may have struck out at a ball on a grass pitch, Mary thinks, toes pointed nicely toward the target. The glass breaks into thousands of pieces. The painting inside, an original oil on canvas Michael bought years ago, a prairie landscape, crumples and splits. Jilly says, "There," as if bringing some unfinished business to a close. "There."

"Get out!" Mary screams.

Jilly screams back, "Fuck you!" She points the end of the stick at Mary and moves forward, locking her eyes on Mary's.

Mary is glad now she brought the wine bottle out of the kitchen when she heard the noise at the door. It feels substantial in her hand. Heavy. She has no idea what is going on in Jilly's head, no idea what is going to happen in the next few moments, but she knows the wine bottle is her ally. She holds it out in a menacing gesture, the little liquid remaining in it sloshing into the cuff of her sleeve and down her arm. She can't believe the words that come out of her mouth. "Back off!"

Jilly laughs. "Yes," she says. "Got you." She dances

forward. With a flick of her wrist she swings the stick at the bottle, hitting its green glass square in the bottom and knocking it out of Mary's hand. It strikes the wall and thuds to the floor, sloshing wine over the carpet. Mary feels her knees give way. She drops to the carpet, crooking both arms over her head. "Stop," she cries out. "Mom!" Meagan shouts. She is in the kitchen, her big body moving with furious agility across the space between the two women and herself. She does not speak another word, does not stop over Mary's crouching form. She barrels into Jilly, knocking her backward. Her arms are out straight in front of her menacing body, her hands vise grips clawing at Jilly's throat.

"Stop!" Mary screams.

Meagan hesitates, turns for a moment toward her mother, and in that tiny gap of time Jilly rights herself, curses, and bolts out the door. Then there is silence, broken only by heavy breathing, Mary's and Meagan's. After a few minutes Mary stands and stumbles toward the front door. She hears first the wind in the trees outside, and then the wrenching sobs coming from deep in her chest.

Michael stumbles out of the Westin, feeling the cold blast of a northern wind on his cheeks. He tilts his head upward, face to the heavens. The sky is clear, the stars cold and remote, the moon a bright quivering crescent above the streetlights and office towers of the city. The icy air stings his skin, but feels good. It feels clean, and Michael stops at the edge of the parking lot and runs both hands through his hair, then extends his arms toward the heavens. Lines of poetry pop into his head: "To stay our minds on and be staid." Michael laughs. His hands fall to his sides with a slap. His underarms feel clammy and he can smell dense, musky perfume, the odor of the woman on his body, God, awful. He needs a shower. As soon as he gets back to Willow Island he will have a shower. One large Scotch and then a shower. He glances around. On the street lines of cars move slowly toward the stoplight at Portage Avenue. A siren is screeching over the bridge in Saint Boniface. Taxis are purring in front of the entrance to the hotel. The city is alive and noisy.

Michael fishes in his pockets for the keys to his truck. On the sidewalk a little ways down two men in soiled clothes are arguing in slurred voices. He hopes they will not approach him and moves quickly to insert the key into the lock so he can put the door of the truck between himself and their scruffy bodies. He starts the engine, making sure both doors are locked, and then leans back in the seat with a sigh. It is 11:17, the digital clock on the dash indicates. In an hour, at most an hour and a half, he will be under the duvet at the cottage. He will be clean and safe. His stomach will be warm with Scotch. Frost's poems will be at the bedside but Ethena will be behind him. He adjusts the rearview mirror so he can study his own face. There is a welt in the shape of a half moon below one eye, his nose is red, and his lower lip is slightly swollen, so little no one would notice. All in all he has come out okay. By morning even he will not be able to tell he has been attacked. He shakes his head. For a moment in there he believed he would die. *Mark*, he thinks. He shakes his head again. There are times Michael wishes he still smoked and this is one of them. Instead he fishes in the ashtray for the mints he keeps there. When he finds the plastic bag he pops three into his mouth.

That's when the cellular phone bleeps. He looks at it for a moment. He has begun to feel the same way about the cell phone he feels about registered mail: it can only be bad news. All his best instincts tell him to let it bleep itself into silence, infernal piece of electronics. What he needs now is a long quiet drive back to the country. He will roll the windows down and feel the ice air searing his cheeks and clearing his mind. He will think about the stars and repeat lines of poetry over and over as the tires whir across asphalt.

He picks up the phone and pushes *send*. "Yes," he says flatly.

"Daddy," Jane says, "I'm so glad you answered."

"It's late," he says.

"I been trying you for nearly an hour. Where were youse?"

"I was—well, it doesn't matter, does it?"

"You're supposed to take that thing with you even when you go walking on the beach. That's why you bought it."

"You don't drag the miserable dregs of technology with you on a bucolic walk. I've told you that."

"No, instead you leave your family dangling. It's selfish, Daddy."

Michael takes a deep breath. *You would know*, he thinks. The two men have moved closer. They are arguing, it appears, over a bottle one of them has in a brown paper bag. He asks, "What's up?"

"Daddy, it's Brad."

In the silence she leaves, Michael feels a flush spreading from his throat into his cheeks. "Are you okay?"

"Yeah," she says. "But, Daddy, he hit me."

"Shit." Michael puts one hand over the lower part of his face, pinching the flesh beneath his eye sockets in toward his nose with his thumb and index finger. "I thought this would happen," he mutters. He brings his hand away, takes several deep breaths, and then says, "Look, I'm on my way over there."

"Christ," she says. "You're hours away."

"I'm in the city, actually. On—here on business." Michael puts the truck in reverse and glances over his shoulder. The parking lot is almost deserted. "God damn," he mutters, "I told you it would come to this."

"You what?"

"I told you he would turn violent."

"Bullshit. You said it would be all right."

"I said to move out to the cottage. You and the kids."

"You didn't mean that."

"I said it and I meant it."

"Bullshit."

"I know what I mean. Are you saying I don't know what I mean?"

"I'm saying you hear what you want to hear."

Jane leaves a silence and in it Michael makes the light at Portage and begins driving north toward Jane's place. He says, "Let's not argue about it."

"That's just you all over again, Daddy. He tells you he's had a few bad drugs and you believe him. You want to believe him because it suits you. That way you don't have to get involved. So you can walk on the beach and talk to the fucking pelicans or whatever it is you do out there."

"I live a life," Michael says. "My life."

"You run away. You duck involvement."

"Jesus, kid, I *am* involved. And you were the one who said it would be okay. Remember, out at the cottage—and after that when I came over?"

"What did you think he was talking about, marijuana?"

"Yes." Michael glances down at the speedometer, slowing for the underpass where the CP station used to be. He cannot remember passing city hall. That's how you get in accidents, he thinks. Distracted chatter on cell phones.

"That's just what I mean," Jane is saying. "He tells you something but you're not really listening. What he meant was he was mixing marijuana with the antidepressant the doctor prescribed."

"Jesus."

"He's like fucked up bad. He takes these drugs so he won't end up the same as his cousin and uncle."

"You never said anything about that."

"That's what made him go off the deep end before."

"But you never told us anything."

150

"And you just chose to ignore it. *Hey, he looks okay now,* you're thinking, *no big deal, Jane's just imagining things as per usual. I'm all right, Jack. I'll just stroll the beaches and putter around the cottage.* Well, it's not all right, Daddy, when he comes home calling me *slut,* busting up the chairs, punching my face in, and where are you? Out on some nature fucking ramble!"

"You," Michael says, "you never told me. Us."

"You just go on seeing what you want to see. Long as you're out of it."

"You didn't tell us. You were busy doing what you do best, hiding stuff from your parents. Deception, lies."

"Fuck you."

"Fuck you."

"Oh duh, Daddy."

Michael slams on the brakes. At Hespeler Avenue some jerkwater in an old beater is attempting to make a left turn from the middle lane without signaling. The two vehicles are so close to each other Michael holds his breath, anticipating the crash, the crunch of metal on metal. But the bumper of the swerving Mazda slides past the beater, it cannot be more than centimeters. Still, the truck bucks as Michael pumps the brakes, the tires screech, the engine coughs and then dies. A tousled greasy head of hair pokes out of one of the car's back windows. "Hey, asshole, watch where you're driving!"

"Fuck you!" Michael screams back. He restarts the truck's engine.

Though it is dark, Michael sees every detail clearly. All four heads in the car swivel, the heads of young men with cans of beer to their lips. Ugly men, angry men. Men with greasy hair, with missing teeth and soiled T-shirts, men with nothing better to do on a Saturday night than get into a fight. Not college kids, not the kind Michael is used to cajoling and molding to his view of things. These greaseballs grimace and curse words he cannot hear as the distance between the cars grows. Michael is thankful they were turning at Hespeler.

He checks the rearview mirror at the next two intersections, but no sign of a rusted-out blue Belair.

In the half minute that has elapsed Michael has continued holding the phone in one hand. His heart is in his throat but he manages to say into it, "Look, that doesn't matter, does it?" He waits and when Jane does not answer he adds, "What matters, honey, is that I'll be there in a couple minutes."

"He said he was coming back," Jane says. "That's why I called."

"A couple minutes," Michael says. "Just sit tight."

"I know this is terribly unusual," the voice on the other end of the line says, "but could I have a few minutes of your time?"

Mary looks at her watch. Twenty minutes past midnight. "I guess," she says. "It's been a long day." She sighs and absently lifts the wine glass off the counter, noting that it is happily full.

"I appreciate that."

"A long day and a long night. But okay, go ahead."

"Good. It's Dr. Jackman, Dr. Leanne Jackman."

"Yes. I got it the first time."

"About Jilly Thomson."

Mary swallows. "Right," she says. She holds the wine glass up to the light and then takes a sip.

"She's here," Dr. Jackman says. Her voice is low, with a husky timbre to it, something Mary likes. She imagines a small woman, a fine-boned woman with wire-frame spectacles and thin lips. An intelligent woman. "Jilly is here with me," Dr. Jackman adds. "I'm her, well, her therapist."

Mary wonders if the two of them are in Dr. Jackman's office, Jilly on the ubiquitous couch, the doctor behind her oak desk. "I see," she says. Deep inside she feels a sudden relief. She'd been wondering where Jilly went. She'd been hoping she hadn't done anything reckless, injured herself, or caused an automobile accident. In the time that has elapsed since Jilly left, Mary's mind has been buzzing with thoughts and she has decided to bring things to an end with the girl. It was a rash beginning between them, and fittingly, they have come to a rash ending. Chalk one up to experience. Beware the girl bearing the field hockey stick.

"Jilly is upset," Dr. Jackman says. "Very upset."

"So am I," Mary says. She did not intend to sound petulant and her first instinct is to apologize, but then she thinks *I have a right to be angry. Why the hell not?* She adds, "She came to my house tonight. She frightened me." She hesitates, then adds, "Scared the shit out of me, actually."

"Yes."

"I suppose she told you about that."

"She told me you were lovers."

Mary swallows hard. *Lovers* is not a word she would use about herself and Jilly, certainly not now. Hardly a word she has let enter her thoughts. She feels a hot flush surge from her abdomen to her face. *Furnace face*, she thinks. *Sauna, steam.* Her thoughts leap to Meagan in the basement. What if she has picked up the phone down there?

When Mary does not answer Dr. Jackman says, "You have no cause to be alarmed. I'm just getting things clear. Groundwork."

"I understand," Mary says. "It's just that it's been an upsetting night."

"Jilly has her bad days," Dr. Jackman says.

"She sure as hell does."

"Like all of us."

"All of us don't come after people with weapons."

"You'd be surprised," Dr. Jackman says. She pauses and Mary can hear an intake of breath over the phone line. This she hadn't expected: Dr. Jackman smokes. Mary thinks *nicotine, cancer*. She feels an itch under her contacts. In a moment Dr. Jackman continues, "Jilly is really sorry about what happened. Sorry and frightened." It seems as if Dr. Jackman waits a moment for Mary to respond, but just as Mary opens her mouth to speak, she adds, "Our Jilly is completely undone. At this moment Jilly wishes she could find a hole in the ground and crawl into it. That's what she has been telling me. She is in despair. Jilly is concerned that she hurt you. She has convinced herself she did you irreparable physical damage."

"I am all right," Mary says. "You can tell her that. Perfectly all right. At this moment I am enjoying a glass of white wine."

"More than that, Jilly is now convinced you will never speak to her again. That she has damaged your relationship. Which is why I have taken the liberty of calling you."

Mary sighs. "Hey," she says, "I'll talk to her. Right now if you want."

Dr. Jackman clears her throat. "Perhaps not this very moment."

"No," Mary says. "It can wait. If she can't handle it or whatever." She takes a deep breath and senses again the stench of ditch water in the air. She'll get out the Mister Clean as soon as she can bring this phone call to a close. Lemon. Antiseptic.

Dr. Jackman inhales and exhales again and Mary takes a sip of wine. "A little while ago," Dr. Jackman says, "Jilly hit rock bottom. Fortunately I was with her at the time." She pauses a moment and then adds, "Jilly's rock bottom is very rock. I am telling you this in the strictest of confidence, as someone near and dear. Has Jilly told you what she does when she hits rock bottom?"

Mary hears a groan from the background of Dr. Jackman's office. Then she hears Dr. Jackman speaking in hushed but urgent tones away from the phone. When she comes back on the line Mary says, "No, she has not."

Dr. Jackman says, "Jilly mutilates things. She had a cat once. That's not the worst of it. She pokes her own flesh with the red-hot end of a hunting knife she bought especially for the purpose."

"My God."

"I have not been able to get this knife away from Jilly. No one has."

"Jesus."

"She took a sledgehammer to her father's car. A new Mercedes."

"I get the picture," Mary says.

"The reason Jilly does these things is she feels rejection. Jilly is extremely vulnerable in that regard. I won't go into all the details but Jilly's mother left her and Jilly's father when Jilly was going through puberty. Not a good time for any of us. I don't suppose Jilly told you about this."

"No."

"No." Dr. Jackman sighs. In the pause she leaves Mary hears Meagan moving about in the basement. She has not slept well since coming home from St. Louis. Her appetite has been off too. Everyone is fucked up in some way, Mary thinks. Her too. Now she finds out about Jilly. Dr. Jackman is saying, "Jilly was devastated. So it goes without saying—well, almost, since I am saying it—that Jilly should not get involved with married women. The risk is very high. Of rejection."

Mary takes another sip of wine. She liked Dr. Jackman's voice when she first heard it, but now it's starting to grate on her nerves. Dr. Jackman seems to enjoy ordering people around. Her voice is brassy. She's the pushy sort. In a moment she'll be telling Mary what to do. Mary says, "I get the point."

"The potential for disaster is—well, is enormous. I cannot emphasize that enough. Enormous."

"I think we had just about run the course," Mary says.

"See, I was afraid you were going to say that." Dr. Jackman inhales and says, "That would be precisely the wrong thing to happen now. To end things—your relationship. That could tip Jilly over the edge."

"You were just saying I shouldn't have gotten involved with her!"

"You are taking this too personal, Mary. May I call you Mary? I was saying Jilly should not as a rule involve herself with people who are bound to let her down. People with prior emotional commitments. Married women, in this instance. Or men, if that were the case."

"But now that she's coming after me with a hockey stick I have to hang in there with her?"

"That seems an unnecessarily cruel way of putting it."

"It's the facts."

"What I meant was, if you care for Jilly. In the long-term sense."

"Of course I do."

"I know that." Dr. Jackman pauses. "I think Jilly needs to hear it. Don't you agree, Mary?"

"I suppose."

"Otherwise—well, I don't want to contemplate otherwise."

"Right. I don't want to be responsible for . . ."

"It's not just a case of responsibility."

"Jesus," Mary says. "I *know* that. Give me a break here. I'm a grown woman, I know what people feel. How they think. How they react."

"Yes," Dr. Jackman says, "of course you do. I'm sorry. I just want to do what's right for Jilly. What's best for her."

"So do I," Mary says. She pauses and has another sip of wine. "Look," she adds, "I have no intention of dumping the girl or anything of that nature. I give you my assurance. I like her, I love her. I'll stick it out until she's level again. Okay, doctor?"

"Okay. Although I wouldn't put it quite that way. *Level.*"

"Put it however you wish. She didn't come after you with a weapon."

There is a long pause and then Dr. Jackman says, "I think

I'll put Jilly on the line now, Mary. She has some things she wants to say to you. And I'm sure you have some to tell her."

"Right."

"Right. Good talking to you then, Mary. We'll keep in touch."

Jane says, "And the blankets. The two in Randy's bedroom." She tips her head in that direction. Sweat has matted one lock of hair to her forehead. In her arms she's carrying a box filled with toys—games, dolls, plastic models.

"We've got plenty of blankets," Michael says. He means there are more than enough at the cottage, where they're heading as soon as they've put in the back of the truck all the things Jane thinks necessary for her hasty flight.

Jane has almost reached the door. She calls back over her shoulder as she fumbles for the latch with the fingers of one hand, "Their special blankets, their blankies."

"Right," Michael says. He moves down the hallway toward the boy's bedroom, glancing into the living room where the kids are curled up together on the sofa. Ali's bare feet stick out from under the quilt Jane threw over them when she moved them out of their bedrooms, sleepy-eyed and groggy, an hour ago when Michael arrived. Randy is lying with one arm sticking straight out over the edge of the sofa, the other crooked under his head. How do kids sleep that way? He stands looking at them for a moment. He wants to cross the room to them, take them up in his arms, tell them they need never worry again. Grampa is here. Grampa loves you. Grampa would throw down his own life for yours. He swallows hard. Tomorrow he will take them to the McDonald's where they have the play structure, buy them each a new toy. He forces his feet to move on. Michael finds the two blankets folded neatly at the door of the bedroom and pauses for a moment, surveying in the dimly lit room the boy's collection of posters: Batman next to the logo of the Anaheim Mighty Ducks, some teen idol Michael doesn't recognize beside a Tyrannosaurus Rex. When Maurice was a kid he had a collection of scale-model dinosaur skeletons which Jane smashed to pieces with a shovel after one of their childhood fights. She broke up a set of Patricia's china too, and drove the Tercel into the back of the garage when she was a teenager. Jane's life story has been one of smashing up things and waiting for Michael to pick up the pieces. He sighs.

"I know," Jane says at his shoulder, "it's been one mother of a day."

He puts his free arm around her. "You're doing okay, kid. Great."

She rests her head against his shoulder for a moment. "Should I bring food? Milk and stuff?"

"There's plenty out there. But milk, sure. Or if the kids have a favorite breakfast cereal."

"Yeah. And fruit snacks. Bet youse don't have those."

"No. Not too many." Michael has brought the index finger of one hand up to his nose to scratch an itch and he smells again the spicy perfume of the woman at the Westin. He blinks his eyes.

"Or Dunkaroos," Jane is saying. "They have to have Dunkaroos." She sighs. "Would you like a drink?" she asks. "Before we take off?"

"No," Michael says. He would, that's exactly what he would like, but now the truck is nearly packed, he's anxious to go. He just wants to be on the road, taking Jane and her kids away from all their grief. Though he knows he can never protect them from grief and heartache in any final sense.

"All righty," Jane says. She pulls away from him and crosses into the kitchen. Before she gets to the refrigerator she glances out the window over the sink, whether out of habit or because she sees something, and then she whispers almost inaudibly, "Oh shit!"

"What?" Michael has crossed to her side and is peering out the window, too, though he cannot see anything in the gloom.

"It's the van," she says, "Brad."

"Damn."

Jane looks at him. "Maybe you should go wait in the truck."

"And have him smacking you around again? Hitting the kids? No way." Michael can hear footsteps on the back stairs and he pulls himself up to his full height. *If I have to*, he thinks, *I'm ready*.

Jane says wearily, "Oh, Jesus." When the door swings open she moves forward in the room between the two men, her narrow shoulders blocking Michael's view for a moment.

Brad seems surprised to find them there. He pauses and looks around, eyes blinking. When he spots the box Jane has placed in the center of the room, a cardboard box containing two packages of Cheerios as well as a half-dozen packets of Fruit Roll-Ups, he asks, "What the hell's all this supposed to be?" His voice is slurred. He swallows and glances around.

"You've been drinking," Jane says. "You're drunk."

"And you're ugly. I'll sober up."

Jane snorts. "And you wonder why I'm splitting."

Brad looks around again and then says, "What's he doing here?"

"Bloody typical, that. Drinking to get up the courage."

"Duh." Brad has not moved since he spotted Michael, but his hands are working furiously at his sides, fists clenching and unclenching. He's wearing a soiled and rumpled black T-shirt with the name of a rock group stenciled on it in silver gothic script which Michael cannot decipher. "Yeah," Brad spits out, "you should talk, you little bitch. Packing up and running away."

"Running for cover."

"On the phone to the old man, you little suck. When are you going to grow up?"

"When you become a man. When you don't have to hide in a bottle."

"Fuck you," Brad says. "You and your old man."

Michael clears his voice as if he meant to speak, but before he can Jane says, "Now you get the whole place to yourself." Her voice is brassy and loud. She has raised one hand and waves it in the air between their two faces, though she has not moved, either. "Isn't that what you want?"

"I want you out of my sight. Out of my house."

"Fuck you."

Brad raises one clenched fist and then reaches back and strikes the wall behind him, an impotent but noisy gesture. Dishes rattle in the cupboards. A tumbler on the counter tips over. "Yeah," he shouts. "And you too."

"All right," Michael says. "That's enough." He steps forward, he is not sure to do what, perhaps to pull Jane back, perhaps to restrain Brad, but just then Randy runs into the room, bumping into Michael's leg from behind.

"Dad!" Randy cries.

Jane turns and kneels, gathering the boy in her arms. "Hush now," she says. "We're just talking with—talking with your father. Everything's okay." She runs her fingers through the boy's hair, whispering to him, making him stop squirming and reaching out to his father, and then she turns him around in a half circle and gives him a light push on the bum. "Go and lie down again."

"But I want to see Dad," he says.

"No," Jane says. "Not now."

Her voice sounds harsh to Michael. He sees the boy wince. He pictures himself crossing the room and holding the boy to his chest. There, there.

The boy wriggles and squirms, his red pajama top bunching around his stick neck. "But I want to show him—"

"No," Jane says, her voice rising. "Go now," she says. "Now."

Brad snorts. "Turning my own kids against me." His black hair is long in back and stringy, greasy and unwashed, like the hair of the four guys in the car that cut Michael off at Hespeler Avenue. He sneers the same way, too, out of the side of his mouth.

"Protecting them," Jane says, "*from* you." She is standing again, a foot or two between her and Brad. "Telling them a damn sight less than I should."

"Fucking slut."

"Asshole."

The punch Brad throws is feeble, more a slap, but it strikes Jane in the side of the head behind the ear and she staggers backward. Michael's hands reach out to steady her, but the moment she has caught her balance he moves past her. Rage races into his face, rage he has been carrying since Ethena hit him in the face, since the greaser in the beater yelled at him. He is a big man, six three and 220 pounds. Two winters ago he was bench-pressing eighty-five kilograms in the gym. He doesn't so much punch Brad as push him, and the smaller man stumbles backward, striking the door with both elbows before losing his balance and sliding to the floor, his neck twisted awkwardly to one side. He grunts. Michael stands over him, bewildered by what he has done, his hands clenching and relaxing. He knows hitting a man in the face hurts his feelings, but if you really want to hurt him, you punch him straight from the shoulder in the sternum—or swing an uppercut into the bottom of his rib cage. That knocks out the breath, too. And then you can do the real damage. Michael may be half expecting to deliver one of those blows, but Brad wriggles up from the floor in a moment, and then wrenches open the door and is gone.

"Leave him," Jane yells.

But something compels Michael's feet out onto the landing. He feels Jane behind him, tugging at his shirt. "Stop!" she cries. "Stop now. Please."

They stumble together on the landing, watching Brad wrench open the door of the van. The engine starts. He sticks his head out the window. "Slut," he yells above the roar of the motor. "Cunt. Assholes."

The van jerks into reverse, and that's when Michael sees the boy run out from behind the garage. He's waving something in his hand, holding it up for his father to see. Michael opens his mouth to yell, to scream, but he does not hear anything come out of his throat, only the thunk the rear bumper of the van makes as it contacts the body of the boy, the tiny, tiny body that flips through the air as if in slow motion, the red pajamas caught for a moment in the red glow of the taillights before the boy lands in a heap on the dark concrete of the back lane, one hand still clutching the rolled-up and now crumpled poster the son was so eager to show the father.

When they reach the junction where the winding residential road splits into two, the tributary leading into the private school while the main branch continues on its arc around Woodydell, Mary pauses and Meagan does too. They have been silent for some time, their footsteps crunching on the asphalt, ghosts of breath puffing up from their mouths. Meagan is wearing a heavy wool sweater which buttons down the front, Mary a fleece pullover with a high collar. At midnight the temperature was hovering around the freezing mark. By dawn, Mary thinks, it will drop below. Ice diamonds on windowpanes. Crack of hardwood floors in the night. Motors cold. Noses red. Mary tugs at the sleeve of her pullover and glances at her watch: 2:11. They have been walking for almost an hour. The air is chilly but refreshing. Just what Mary needs. Something to clear the gray matter, something to remind her she's alive and sane. That and many glasses of water for the headache she feels rolling toward her skull like summer storm clouds. She turns to Meagan.

"Quite a moon," she says, "rattling around up there."

Meagan tilts her head this way and that, her lips working as she studies the bright crescent above them. Finally she says, "White light."

Mary grunts. They are both happy to leave it at that. Mary wrinkles her nose. She has a tissue in the back pocket of her jeans but she does not reach for it. They resume walking, side by side, along the road that takes them in the arc past Woodydell. Meagan's breathing is heavy. She should exercise more, Mary thinks. Exercise, period. From time to time a motor can be heard in the distance, thrumming the cold air. When they near the junction where the dirt path runs along the river, they can see the headlights of cars gliding through the suburb on the far bank. Mary pauses. "It's odd," she says, "isn't it, the city in the dead of night?"

Meagan nods. "Eerie, eh? Like a whole other planet."

"Frightening."

"Most people find the country strange at night, you know, because it's empty, eh." Meagan clears her throat. "The silence. But the silence of the city is what's weird. All these lights, these houses, streets, signs, stuff that's usually so alive—noisy somehow—suddenly silent."

Mary says, "Let's take the river path home." They descend the grassy slope from the street and find the beaten trail through the woods along the bank of the river. Most of the leaves are down. Bare branches overhead. At this proximity Mary can hear the swishing of the water. Nails on sandpaper, she thinks. The path is just wide enough for two. Their shoes thud over the mud.

Then Meagan stops. "Listen," she says. High above, the call of geese, heading south. They look up through the trees but cannot spot them.

"Magical," Mary says.

"Eerie," Meagan repeats. "So non-human."

"I guess," Mary says.

"They're like prehistoric dinosaurs or something. If you didn't know they were geese they would scare the hair off you."

"I used to think of them as noisy creatures," Mary says, "but they're not. They're tranquil, actually, serene. Magical. With the wisdom of passivity."

They continue walking, climbing the slight slope that loops past the clubhouse where the kids play hockey in winter, soccer in summer. Soon they will rejoin the paved street that takes them home. Home, Mary thinks. Recalls the game they played as kids: *home free!* For some reason she thinks of Mark, the look on his face the night he told them about his cancer. When they pause at the crossing, Meagan fishes a cigarette out of a pocket in her sweater and lights it, cupping her free hand over her mouth. Mary studies the flare of the lighter's flame and the way Meagan's cheeks puff in and out as she inhales and exhales. After she has blown smoke into the air Meagan says, "So, you had—what?—an affair with this Jilly?"

No point in lying, Mary thinks. Puts one hand up to her face. She must be blushing. "You could call it that."

"I've always liked the word *fling*."

"Not *romance*?"

"Naw," Meagan says, "too romantic." They both laugh, little gasps that are swallowed up by the swishing of the river.

"I guess it was crazy," Mary says. "But it was something I had to do."

"Try it out, you mean? With a woman?"

"Jilly wasn't a new brand of detergent, darling."

Instead of answering Meagan kicks at the dirt on the trail, spraying their shoes with tiny hard lumps of mud. They climb the steepest part of the path and continue in silence for a few minutes. Mary's heart is beating fast, her face feels hot. She read in one of the magazines lying around the club that walking—walking long distances at a brisk pace—is a demanding exercise, very underrated. Excellent for cardio-vascular. Muscle toning. Maybe she'll give up all that huffing and puffing on the bicycles and stair-masters and just walk three or four miles a day. That way she could avoid Jilly, too. The club. But walking would take a lot of time, it's a retired person's exercise. She is calculating whether she can afford that much time away from work when Meagan says, "But it's over now? The thing with Jilly?"

"That part is over, the—the intimate part. Though this doctor says I should continue to give her support and so on. Her therapist."

Meagan inhales and studies the glowing cigarette in her fingers before saying, "Hold her hand, you mean."

"Exactly." They are walking with their heads down now, speaking in subdued tones. Mary says, "I shall tell Michael soon. In my own good time."

Meagan is breathing heavily. This walking is hard on her. "Sure."

"It was crazy," Mary says again. "And it turned out a mess. Krikey."

"But you're not thinking . . . you're not going to . . ."

"No, no. Nothing like that. I was just—I don't know— bored, restless. A marriage goes through these phases. Up and down."

"The old roller coaster."

"Exactly. No, nothing like that, separate lives and all the rest. I love Michael. We love each other."

"Well, Jilly was not boring."

Mary snorts. "She certainly was not that."

Meagan has slowed her pace and Mary slows hers too. Leaves crunch underfoot. Twigs. Finally Meagan asks, "And did you enjoy it, being with a woman?"

"I did," Mary says. She laughs and then adds as if she's only just thought of it, "Women understand women intuitively. We're at ease with each other." She hesitates. "Women know how to please each other."

"I know."

165

The way she says it brings Mary almost to a stop, though she wills her feet to keep moving. Ruts worn in the mud beneath the soles of her shoes. Brown corrugation. After a minute she says weakly, "You do?"

"Yes," Meagan says. She breathes deeply through her nose, sending streams of smoke into the air. "You remember Melody and Tanya?"

"That was in high school. I thought you were just chums."

"Well, yes, that too. And Cheryl and CoraLee."

"The one at the office where you worked last year?"

"The dispatcher at GI, yeah."

Mary says, "I should have guessed." She wants to look at Meagan, to peer into her daughter's soul, but she keeps her eyes fixed to the ground.

Finally Meagan says, "You should have, Maw."

"I feel like an idiot."

"No. I worked hard—we worked hard—to keep it from you."

"Why did you do that?"

"Why?"

Mary blinks her eyes. Sometimes she can't believe the words that come out of her own mouth. She touches the sleeve of Meagan's sweater. "Stupid," she says. "Stupid question." They have turned at the fork where the path over the grass angles back to the asphalt. "Have I been such a terrible mother?"

"You're a good mother." Meagan pauses. She flips the cigarette butt into the air, and when it lands she grinds it under her boot. "Just a little too helpful from time to time," she adds.

"Pushy, you mean."

Meagan sighs. "I have to decide things for myself, eh? That's all." She reaches out for Mary's hand, fumbling with the bulky sleeve of her pullover before she finds the fingers. Squeezes once. "Like I've decided to move out."

"Darling."

"Maw. Don't start."

Mary groans aloud. They've been all through this. Diabetes is not the flu. "What if—"

"Damn the consequences," Meagan says. "You can't let fear about what might happen rule your life. You know that. You taught me that." Her breath is coming in short gasps. They cross the patch of remaining grass in silence. "Like," Meagan continues, "going to a psychiatrist to see if I can get a handle on my life, eh."

"But we tried that."

"Ten years ago we tried it. Ten years ago, Maw, and on your terms. This time I'm going on my terms and because I want to go."

"I see."

"I don't think you do, Maw." Meagan stops on the asphalt. They are only a city block's distance from home. The chimney of the house is visible through the denuded trees. She looks into Mary's face. "I'm angry," she adds. "I don't mean right at this very moment. I mean I'm an angry person. That's something I've discovered about myself. I'm filled with this rage, this boiling anger. Like your friend Jilly, eh? I want to hit things, smash things up. You. For one. All the kids I went to school with, the Sarahs. I'd like to choke them with my bare hands, I'd like to—well . . ." Meagan pauses. She is still holding Mary's hand in hers. "That's no good," she says, "anger that goes so deep."

"No." Mary swallows hard. Squeezes Meagan's hand. "All right."

"So CoraLee told me about this Dr. Shand."

"The psychiatrist?"

"Psychoanalyst, actually. I'm starting next week. First I have to get a new apartment. Get my living space in order, eh, then my head space."

"You're sure?"

"I am absolutely certain."

MEAGAN

I am at the counter at the dispatch office at GI, and Tara is there, this big woman who worked there on the files and stuff, she is trying to rape me. She has me pinned against the counter. Her hands are on the waist of my jeans and she is jerking down on them, jerking so hard she rips the seam running up the back of the crotch. She has a big mouth with bright red lipstick painted on it crookedly, as if she didn't have a mirror to look into, and her pink tongue is sticking out the way Michael Jordan's does when he goes in for a dunk. There are other people in the office, women, secretaries, but I don't know who they are and they don't seem to be concerned about what is happening. I am not that concerned about it either, not scared or anything, just wanting to get Tara off me. Her breasts are huge, like pillows, and soft and spongy against my face and neck. I push at them with my hands. I try to remember what you are supposed to do when being attacked but all I can recall is *knee him in the balls*, and that won't work with Tara, will it? I push and struggle. Suddenly I have escaped enough from her clutches to free my arms and I am throwing punches in her face. One, two, three. Tara's nose is bleeding, gobs of red blood dripping down the front of her white blouse, streamers of it, where I see now milk is leaking from her breasts too, white, and mixing with the blood as it runs down her legs. She is saying *fuck, fuck*, but I continue throwing punches at her face, punches which now are not landing though I am exerting enormous strength to throw them. I am very excited, it seems. My heart is pounding. I feel sexually aroused. And then without my having noticed him arrive, Jerry, my boss at GI, is choking Tara, he has her by the throat with both hands and she is sinking to her knees, gasping and flailing her arms above her head like a drowning swimmer. I want to say *no no, don't hurt her, she wasn't really hurting me*, but I wake up.

This is not my idea, this is what Dr. Shand—Rosie—says I am supposed to do, write down the dream as soon as I wake up, I'm not sure I'm even doing it right, and then I'm supposed to read it over and jot down whatever thoughts pop into my head. Like, I guess, why Tara? I always liked her. She didn't give a damn that she was overweight. She wore tight clothes the way you are not supposed to when you're fat. She was loud, too, with a hooting laugh you could hear all over the terminal. CoraLee says it's going to get her fired. But now that I think about it Tara had blonde hair the same color as Mom's except cut in a different style, shoulder-length flip, only in the dream it was the same style as Mom's, bobbed. Does that mean I want to kill Mom? I guess part of me might, I even said so a week or so ago when we went out walking down by the river. And here's another thing. When I was a little girl I always thought her breasts were huge, Mom's, like Tara's were in the dream, and I wanted to have big breasts like that when I grew up, big smothering breasts, except when I got them I hated them, I used to imagine cutting them off with a knife so they wouldn't be so obvious and embarrassing, flopping around on my chest that way, only I imagined they would bleed down the front of my body if I hacked away at them, and that made me sick to the stomach. But that was an enormous bummer for me in high school, my breasts, I always imagined the Sarahs and Heathers were laughing at me behind my back. You know the type, simpering blonde bitches with simpering laughs. Sara Templeton. I wanted to choke her to death every day during high school, and now I think about it *Sara* sounds the same as *Tara*, except not pronounced quite the same. And I told Mom that crazy night when I said I wanted to hurt her sometimes that throughout high school I wanted to choke the

Sarahs and Heathers with my bare hands the way Jerry was actually doing in the dream. I told Mom I had all this anger inside me, and I do. I told Rosie the same thing and she said, *let's start there then*, so my subconscious maybe took note and threw up this dream. Only there's a lot I haven't touched on. Why Jerry? How about that blood and milk running down Tara's (Mom's? Sara's?) shirt? It's a start. (October 21)

I'm in the rig down a gravel road somewhere. I'm frightened because we never take the rig off paved surfaces, it's danger-ous, and I know I'd smash it up trying to maneuver. It is night, the headlights of the rig shine down the gravel road, which bends away in the bushes. I can't see very far ahead. I want to get moving, get the rig back on the highway, but it is rolling backwards. I press on the brakes. This is weird because the brakes in the rig don't work that way, but no mat-ter how hard I push down with my feet, the rig keeps moving backward. Then it picks up speed in reverse. My heart is rac-ing, and I jam my feet to the floor, but the rig rolls backwards, I know it is going to crash into the bushes behind but I can't do anything to stop it. We are traveling faster and faster, an enormous speed, and I am scared, real scared, knowing the crash is coming any minute, and I am looking back feeling my elbows strike the window glass, and then I am in a wheelchair, not the cab of the rig, and my elbows are sore from lying on the armrests. I'm on a path in the woods, a rutted mud trail, and the wheelchair is rolling forward faster than I want it to, but again I can do nothing to stop it. I know my legs are use-less, so I don't even try to use them. My fingers hurt where I am squeezing them on the wheels to slow the roll of the chair. And now I see the path leads down to the river and I am hurtling down a slope toward the water. Trees and bushes are flying past, branches strike me in the face and cut me, so I raise my arms to protect myself. I feel blood running down my face, I look and my hands are covered in blood and I think *how can that be, my skin has only been lashed by leaves and branches but I'm bleeding like a stuck pig*, and then I see the water below me and the cliff the wheelchair is going to go over and I say *okay this dream has to stop now, open your eyes Meagan, open your eyes*, and I force my eyes open and just as the wheelchair goes over the cliff, I awake.

I've had this dream before, about the rig going backwards, except I never remembered it until this time. I always wake up in a sweat, thinking *thank God that was just a dream*. This time, though, when I think about it, I know that gravel road, it's the road out to the cottage at Willow Island, even in the dark of the dream I recognize it because of the squiggly little bends in the road and the willows growing along the ditch. When you drive up there at night they switch around in the headlights of the car, and when I was a kid I thought they would close over the car if it wasn't moving at a good speed and I would be buried in the car, alive, like. I used to say to Michael *go fast go fast or we'll all die*, and Mom would look into the back seat and say *oh darling, you can't be scared by a silly old dusty road*. She was always saying don't be afraid of this, don't be afraid of that, but I was, I was afraid of everything from bugs on the sidewalk to the clap of thunder, I think that's why I took up driving the rigs, to prove to myself and to her that I could handle the most dangerous job a woman can do. Only in the dream it was all slipping away from me, the rig was going to crash, and that would prove I was incompetent after all, wouldn't it? And then that bit about the wheelchair that got confused with the rig somehow. As soon as the doctors in St. Louis said it might be something wrong with my nervous system I thought *oh no, not paralysis of some kind, the rest of my life in a wheelchair*, I've always pitied people in wheelchairs, though I recognize they're really brave and amazing for the way they manage in spite of their problems. I have always been afraid of drowning, too, from the time I was a kid, choking in water seemed worse than being choked to death by pillows, and now I see both these dreams are about me suffocating, drowning in water and drowning in breasts, and I remember screaming at Mom a long time ago when I was a teenager *you're suffocating me!* It was one of our big fights, a real blowout, about dropping out of high school and what was I going to do with my life and whatnot. *You'll end up slinging fries and gravy in a truck stop*, she shouted, and that's when I decided to show her, that's when I decided to drive trucks for a living. And I went from that to being a roadie. That seems a long time ago now, but I see the chickens have come home to roost, as they say. Only Rosie says every dream is a wish fulfillment, even the bad ones like this, and I see now how this one can be. I woke up thinking *I'm not in a wheelchair, thank God, and I am still driving the rig and throwing gear for the band, so that goes to prove I am in control of my life, right?* Which is what I want, to be healthy and in charge of my own fate. (October 23)

I am sitting on a bench, the kind in parks, but this bench is in the tall grass that grows in ditches alongside highways. The bench is across the ditch from the road and is facing the road, but there are no vehicles going past. In the trees sit birds, huge black birds, like vultures, and I know they are going to swoop down and peck my eyes out. I am thinking *I don't want to be blind, not that*, and trying to get up off the bench, but in the tall grass beneath me a man is lying on his side and he has his hands on my legs. He is running his fingers up my thighs and into my crotch, the middle fingers of both hands pushing back the lips of my vagina and touching my clitoris. I am becoming aroused, very aroused, and yet I am thinking about the birds, I know that at any moment they will swoop down on me. And yet I am moving my groin rhythmically to the pressing of the fingers on my clitoris, spreading my legs and pushing down hard. My eyes have been fixed on the birds the whole time, but I glance down briefly and I see that it is not a man in the tall grass but Joycey, one of the backup singers in the band, she has black beautiful hair and lovely full red lips, I have had a crush on her for ages. But looking down I see, too, that a white fluid is running down my legs, and I think to myself, *that only happens to men, not women*, and just as I think that I realize my socks are on fire, orange flames are leaping up my legs, and I try to stand and beat the flames back, they are racing up my legs, licking at the tails of the blouse I am wearing, and I think *I don't want to die, I'm too young to die*, and then I wake up.

I know what this is about. When I had that first attack on the road and had to pull off the highway just past St. Louis I thought right away that I was going to be blind and it terrified me. As kids we sometimes played that game, which would you rather be, deaf or blind, and I always said deaf. To never see things again, the colors of flowers, the smiles on faces, that purple and orange on the horizon when the sun is setting, I could give up music and talking and the other things the other kids said they couldn't live without as long as I could see those colors every day of my life. And I think too, *I'm too young to die*. I think it all the time. The doctors say no one dies of diabetes, but they do, and everyone who has it dies of it sometime. It kills you. And when you get it the way I have, in your late twenties, then you've been given a death sentence. Maybe you'll live to fifty, maybe if you're really lucky, sixty, but you can kiss seventy goodbye, and even though that's a long time from now it still scares you. Everyone wants to live as long as they can, eh? You wake up every day and you think about it. My pancreas doesn't work any more. I'm going to go blind someday. Slowly, maybe, but it's one of the things that happens. So now every time I take that tiny bite of chocolate bar to stimulate the body to make insulin I think *one step closer to my death*. And that's what the birds are all about. There's something hanging around on the edge of my life, waiting to make me blind, the way those crows are in the dream. My executioners. And opposite to that is my life urge, my sexual drive. Sometimes when I go for weeks without having sex I nearly go crazy, and now that I have this disease hanging over me, it's even worse. I want sex all the time. I have to have it to know that I'm still alive, still kicking, so when I look at someone like Joycey, who I know kind of likes me but thinks maybe I'm not her type, too fat or too loud or whatever, not sophisticated enough, I just get sick now. I have to masturbate, using my own hands the way she was in the dream, and it's sickening, I want to lie beside her and feel those things, I don't have time to hang around waiting for her to take an interest in me. I'm burning up with desire. I'm, like, on fire, you could say. (October 25)

I am walking along the shore at Willow Island. It is summer and I have a long walking stick. I am stabbing at bugs running along the sand, ants and beetles, squishing them with the stick. Tiny droplets of blood squirt out of their bodies. I stop and sit on the beach. My knees stick out of the shorts I'm wearing. Then I'm lying on the beach, reclining, and I feel the coarse grains of sand on my elbows. I shift to decrease the discomfort and find I am stretched out on top of Penny McGibb, the girl I first went with in high school. We are naked. I am sucking Penny's breasts. They are small, I can almost suck the entire orb into my mouth, which is working intently, like a baby's. I can see this clearly, as if I am standing outside of myself watching myself. Penny is stroking my hair and murmuring to me. High above in the sky there are birds circling, gulls of some kind, circling and crying. Penny's one hand is stroking my hair. The other is lying between the pubic hair of our bodies. I want her fingers inside me and I try to move around on Penny's body so she can touch my clitoris, rub it until I come, but for some reason I cannot get the right angle. I grind my crotch against her hand. Then I feel the dream slipping away, I know that I will not come and I try harder to position my crotch over her hand, but it does not work, and instead I find myself under the quilt which was on my bed at home when I was in high school, the duvet with the red rose pattern. I feel cheated but I also feel warm, so I pull the quilt over my head. I wake up.

It's funny that I would have that walking stick because it was the one I kept at the cottage for my beach strolls when I was about twelve or thirteen, a long time ago, yet in the dream it is the now me, the thirty-year-old me, I know this, except I haven't taken a walking stick with me on walks at Willow Island for a long time now, that particular stick disappeared ten years ago. I used to hate the bugs on the beach out there, and I enjoyed squashing them with that stick. Sometimes I counted how many I squished in one walk, seeing if I could better the previous record. Which reminds me of my feelings about strangling the Sarahs and Heathers. Once when we were going together Penny and I drove to Willow Island on an afternoon when we wouldn't be discovered and spent the afternoon there, undressing each other and touching and masturbating each other in the cottage. I felt nervous the whole time and guilty afterwards, because we had to sneak around behind Mom's back, not because of what we'd done together. I liked what we did together. The taste of her mouth, the way she touched my clitoris. I'd been with boys before and they were either too rough, rubbing your clitoris hard, or too shy, afraid to put their hand there at all. Mom is right about this. Women know the female body from the inside out, so they know what makes the other person happy. Penny was that way, except in real life her breasts were large, like mine. We used to lie on the bed in her room when her mother was out, sucking each other for what seemed like hours. My mouth hurt afterward. But I didn't really care for Penny, so I don't know why I dreamt about her. She was prissy in her way, the same way Mom is, always straightening furniture out and wiping things up and so on. We had big fights where we yelled names at each other, *cow, slut, bitch*. In the past years I've grown to prefer softer women more, women who take my head in their lap and stroke my hair, and talk to me quietly for hours, the way Penny did in the dream, but never did in life. She told me I was too immature for her one day and just took off for Vancouver. I haven't heard of her again. So maybe it's not really Penny in the dream after all, but CoraLee, who I'm with now, and who does have small breasts. She makes me feel like I'm a girl again, secure and safe in her arms. She makes me feel like I'm the little girl who used to love curling up under the rose-pattern quilt on Saturday mornings, wishing the hours away until Mom called up that it was the last time she was calling me down for breakfast. This all doesn't make much sense, I know. I'm confused, more confused than usual when writing about my dreams. But I do see some things clearly: that Mom is in a lot of my dreams, one way or another. That who I am is somehow tied up with the idea of what makes a woman that Mom impressed on me all those years we lived in her house together. That I can't live her life over, re-creating the model she set for me, and that one part of me wants to kill that woman, so to speak, before the woman I am can emerge. It's complicated, and I've probably got everything all wrong, what the hell are dreams anyway, but maybe Rosie can help sort it out. Yeah, right. (October 27)

Part 4

Pinot Noir is the grape variety wholly responsible for red burgundy. Pinot Noir demands much of both vine-grower and wine-maker. It is a tribute to the unparalleled level of physical excitement generated by tasting one of Burgundy's better reds that such a high proportion of the world's most ambitious wine producers want to try their hand with this capricious vine. If Cabernet produces wines to appeal to the head, Pinot's charms are decidedly more sensual and more transparent. The wines are decidedly more charming in youth and evolve more rapidly, although the decline of the very best is slow. Pinot Noir has for a long time been grown in Burgundy but it is particularly prone both to mutate and degenerate. The vine is also more prone than most to both sorts of mildew, rot, and to viruses. The best Grand Crus are intense, fleshy, vibrant, fruity wines with structure but oak influence that is never obvious.

THE AUTOMATIC DOOR springs open in front of him with a pneumatic woosh when the soles of Michael's boots contact the rubber mat reading Children's Hospital, and he steps quickly through the narrow space into the corridor and heads for the elevators. He touches the top button and stands back to wait for the ping that indicates the car has arrived. The corridor is not crowded at midday. Two native children are riding a tricycle around in circles, an old man is using canes to make his way to the exit. He is wearing an orange windbreaker with Oilers written on the back in blue letters. Michael feels overdressed. In addition to the black leather boots, he is wearing a three-quarter-length camel-hair car coat with a silk scarf round his neck, an outfit reminiscent of the way his father dressed in the fifties. When the elevator car arrives he steps in, the lone occupant to the fourth floor, where he takes the first corridor right and then swings left past the nursing station, nodding briefly to the nurse on duty, before stopping in front of Room 433. He peeks in the window glass. Jane's stockinged feet are sticking out past the end of the fold-down chair, but he cannot see her body because it is obscured by the high bed where Randy is lying motionless under the starched whites of the hospital laundry. Michael turns the door handle as quietly as possible and sticks his head in. "Jane," he whispers.

Her head comes up immediately from behind the bed. "Daddy." She glances at Randy, asleep apparently, and puts one finger to her lips as she rises quickly but quietly and pads across the tiled floor to the door.

Michael wants to go to the boy, to touch his face, but instead he steps backward into the corridor. "I woke you," he says.

"It's okay," Jane says. She's running her fingers through her matted hair and blinking the sleepiness out of her eyes.

"You look tired. Maybe this wasn't such a good idea."

"No." Jane blinks again. "Just give me a minute." She glances back into the room and then rubs her eye sockets with the palms of her hands. She groans and stretches. When she brings her hands away from her face Michael sees the black pockets beneath her eyes, the map of red lines criss-crossing her scleras and rimming the irises. Finally she says, "I'm glad you came."

"I had to see Randy."

"Of course."

"I've just been over at Patricia's with Ali. She's fine. She's a real little trooper."

"She is. I know."

"You bet," Michael says. He waits a moment. It's his day for hospital visits. First here, then across town to visit Maurice in the psych ward. If he had time he'd stop in and see Mark. He glances at his watch: 2:15. Maybe there will be time to call and chat on the phone. "I thought you could use a cup of coffee," he says. In the overhead lights of the corridor the skin of Jane's narrow face looks washed out, sickly and gray.

"Yeah." Jane looks up at him. "It's good to see you."

"Should I go down and get us one from the cafeteria?"

"The nurses have one of those brew things behind their counter." She steps past him across the corridor toward the counter and pushes open the swinging door. "Eileen," she says, "I'm just going to grab us two coffees."

The nurse looks up from the computer screen she's studying and smiles at Michael. "It's been a long night," she says, tipping her head at Jane.

Michael grunts. He takes the Styrofoam cup Jane offers him and stirs with the swizzle stick for a moment. "How are you?"

"Dragged out," she says.

"You look tired."

"Exhausted." Jane takes a sip of her coffee. "Randy was moaning and groaning all night. I asked the nurse to give him more of the painkiller in the intravenous drip, but she can't give him nothing the doctor hasn't ordered."

"Jesus."

"First he flips around like a fish out of water. Then he starts crying. The kid's hurting, Daddy, really hurting."

"Jesus." Michael looks around. The pain of his grandchildren hurts him more than the pain of his own children. What an odd betrayal, he thinks. But what he says is, "When does the doctor come in?"

"He can't sleep," Jane continues, as if she hasn't heard him, "and then I can't sleep. By the time morning comes around we're both a wreck. Thank God he drops into these blackouts every couple of hours."

Michael has been sipping his coffee, but he puts it down on the counter and places both his hands on Jane's shoulders. "We'll get that all straightened out," he says, "when the doctor gets here. If he won't do anything, I've got some stuff at home, 292s, tranquilizers I never used, we'll at least get the two of you some rest."

"Tranquilizers?" Jane says. Her green eyes are suddenly large.

"Yeah, diazepam. Dr. Fayyaz gave them to me when my stomach started acting up and I couldn't sleep." Michael thinks of the mornings he tossed away restlessly a summer ago, worrying that he had an ulcer. He's sure that's how it begins, the sudden decline down the slippery edge, with something as ordinary as ulcer.

Jane interrupts him, saying, "I haven't seen Ali in two days."

"She's fine," Michael repeats, "she's wonderful." He can still smell the girl's hair and feel her thin bones beneath her skin when he lifted her to kiss her cheeks. Now maybe, he thinks, there will only be the one.

"She *is* great," Jane says. "My Ali."

"Maybe I could stay here while you took the car and—"

"No. Patricia's going to bring her over here later." Jane has finished her coffee and put the Styrofoam cup on the counter. "Or Brad will bring her with him," she adds.

Michael grunts. "I'll make a mental note to get you those 292s."

Jane nods. "And I'll talk to Dr. Pankratz as soon as he comes in."

"Right," Michael says. He reaches out and takes Jane in his arms. "In the meantime," he says, "I'm going to give you a back rub. Get rid of some of the tension in your body."

"Oh God, would you?"

In response Michael places his fingers on Jane's neck, reaching around as if he meant to choke her, at first massaging lightly in circles, then moving upward to the base of her skull and down again. When he encounters knots, he presses slightly harder. Jane moans. With a shudder and a sigh she lets her head fall forward onto his chest. He smells her thick hair, permeated with the odor of institutional cleansers and antiseptics. Jane sighs. He moves his hands in wider and wider circles, his muscular fingers applying greater and greater pressure as he digs deep and deeper into the tissue of her neck muscles. When he stops he whispers, "How's that?"

"God, better. So much."

Michael clears his throat. "And with Randy?"

"Nothing," she says. "In and out. Dr. Pankratz says it may be days yet, before he comes to, weeks maybe. It's the body's way of healing, he says, making space for itself to heal. Shutting down on the conscious level."

It will be only one, he thinks. His heart can hardly stand it. He says through a dry mouth, "And all that's coming along okay? The healing?"

"As far as they can tell."

"Yeah."

Jane looks at him. Her green eyes, usually so filled with sparks, now are dull and remote with exhaustion and fear. Michael prefers her the other way, angry, angry at him, even. She says with a sigh, "The bones will heal. I'm not worried about that. It's the other stuff, the internal organs and so on."

"He'll be all right. Kids. They heal."

"That's what Dr. Pankratz says."

"They heal. Remember when you fell out of that tree?"

He laughs, trying to bring her around with humor, but Jane says dryly, "A broken arm. That wasn't nothing compared to this."

Since the moment the van struck the boy Michael has felt that he has betrayed Jane somehow. Now even his attempts at humor are failing. He puts his arms around her again. His coat is open and her face is pressed against his cotton shirt. "Don't worry," he says.

"It's hard not to." She takes a deep breath. "With everything so . . ."

"Don't worry," Michael repeats. He sees Ali sitting on the edge of the bed when he visited her at Patricia's, little hands folded in her lap, eyes round with fear. Michael swallows hard. "We're here," he says. "We'll take care of it."

Jane lets out a deep breath, which Michael feels as warmth through his shirt. In the pause she leaves, he hears the ticking of the heating system in the ceiling, the clicking of fingers on a computer keyboard, and voices down the corridor. Over it all, the smell of hospitals—antiseptics, alcohol, sickness. He hates it. Finally Jane says, "Brad was here again."

Michael bites his lower lip and says as neutrally as possible, "And?"

"He's entirely different now, Daddy. He's changed. It doesn't matter what he done in the past."

Michael takes a deep breath. He closes his hands over Jane's shoulders and pushes her backward, looking into her eyes again. "I'm listening."

"He says so himself, Daddy. He was crying the other night, sitting here holding Randy's hand and crying. You should have seen him. Tears running down his cheeks. He says he never realized how much we all meant to him, me and the kids, how stupid he's been to behave the way he has. He's really different, Daddy, he is. He's grown up overnight, the way people do when there's a tragedy and they're suddenly forced to look into themselves."

Michael sighs. "Jane," he begins, "listen."

"No. You listen. I may not love him the way I used to but I need him, and the kids need him. He's my husband. We're a family."

"These are his words."

"They're what we both think."

"You're so soft. Too soft."

"You're always saying I'm too tough. Too tough on people." Jane has stepped back from Michael and for a moment her eyes flash in the old way.

"On Patricia, on Mary, on me. With him though ..."

"Daddy, we're a family and we got to stick together. Especially now."

"Oh, peanut."

"Don't call me that!" Jane's voice echoes briefly in the corridor and both of them look about, startled and guilty, but the nurse is busy at the computer and the corridor is otherwise empty.

"All right," Michael says. "Okay." He breathes in the anesthetized air of the corridor, wishing he were at Willow Point, the bite of autumn wind at his cheeks, blowing guilt and anger and weakness into nothing.

"Whatever happens we're a family." Jane exhales deeply.

"We are. We got to get through this together."

"All right."

"We got to, Daddy."

Michael clears his throat. "All right," he repeats. He waits a moment and then adds, "Which means moving back, I gather, to the house on Munroe Avenue?"

"Yes. Yes, it does mean just that."

"Oh," Mary says, "oh, oh." Her voice is muffled in thighs and pubic hair but she feels the urgent thrust of Jilly's wet mound against her tongue and lip at the same time as she drives her hips up, seeking her own climax. Stars. Taste of lemon. Jilly grunts, grinding down on Mary's mouth one last time. Then her thighs spread as she rolls off, reaching her climax with a prolonged groan mere seconds before Mary. They lie silent. Mary opens her eyes and looks at the ceiling. Flecked with stipple. Coral paint. Jilly likes tropical tones. Lime trim around the windows. Mango pillow slips.

Jilly clears her throat and asks, "You too?"

"Yes."

"Good."

"Um."

Jilly moves about on the bed, making a half circle like a dog before she curls into a fetal ball, one arm crooked over Mary's waist. "Mary Moo," she whispers in a sleepy voice. She closes her eyes.

Mary glances at the clock radio on the bedside table.

3:12. She should get up. She promised to meet Michael at
the hospital at 4:00. Just five more minutes, she says to herself. Eight. Closes her eyes. Listens to Jilly's hoarse breathing. Scent of apples. Asks herself yet again *what am I doing
here?—what are you doing, Mary Mitchell?* To which she has
no answers. Except the feeling that if Dr. Jackman had not
insisted she be there for Jilly, to hold her hand when she
came out of the psych ward, to comfort and care, she would
have broken it off. Yes. She wanted to, she tells herself, she
knew that was the best course of action—the only one—to
take with Jilly after the night of the hockey stick. She has
always believed in nipping things in the bud, in making a
clean break. That's the right way to do things, the tidy way.
In her mind she pictures herself standing in the kitchen with
her mother when she was a girl, a bandage being ripped off
her skinny arm. Hears her mother's voice: *one quick motion—
right off!* Mary does not like dawdling over decisions and has
nothing but contempt for the shilly-shallyers of this world.
Should I, shouldn't I? It's ridiculous to dawdle. But Dr.
Jackman insisted, so here Mary is, drinking wine on stolen
afternoons of lust, sharing Jilly's futon, making up elaborate
stories about where she's been. Lying to Michael. Lying to
Freddo. To Meagan. A list, actually, of betrayals too lengthy
for Mary to rehearse—and too painful. It's Dr. Jackman's
fault, if anyone's.

Lust, yes, she thinks. Lust plain and simple, now that the
air has been cleared between them, now that it is clear to
Mary, anyway, what brings her to Jilly's bed. No illusions
about that. She does not love this girl, this woman, at least
not in the way she once imagined: romance, passion.
Desires, certainly. Cares for, maybe. All the rest you can
chuck out with yesterday's diapers. After the romantic talk,
the bullshit, little more than carnal desire remains. Her
strongest feeling, actually, is fear. She realizes now she has no
wish to hurt Michael. No. She fears bringing pain. And she

fears that she and Jilly will be discovered. If they continue, they are bound to be discovered—aren't you always?—and there are bound to be repercussions. She has no taste for that. She fears that Meagan will no longer trust her. The idea sickens Mary. Her own child. Besides, she has no idea what Jilly is capable of in a moment of rage—murder, probably—and she, Mary, would be the victim. It's all sickening—and demeaning. And yet this is where lust brings you.

One thing she knows for certain. She is done sermonizing about what is right and what is wrong. Without quite realizing how or when it occurred, she has become judgmental in the past few years. Stupid at her age. Everything she has experienced was telling her the opposite, she realizes now. Telling her to let things be. And if there was one thing she should have learned it was not to judge others. But do we ever learn anything? Actually learn?

She opens her eyes.

Jilly is looking at her. "Penny for them," she whispers.

"Just thinking how mixed up life is."

"Me, you mean."

"Me, actually."

Jilly grunts. "I bet," she says.

"The truth," Mary says. "I was thinking about a friend of ours who has cancer. Of Meggy. Of one of my stepkids in the hospital. Life is pretty awful sometimes."

"You're telling me."

"Life is just one big crapshoot."

"And I'm the snake eyes Mary Moo has rolled."

Mary has been stroking the freckled skin above Jilly's breasts with her fingertips but she stops. "Is that bad, snake eyes? I don't know much about gambling."

"It's the worst, babes. Like me."

"Don't say that."

"I'm abnormal."

"We're all abnormal."

"Not you. You're the definition of normal, Mary Moo. Proto-normal."

"I don't know what that means, *proto*."

"Me neither. I just made it up." Jilly closes her eyes for a moment and Mary sees the crow's-feet moving in around the corners of her eyes, the slight pouch under Jilly's jaw. Double chin. Age. The flesh weakening. Mary listens to the twittering of Jilly's refrigerator, the faint hum of the bedside radio. With a sigh Jilly whispers, "I know you don't want to be here. Not really."

"No," Mary says. "I do."

Jilly reaches out and touches Mary's head, strokes her temple with the ends of her fingers, drawing circles which produce that sandpaper sound in the short hair over the soft spot. Jilly says, "You're a terrible liar, you know that?"

"I thought people in my business had a reputation for being good at it."

"Not you." Jilly's fingers slide down Mary's cheek, massaging between the cheekbone and jaw. "Not when it comes to what's going on with us."

"And what is going on with us?"

"Sex," Jilly says. "Not much more. Fucking."

"I care for you."

"I know. And I care for you, babes." Jilly sighs loudly. Her hand has slid down to Mary's throat, the fingers stroking above the collar bone, tickling almost. "Maybe that's enough," she says.

"It's quite a lot. Actually."

"I know, babes."

"Caring is quite a lot."

Jilly sighs again. "Maybe we don't need love, not really," she says. She stops massaging, her open hand resting on Mary's throat.

Mary can feel her pulse throbbing beneath Jilly's flesh and bone. The much quicker pulse along Jilly's fingers.

Electric. "You think?"

"Maybe what we need—really need—is companionship. Someone to be there when you come home, background noise, you could say. A hand to hold in the tough times."

Mary breathes through her nose. "A shoulder to cry on?"

"I don't know," Jilly says. "I understand lust." She has tightened her fingers on Mary's throat. "The occasional expending of lust."

Mary raises one hand slowly to her throat, takes Jilly's fingers in hers, and gently guides both hands into the space between their bodies. Squeezing. After a moment she says brightly, "Hey, I have something for you." She rolls over, fishes in the pockets of her trousers and brings out a velvet box.

Jilly says, "Oh, shit."

"What?"

"You've bought me a goodbye gift, a—"

"Open it," Mary says.

Jilly pries open the top with one finger and lifts out two earrings. "Christ," she whispers, "diamonds."

"They don't match," Mary says, "by design. So you can wear them one at a time, the way you prefer."

Jilly holds them up to the lights, turning them this way and that. "They catch the sun's rays," she says, "beautifully."

"I'm glad you like them."

"I do," Jilly says, "they're nice." She studies the earrings for a moment and then sets them down on the bedside table. "They're still a kiss-off gift."

Mary is lying on her back, looking at the ceiling. She closes her eyes. "When people say *I love you*," she says, "what they mean is *I need you. Me*, not *you*, so to speak. Professions of love are rarely that; they're confessions of weakness. Nine times out of ten."

"That sounds awfully harsh." Jilly has rolled over and is fumbling with a cigarette and a lighter. "I know," she says, "a filthy habit."

"You'd given that up. You'd beat it."

"Not really." Jilly takes a puff, exhaling streams of smoke through her nostrils. "And Jackman is right: whatever gets you through the night."

"And smoking does that?"

"You bet, babes." Jilly puffs again. "And it's working, I'm on the way back. Even Jackman agrees. Soon I'll be on top of this thing." She inhales deeply. "Soon you'll be free of me."

Mary runs one hand through her hair. She closes and then opens her eyes. "I'll tell you another thing. Most people who marry and stay together become pretty self-righteous about it. They think they are pretty virtuous. But they're not. They're weak. They may say *I love you* over and over to each other but what it mostly comes down to is they cannot imagine living without the other person. No, they can imagine it but it scares the shit out of them. So what it boils down to is fear. The cement of marriage is terror—terror of ending up alone. There's no virtue in that, is there?" Mary exhales again. She is not used to making speeches but she plunges on. "But mostly what we call love is little more than the mating rituals animals go through before breeding. Look at my plumage, smell my ripeness. Strut, strut. Then fuck, fuck."

"Pretty primal, babes, pretty base."

"But not bad. Just not to be overestimated. Just not to be mistaken for what it is not. For caring. That's a different thing. Caring is what you feel for your child—naturally—and what you *can* feel for someone else—if all the signs are right or whatever." Mary lifts her arm and looks at her watch. She closes her eyes and sighs. "Excuse the speechifying."

"It's okay," Jilly says. "We all rattle on some days."

"Umm." Mary glances at her watch again. "I've gotta run," she states.

"Yeah," Jilly says. "So much for romance."

Mary lifts herself on one elbow. "I thought we just decided about that?"

"You did," Jilly says. "I'm still coming around to it."

Mary has stood to begin dressing, but she leans over and kisses Jilly on the cheek. "You will," she says. "In your own good time."

Mark says, "It's not such a coincidence, really. I seem to have taken up permanent habitation here." He smiles and sweeps one arm round the corridor of the hospital. The ring on the middle finger of his right hand flashes, the ring, Michael recalls, that Mark's father left him when he died suddenly a few years ago. Mark is standing beneath a sign with green lettering reading Nephrology, and Michael has been wondering since he and Mary bumped into Mark a few moments earlier what aspect of medicine that is. *Nephros*, he thinks, *kidneys?* Maybe. They are in the hospital across town from the Children's Hospital, a rambling institution operated exclusively at one time by the Grey Nuns but now part of the state-run medical services. Mary and Michael have just come from the psychiatric ward, Mark from oncology.

"You look great," Mary says.

"I feel good," Mark says. "Except I get these headaches."

Michael nods. He's imagining a tumor the size of a golf ball somewhere behind Mark's ear. He's been imagining lately that something's growing in his abdomen, a cancer that will end up big as a cauliflower. He swallows hard and asks, "And how do things look?"

"Now they've scheduled me for early next month," Mark says, laughing. "First they were renovating the operating rooms, and then they had to perform the surgery on someone more urgent than me." He shrugs his shoulders.

"Krikey," Mary says. "Renovating. Your life is on the line."

"State medicine," Mark says. "It's the price you pay."

"Lineups," Michael says. He's been studying Mark's face. There's a nervous twitch around Mark's mouth when he speaks. He's having trouble sleeping, Michael guesses. He lies awake, wondering: *will they get the tumor, will they get it all, will I die on the operating table?* He adds, "With our system you pay in time rather than money."

Mary asks, "And what then? After the operation?"

"That's the scary part," Mark says. "They may not get it all. Even if they do, I could lose some motor functions, some aspects of memory."

God, Michael thinks, *vegetable, wheelchair.* "Not you," he says, "you'll come through flying colors."

"Sometimes," Mark says, "it takes months to recover—if you do." There is a silence and then he adds, "But I'm okay. I played tennis this morning and we're going on a cycling jaunt this weekend. I feel good, really, and Alix has been great. We're looking on the bright side of things. Planning to do the tour through the Cotswolds next summer."

Mary says, "I admire you." She is clenching and unclenching her fists, shifting from one foot to the other. A little dance. "You're so brave."

"That's kind of you to say," Mark says, "but I'm not brave. There is no such thing as bravery. I've learned this in the past few months. There is merely the will to survive."

"Pish," Mary says. "You're such an example to those of us who think we have problems. All of you are."

"If there is bravery," Mark says, "it's the kind everyone gets in moments of crisis. You gird yourself up. You take responsibility for your fate. That's something else you learn. If you don't, no one else will."

"Not everyone," Mary says. "Lots of people just cave in."

"That's right," Michael says. He's been watching Mary watch Mark, her eyes darting from his face to his hands and back to his face. Michael says, "Their disease becomes an excuse to give up on a life they didn't think worth living to begin with." He breathes in through his nose, trying not to taste antiseptic on his palate.

"I don't believe it," Mark says.

There are black pouches beneath his eyes, Michael notices. He has lost weight on his cheeks, which once were fleshy. Michael wonders, *is this the face of death? Am I looking at death?* In the past weeks he's dreamt often of tumors, white masses of swirling cells he saw once on the Discovery Channel, gradually ballooning in a monkey's heart. Michael touches his fingers to his lips. "You're the rarity," he says. "Changing your diet, the course of vitamins and herbs you're taking, meditating, going for massage therapy. That takes a lot of effort, it means investing a lot of psychic and physical energy. Most people don't have the strength to do it."

"You do what you have to do," Mark says.

"The strength of personality, I mean."

Mark nods and shrugs his shoulders. "You do something."

"Most people are resigned," Mary says. "They say to their doctor, *all right, I'm sick, you fix me. Give me the drugs or whatever, I'm in your hands, but don't expect me to do anything. Cure me.* They're passive, inert."

"Those that don't give up entirely." Michael has taken Mary's hand, he realizes. The smoothness of her cool skin comforts him, reminds him of the morning when she stroked his temples as they talked about their plans for this day. They are both staring at Mark, whose face has flushed slightly in the past few minutes. "That's why you're going to survive," Michael adds.

"Your cousin, you know," Mark says, "has given me some useful tips. Showed me how to access some stuff on the Web."

"Great," Michael says. "He's a smart guy."

"A nice guy too," Mark says. "It's guys like him that keep you going." He is silent for a moment. Finally he adds, "And people like you two."

"I don't think so," Mary says. "That's something in you. Courage."

"Something admirable," Michael says. "A spiritual thing, really."

"Well," Mark says, "sometimes you just have to go deep into yourself, find out what's really there." He looks over their heads for a few moments. He is wearing a light green jacket, a barn jacket with a leather collar and cuffs, and he has his hands thrust deep in the pockets. "Well," he says finally, "how's Maurice?"

"They're releasing him Monday," Michael says.

"He's got over that terrible patch," Mary adds. "Thinking everyone was against him. Wanting to kill himself." She glances down at her feet.

"It was bad," Michael says. "But he's over it now."

"Gouging himself with glass." Mary shivers dramatically. "Ugh."

"It's weird," Mark says, "isn't it, this whole existence thing? Here I am in a dogfight to extend my life, doing everything possible to survive, and then there's people who want to throw theirs away."

"Maybe not willingly," Michael says. "Maybe it's more . . ."

"I know," Mark says. "I didn't mean Maurice . . ." He shuffles from one foot to the other. In the pause he leaves, Mary slips her hand out of Michael's and pushes back a strand of hair which has fallen into her eyes. She glances at her watch. Mark says, "I don't think now I could ever consider suicide."

Michael grunts. "Did you ever," he begins, "have you ever had suicidal thoughts?" He drops his eyes to the floor—row on row of off-white tile flecked with black triangles.

"I don't know," Mark says. "Not really."

"I have," Mary says. She's started to rub her thumbs and index fingers together, making a slight rasping sound, and she looks down at her hands now, willing them to be calm.

"I mean," Mark continues, "I've considered the possibility of suicide, but I don't think that really counts. I've never had the gun in my mouth or the pills in my hands, kind of thing. It's never come down to that very moment." Mark pauses. "I think to qualify as suicidal thoughts, really qualify, you have to have come to that point. Otherwise it's, I don't know, thoughts and little more. Like thinking I'd enjoy traveling to Chile someday."

"I've held a knife to my chest," Mary says.

Mark studies her a moment. "Well then you have. You've been there."

"Maybe not," she says. "I know what you mean. What is posturing and what is the real thing? Reaching the final desperation."

Michael has taken Mary's hand again and is holding it tight. "Perhaps," he says, "it comes down to this: the only people who have suicidal thoughts are those who commit suicide."

"All the others," Mary says, "are cries for help."

Mark grunts. He lifts one hand to his face and scratches along the side of one nostril with his index finger. "Anyway," he says, "Maurice is past that."

"Thankfully," Mary says.

"I don't think he was ever that down," Michael says. "That low. Or I don't want to believe he was. You don't as a parent. But the doctors up in the psych ward say we have to be vigilant now. It's a critical period."

Mary says, "He's a strong man. He has resources. He's loved."

"Right," Michael says. He's been feeling one of those burps coming on and inhales deeply, hoping to hold it down.

"He has you guys," Mark says. "And Victoria."

"Right," Michael says. "Still, it's going to be a long haul seeing him all straight again—but then what isn't?"

"And he—what?—he just set himself on fire?"

"Apparently."

"Jesus." Meagan slows her pace for a moment, glancing first right and then left, before they cross the asphalt and start up the grassy slope to the top of the dike. It is just eight o'clock, but dark already, an early November evening with the bite of frost in the air. Meagan is wearing the charcoal Irish wool sweater that Mary brought back from Donegal for her several years ago. Mary has on a brown leather bomber jacket with a sheep's-wool collar. The moon seems low. Shimmering. It is quiet in Woodydell. The traffic on Grunwald Street, which lies below the dike and to the south of where they are walking, is light at this time of night. A few kids are out on bicycles, shouting and calling phrases back and forth, their voices resonating like crackling ice on the still air. When they reach the crest of the dike and begin walking along the gravel path west, Mary stops to adjust the collar of her jacket. Fingers shaking. She feels chilly, but whether it is because of the air or because of the news of Freddo's suicide, she is not sure. No. She knows. Her insides are trembling almost as much as her hands. *Butterflies*, her mother used to say. These are hummingbirds.

"This is what Tony told me," she says. "He drove out to the track, he sat down in the straw of the stable the horse occupied, and then he poured a can of gas over himself, and before anyone could do anything, that was it."

"Ugh. The horse had—what?—had to be put down?"

"It was something in the leg. You know how it is with horses. It had bone chips or whatever and Freddo didn't want it to run but the trainer talked him into it and then it broke its knee or ankle or whatever and they had to put it down. He was devastated. He blamed himself."

"But it happens all the time—eh—with horses?"

"It must have meant more to him than he let on. Poor guy."

"I guess." Meagan sighs. She glances up at the stars and Mary's gaze follows hers automatically. The Big Dipper, Orion. Mary looks for the North Star, but cannot find it. Feels disappointment out of proportion to her failure.

"Maybe it was the last straw," she says. "The condo thing really got him down. He was drinking a lot. More than I knew. And he was never really the same after his wife died a couple of years ago of cancer."

"I thought he remarried."

"Yeah, but it was one of those convenience things. Someone to share the house and all that. Go on trips together. It wasn't much love with Cassie." Mary sighs. The air tonight is filled with gentle odors, river smells, leaf, bark, grass. "He just started to unravel," she adds. "He would forget things at the office, make mistakes even a rookie would not make. Then he started hanging out with those guys at Picasso's. Drinking, gambling. I should have been more aware of what was happening. The condo thing never should have occurred. But it did and he was a terrible one for blaming himself."

"Look who's talking."

"No. He always thought he had to prove himself, being the man in the partnership, and when he made mistakes it ate him up inside. He kept a bottle of Maalox in the bottom drawer of his desk—along with the rye."

"Still," Meagan says. She exhales loudly, puffing out her cheeks. "To pour gas on yourself. It's a hell of a way to die, eh?"

"It's taken the wind out of my sails too."

"Yeah."

They have come to the western end of the dike and turned north onto the road that skirts the golf course. Mary looks at her watch. It is hard to believe that Freddo was alive twelve hours ago. She wonders what his final thoughts were that morning as he put the gas can in the trunk of his car before driving out to the Downs. His wife? Disappointments as a teenager? Trips he took to Greece with his first wife? Maybe he wasn't thinking at all, not in the usual way. Maybe he was just going through the motions, sleepwalking, and the final motion was striking a match to his clothes. She wonders if she will ever be able to go into the office again. What the point of that would be. Maybe she should look for a new partner, or join one of the mega-firms and get lost in the crowd. Try a different line of work, a shop in Osborne Village, maybe not work at all. Now that there's insurance money to pay out the lawsuit over the condo fiasco she would have enough to do that too.

She reaches out and takes Meagan's hand. "And you," she says, "how's it going with you, darling?"

"I'm okay."

"You lost some weight there."

"But I've put it back on." Meagan laughs. "Mostly."

"That's good. Isn't it?"

"I guess. It would have been nice to keep it off forever. It would have been nice for this disease to have one positive side effect."

"You don't actually mean that."

Meagan laughs. "No. I'm not sure."

"No, you don't." Meagan releases her hand as they turn onto the asphalt road running down the center of the golf course, heading east. Mary says, "How about the injections? They hurt?"

"No. You just pinch up some fat around your waist and jab yourself."

"Ah." Mary grimaces. "I don't think I could do it."

"You could. You *would*."

"No bruises?"

"Nothing so far. It's not like shooting up heroin or getting an injection at the hospital. No veins involved. It's subcutaneous. Like I say, you just pinch up some fat, eh. No problem for me there."

"Um," Mary says. They are walking side by side, swinging their arms as they pick up speed on the gentle slope down toward the river. "And how about the other? Your personal life?"

"CoraLee's been great, eh." She leaves a pause and Mary listens to the squish of their rubber-soled boots on the dew-damp asphalt. It's a pleasant sound, she thinks. She inhales deeply. It's a pleasant night. Good to be alive, good to be here. Life. Blood pounding in the veins. A little tug of hunger in her abdomen. Good to be alive. Good to be with Michael, his thick arms to hold her. Meagan is saying, "But I'm going to have to find something else to do." She pauses again, then adds, "Being a roadie was kinda cool but the band wasn't going anywhere, not really." She pauses again, and then adds, "I was thinking of construction, framing houses, maybe. Nails and boards and hammers. I have to work with my hands, eh?"

"You wouldn't get run-down? Sick?"

"It's healthy. Outdoors, sun on your face. Moving around."

"Ice, wind, snow. We've got six months of winter here. Coming."

"I wasn't thinking of here, actually." They are walking with their heads bowed, and Meagan is looking at her feet. "The thing of it is," she says, "we want to move in together, CoraLee and me, and we thought we'd be better off starting up fresh somewhere else. Vancouver, we were thinking."

"Oh, darling." Mary hesitates a moment, but Meagan continues striding on, so Mary does a quick skip step to catch up. She says, a little out of breath, "We thought you should be here right now. With us."

"We'd both just feel—well, awkward. Running into people on the street, in restaurants and so on. High school friends. Your friends. We could never be ourselves here. Not really. We'd always be looking over our shoulders, eh? So we have to go where we can disappear in the crowd. At least for a while."

"Gosh," Mary says. "It's so sudden."

"Not really. I'd moved out. It's just another step, Maw. A little step."

They have passed the dike and are on the grass path that runs along the fields of the community club. Sodium arc lamps overhead. Mesh fence of the ball diamond. Deserted now. Empty. Mary says weakly, "I could come and visit. I've always liked the West Coast."

"That's right. CoraLee has a friend who has her eye on a two-bedroom flat for us. Second story of a house in Kits. There's a sofa and rugs and a TV too. We'd need, like, only beds and some furniture to fill the place out."

Mary says, "It's a sure thing, then, this move?"

Meagan leaves a pause before she states, "I have to live my own life, Maw. I thought that's what you wanted."

"It is. It's what we both want. For you."

"So there you go then."

Mary stops for a moment. Meagan has said the words exactly the way Freddo used to say them, and she feels for a moment the way she feels when she hears "Cathy's Clown" on the golden oldies station, transported backward suddenly into emotions she thought she had traveled beyond forever, falling into a vortex of not entirely pain-free memory, spiraling down into regret and shame and fear. Freddo. Hands, eyes, lips. Gone. She clears her throat. "So there you go then," she says.

Michael grunts as he penetrates deeper into her, arching his back by digging both sets of toes into the mattress so he can thrust forward with maximum force. She thrusts back. He feels the sheet beneath his toes give way and start to slide back slightly. He feels her response to his penetration up the entire length of his spine, and when he thrusts forward again his weight hangs suspended over her hips, his bone on her

bone, before he draws back again, his momentary withdraw-
al accompanied by the sucking sounds of their lubricious
organs. He grunts again. She laughs into his face, dancing
gray eyes that urge him on and mock him at once, he is not
certain which the more. Her long legs are sticking straight
up into the air as if she were performing some sort of
stretching exercise, her knees crooked over his shoulders.
Earlier she had reached over and jammed a pillow under her
buttocks, raising herself to meet him. Now she is throwing
her head back with every thrust, banging it against the headboard of the bed. Her close-cropped hair falls forward into
her eyes as they rock backward on each stroke, and flies back
from her face as his weight shifts forward. The back of her
skull thumps against the headboard. She bites her lower lip.
He feels himself huge and stiff in her, painful almost. His
arms are wrapped around her thighs just above the V her legs
form. She lifts her torso upward and toward him, as if she is
doing a sit-up, and she grabs one of his arms below the
elbow. "Choke me," she whispers harshly. When he does
not, she cries ou,t "Choke me, choke me," and wrenches his
arm forward suddenly. Inside her he bends, and he feels himself toppling forward. He nearly loses his balance, but he
adjusts his weight, his fingers coming to rest on her neck.
She sighs. He leaves his palm open but he applies pressure to
her throat, forcing the V made by his thumb and fingers
against her larynx on each thrust. She smiles and lets her
head rock from side to side. She closes her eyes and whispers
softly, "Choke me, choke me." And then he fills big in her,
too big to contain. The tempo of his thrusting takes on a life
of its own. She laughs between gritted teeth as he drives
himself to a finish.

She asks, "You liked that, didn't you?"

He has withdrawn himself and collapsed onto the bed
beside her, arms thrown wide like the crucified Jesus. "Yes,"
he manages.

She laughs again. "See. I know what you want."

He sighs. "Not the hitting. The hurting."

"I did not hurt you. Correct?"

"No," he admits. Though he remembers looking into the rearview mirror of the truck after the first time and seeing red splotches beneath both eyes.

"I know what I'm doing," she says smugly. When he doesn't answer, she reaches for the sheet which became entangled in their legs and pulls it up over her breasts. "I'm a pro, see, and in this business these days you have to know what you're doing. And you have to have an angle. Mine is hurting just a little bit. Enough to get you interested."

From his position Michael can look out the window. The sky is black now, with a bright crescent of moon to the east. There is a small halo around its circumference, that's supposed to mean winter is coming. He says, "That was good."

"See. I've got your attention. You're interested."

"And I'm happy. Utterly."

"Good," she says. "I've done my job."

They breathe in silence. Michael smells the liquor of her breath on his face, feels the warmth of her body. He closes his eyes and feels the pulsing of blood in his temples. He could sleep now if he let himself go. After a while he says, "How do you mean, *angle*?"

"The competition," she says. "It's crazy out there. Everybody's in the game now, it seems. Housewives making extra money. Failed models who are used to having lots of cash at their disposal. More and more college girls every year. High school kids too. They start having sex so young now. And they learn real quick that it's only physical, that sex is just physical pleasure without all the religious claptrap we were led to believe, so if you're not saving it for Mister Wonderful, why not do it with whoever, and why not get paid? You'll still be able to give the guy you marry or whatever all the pleasure he wants, but in the meantime you can turn an easy dollar. Beats waitressing or typing for some bozo who tries to grope you in the back room every day anyway. This way you're getting paid for it. And it's on your terms."

"Um," Michael says. Though his eyes are closed and he feels relaxed, he is filled with energy too, he is brimming with sexual drive. It's remarkable. No more than a few minutes have passed since he came inside her, yet he is thinking about her haunches again, about bending her over the end of the bed.

She lifts his arm nearest to her up from where it is lying on the sheet and places it over his chest, curling up into the space between them. She whispers, "You have to do more than just screw these days, see. You have to have a specialty or you only get one-time hits. Sure, most guys, as you did, try out a few girls, sample what's on offer, going from one girl to another at first, but then they get tired of doing that and want something more steady, so to speak. Then they go back to the one they liked, the one who made an impression on them. That's what I'm talking about. You have to offer something."

"Pain," he murmurs. He inhales deeply. She isn't wearing the same perfume as the first time, but it's just as strong. He wrinkles his nose.

"Danger," she says. "Danger makes things exciting. It gets men—men like you—excited again. After years of predictable and dull screwing. If you pardon my French. Kitchen cunt. Correct?"

"I guess. Though that's not how I would have put it."

"I can tell what a man wants," she says. "Some guys want to be hurt. But then sometimes the guy wants me to be young but experienced, completely experienced, so I'm dangerous in that way. You have to be able to read the guy. I can. That's what I mean."

Michael hears bragging in her voice, but he asks, "Or coy and kittenish? You can do that too?"

"Sure. Those come easily to a woman. That's what most men want."

"A sweet lover?"

"A toy to play with. A little thing to pet and fondle."

"You've given it a lot of thought."

"I have. I think about sex a lot."

"Me too."

"You think about *having* sex. There's a difference, buster."

Michael opens his eyes. The light from the lamp beside the bed makes him blink, and he closes them again, seeing the outline of the woman's head shimmering on the inside of his closed lids. He doesn't like her much, he realizes. She wears vulgar perfume, she is stupidly proud of what she does to get money, she's got a mean mouth. He says, "You have an interesting way of putting things."

"You don't have to go to college to be smart."

"No," he says. "But it helps you become articulate."

"That's what you *are* good at," she says. "You people who go to college and teach people at college in your turn. Twisting other people's words."

"You're not so bad at it yourself."

"Fighting back," she says. "Holding my own." She has placed her right hand on his thigh and is tracing circles in the black bristly hair near his crotch.

"That's nice," he says.

"Am I staying the night?"

"I don't know. What do you think?"

"It's your nickel." She closes her fingers over him, and then relaxes her grip, closes and relaxes. "You're certainly up to it," she says.

"I was thinking of what we did the last time."

"I know," she says. "You should have seen how your eyes bugged out."

"How could you tell?"

"I looked back. Over my shoulder. You were deep into it."

"Deeply?"

"Deep." She laughs. "I should know that." She has moved her hand back to his leg and is running one finger along his thigh to his knee. "If I am," she says, "staying, I'm going to need a drink."

"Me too." Michael blinks. He wonders what time it is. Earlier in the evening he told Mary he was going to Willow Island, to get ready for the last gathering of the gang for the season. Stephen and Colleen have returned from Portugal, Ashton and Petra from New York, Mark and Alix from Vancouver. He wonders what Mark is doing at that moment, and thinks maybe meditating, using inner strength to confront and defeat his cancer. He's a strong man and a good guy. So are all of Michael's friends. They're good. Mary, too, he thinks, whom he shouldn't be betraying with a woman he already finds tiresome. He sighs. God, he's a pig. He'll have to bring it to an end. No more calls on the cell phone to "Tiffany." This, he resolves, will be the last time. It was fun, it was educational; but it has to end.

"I'll take a Scotch," she says. "Ice but no water." She laughs. "Lots of Scotch."

Her laugh is loud and brassy in the little room. He rolls toward her, feeling her moist breath on his face. "Whose nickel did you say this was?"

She raises her hand and places the tip of her index finger on the end of his nose. "I'll make it worth your time," she says. "You know that, buster."

"So the Roughriders are going under," Stephen says.

"Again," Ashton says. When he tips back his glass of beer his Adam's apple bobs beneath his trimmed salt-and-pepper beard.

"And the Lions too," Mark says. "Done like duck."

"The CFL is done like duck," Michael says.

Stephen reaches over and punches him lightly on the shoulder. "Hey, buddy, you said those very words ten years ago."

"No."

"Five, maybe. And if I recall correctly it was in our basement, playing pool." Stephen laughs, a hearty growl echoing round the room. "But you're still here and so is the CFL."

"Well, it's a good thing," Michael says, wiping his lips with the back of one hand, "somebody around here holds consistent opinions."

"I thought consistency," Mark says, "was the hobgoblin of little minds."

When they laugh and tip their drinks back, Mary turns her attention to the saucepan on the stove. She is making a soup to start their meal, and has already simmered the sautéed onions and slices of sorrel in the stock to the point where it is ready for the cream. She carefully pours the cup and a half from the measuring bowl, watching the surface of the soup for bubbles. The liquid must not boil. The cream will curdle. She stirs slowly, waiting for the cream to mix through. At her right hand stands a dish with fresh tarragon and marjoram from Michael's herb garden. They go in next. Then the cayenne pepper—not too much—and finally a dollop of sour cream and a chive flower. She runs through the recipe in her mind, mentally checking off the ingredients, then dips her nose over the saucepan. Sniffs. Perfect.

In the background the men have resumed talking again. Men and sports, Mary thinks. The one constant in their lives. Women come and go, jobs, even other men friends in the shifting world of alliances and acquaintances. But the sports talk remains. Flotsam on their jetsam. Stephen is saying, "Professional teams, I've had it with them. Piss on the lot of them. The capitalist swine."

"One huge money grab," Ashton says. "Players, owners. It's sick."

"Piss on them," Stephen repeats. "We should boycott. Drive the lot of them into bankruptcy."

"The symphony," Ashton says. "Season tickets to the ballet."

"Do your own thing," Mark says. "Cycle, jog, whatever."

"I'm going to work out this year," Michael says. Like the others, he is drinking beer in a glass, an imported beer Mark brought along with two bottles of red wine. "Put some concerted effort into building up the pecs and biceps. Thirty minutes a day on the rowing machine."

"I hate that," Alix says. Mary looks up. Earlier Alix had been putting logs on the fire and had her back to the room, but now she is standing between Stephen and Mark, her glass of wine winking in the firelight. Petra has joined the men, too, leaving Colleen alone on the sofa, flipping through a magazine.

"And I hate jogging," Ashton says. "Slogging around in circles. It has to be hard on the knees. The hips, the ankles. It's punishment."

"Pain," Stephen says, "is what it's all about. The whole exercise thing." He puts his beer glass down on the table and smacks his lips.

"Good pain, though," Alix says. "Wouldn't you say?"

"Give me beer," Stephen adds. "Give me wine. Give me fun."

Alix says, "You gotta burn it off. You gotta burn, baby."

"Stephen's right," Mark says. "Everyone's out there doing exercise these days but no one's having fun. You see these guys pounding by you on their daily jog, they're not enjoying themselves. Their teeth are gritted tight. They are sweating, sure, and that's good for their bodies, but they may as well be at the office. What they're doing is just an extension of work."

"Labor," Stephen says. "Grunt work."

"Exactly," Michael says. "It's work. It's not pleasure."

Mark nods. "Even when I'm out cycling myself, I'm not

listening to the birds or enjoying the color in the sky. I'm pounding."

"Not in the Cotswolds," Alix says. "We stopped to smell the flowers."

"In the Cotswolds, yes, we did stop to smell the flowers," Mark says. "But on my regular city routes, I'm just pounding."

"Pounding?" Alix says. She gives Mark's arm a playful tug.

"What it is," Stephen says, "is another version of Puritanism." He has moved away from the table and is standing in front of the refrigerator, getting out bottles of beer. He asks, "Anyone else?"

"Me," Ashton says, looking about. "And Mark."

Michael glances at his glass. He downs the remainder in one swig and says, "Me too." He comes over to the counter and asks Mary, "Need help?"

"No," she says. "Thanks." She has poured out the sorrel soup and is dropping one chive flower and calendula petals into each bowl.

"Looks good," Michael whispers.

"Tastes wonderful," she says. "I think we're just about ready."

Michael glances back into the room. He is wearing a white cotton shirt, a loose cut which flatters his barrel chest and big arms. Mary thinks he looks good these days. Strong. There is a glow to his cheeks and a readiness in his step she thought had disappeared forever. *Face it*, she says to herself, *sexy. Face it*, she adds, *you're horny, girl.* She looks past his shoulder into the room. Stephen is passing round bottles of beer and saying, "It's all an industry plot, selling all this exercise equipment— skis and bikes and outrageously expensive trainers. It's the health food thing all over. Just another way to put the grab on our wallets—while making us feel virtuous."

"Not just," Alix says. She has moved to the other side of the table and is pouring a glass of wine. "Working out is good for you."

Ashton says, "I read the other day that smokers who exercise have a greater life expectancy than non-smokers who don't exercise." He raises his bushy black eyebrows and then pours beer from the bottle to the glass.

"Okay," Alix says. "But not non-smokers who do exercise."

"What about smokers who don't exercise?" Petra asks. She is standing with her back to the fire, its light making a halo around her head. On their walk to the point earlier she found a tail feather from a pelican and she has wormed its quill through the knit wool of her sweater, making a primitive brooch on her breast.

"They weren't in the study," Ashton says.

"No," Michael says. "They're six feet under."

In the laughter that follows Mary says, "All right gang, time to chow down." She has begun bringing the soup bowls to the table. She raises her voice and adds, "Come on, Colleen."

Colleen drops the magazine on the coffee table and straightens her skirt as she stands. She tosses her brown hair over one shoulder. "All right," she says, "I'm coming." But her voice seems far away to Mary, distracted. Preoccupied. Maybe she's having an affair. Not likely. Maybe Stephen is having an affair. Hm. Probably Colleen's starting to go through menopause.

"It's all a matter of trying to beat time," Michael is saying, "and nothing more." He's seated himself at one end of the table and poured out his beer.

Mark says, "That's one thing you learn when you meditate. That there is no time." He has seated himself between Alix and Petra.

"No time?" Ashton says, startled. "What does that mean?"

"Or rather there's all kinds of time," Mark says. "Meditation time is wholly different from normal time, for one."

Petra squints her eyes. "How do you mean?"

"There's a silence at the center of meditation time. Peace. A place for the wisdom of waiting. The wisdom of the frog."

Michael and Ashton laugh but Mary thinks it's because they're picturing the frog's bulging eyes and leathery skin, not imagining its blinking passivity. Tranquil, serene. Buddha-like.

Mark continues, "People are always asking *how long do you meditate?* That's not the point. The point is where you get to."

Stephen says, "That sounds pretty goal-oriented. Not very Zen."

"The state of mind you reach," Mark says. He's lifted the glass of wine he's poured for himself and is studying its color. "Your mental plateau."

Ashton says, "You're not going metaphysical on us, are you?"

He laughs but Mark says in a flat voice, "You tend to get that way when you have a life-threatening illness." When Michael winces Mark adds, "I know it's a mouthful but it's what my oncologist says and I've kind of adopted it too." He clears his throat. "It makes it easier for people. It's much less threatening than the C word. For most people."

Mary says, "You're worried about their feelings?"

"Of course," Mark says. "They're the ones who have a difficult time dealing with cancer. After the initial shock, you get on with things. With life."

There is a silence in the room. Michael looks down at his soup. Chairs scrape and throats clear. In the hush around the table Mary hears the crackling of logs on the fire, waves slapping up the shore. Earlier, on the walk out to the point and back, Michael had rattled on about the birds and trees, Stephen had made fun of him, Ashton and Petra were holding hands like teenagers. It was a beautiful bright afternoon, with the kind of light in the sky that makes you want to sing. Everybody was laughing. Mary looks around the table at their faces. Glow of alcohol, glow of expectation. This is what she loves. She is about to say so when Mark breaks the silence by adding, "We could learn to live with death much more easily if we didn't think of time the way we do. Chopped up into tiny bits. Portioned out."

"Exactly," Michael says. "Time is our way of parceling out the degree to which we think we're cheating death."

"Control," Stephen says. "The bugaboo of the Western mind."

"That's it," Mark says. "When a dog dies we say he was an old dog. Not fifty-six or seventy-two. We're not concerned about whether he made it to some arbitrary road post. Sixty, say. Fifty. *Old dog.* It means he lived a good long time. If he didn't, we say, *too bad, young dog.* Or *really old dog.* A mark of distinction." He has lifted his beer glass to the light. "If we could learn to say that about ourselves, to think that way, we would be much happier. Free of the shadow of time, maybe."

"Now that's metaphysics," Ashton says.

He is about to add something else but Stephen puts up one hand, waves it in the air and interrupts, saying, "Mystery, not metaphysics." He smiles at Mark and adds, "I prefer to think of magic as the real mystery of life. The way we create magic around this table whenever we gather, for instance. The way we create moments which are so charged with beauty and wonder they remain etched in our minds forever." He looks up and down the table.

"Give me a break," Ashton says.

"No, he's right," Petra says. "Here's to ordinary magic."

Stephen raises his glass and clinks it against Petra's. "Righto," he says.

"Hear hear," Mark says.

"All right," Ashton says, "I'll buy that. Okay."

"Me too," Alix says.

In the silence that follows Michael clears his throat. "Well, this old dog knows one thing," he says. "He's having a fine time with a fine old pack of friends." He raises his glass. "To us," he says.

"To the Willow Island Gang," Mary adds.

And they drink.

Mary and Michael stand side by side on the gravel driveway, their arms raised in a formal gesture of farewell as the red taillights of Stephen's Camry flicker through the willows before disappearing round a bend in the road. They are left in darkness, only the faint glow of the lights of the cottage illuminating their path back to the door. Michael's knees hurt as he climbs the steps to the deck. It has been a long day. And a long night. He runs his tongue around the inside of his mouth, feeling the residue of alcohol and food. At least he doesn't have to drive back to the city. At least he doesn't have to get up before 6:00 in the morning, as Ashton does, to catch a plane to Toronto.

They stand on the deck for a moment, looking out at the lake. The moon is obscured but when your eyes adjust to the darkness you can see the crests of waves beating to the shore. You can hear them rush up the sand and feel the breeze off the water, cool and getting cooler. This is the last gathering of the gang for the season, another summer come and gone. Michael listens for night birds, for sound in the underbrush, but he hears nothing. Silence. Far to the west a big dog is barking. For some reason he thinks of his grandchildren. Randy is home now and recovering. He would like to be holding the two of them at this moment, one on each knee, smelling their hair, listening to their high-pitched voices. He closes his eyes, takes several deep breaths, and then turns his back on the lake.

Inside he follows Mary to the kitchen sink where he rolls up the sleeves of his shirt. Various people helped with the washing up after dinner, but there are still liqueur glasses standing about, several beer mugs, coffee cups. The cottage still feels warm from bodies. Mary runs hot water into the sink, a billow of steam clouding her head momentarily. He thinks of fog, he thinks of his brain. On the counter stands his half-full mug of beer. He takes one last pull. Then he picks up a towel and flicks it open. He studies Mary's head, bent in concentration over the sink. "Thinking about Freddo?" he ventures.

"No," she says. "No." She exhales. "Surprisingly I'm not that upset about it. Maybe I was half expecting him to do something. I don't know."

He grunts. "Poor bastard."

"Yeah." She sighs. Actually," she says, "I was thinking how much I love those guys."

"I know what you mean."

"More and more." Mary sighs. She has put on an apron and it draws neatly at her waist, pulling her blouse down and exposing the tanned flesh of her neck, pearled by perspiration. "I just love having them around."

"I know," he says, "our friends, our pals." He imagines planting a kiss just below her hairline. He's felt sexier about her, he realizes, from the moment he decided the thing at the Westin had to end. He adds, "They make me laugh."

"It's more than that," she says. She pauses to place a couple of liqueur glasses on the wooden rack. "More and more it's clear to me that the only thing we acquire of lasting worth in this life are friends. They abide when all else changes. They endure beyond lovers, beyond spouses, beyond children."

Abide, Michael thinks, *what a lovely word: magical, spiritual.* He says, "We've endured. It's more than twenty years." There is a tone of hurt in his voice, more than he intended, but Mary seems not to have noticed. He wipes the liqueur glasses and picks up one of the dripping mugs. It's amazing they have endured, he thinks, given what they've been through. Or maybe not, maybe they've been able to go through it only because they can always go deep on each other.

"You know what I mean," Mary is saying. "Friends— some—are with you from childhood. Mother and some of her school chums have survived their husbands. They go out on jaunts the way they did before they all were married."

"That's weird. Don't you think?"

"In an earlier time people were close to their relatives. Cousins, sisters and brothers. But now those people move away, or they develop different interests. Now it's your friends who are lifelong companions."

"The person you love," Michael says.

"That too. Them too."

Michael has placed the last beer mug on the counter. He puts his towel down and moves in behind Mary, his face against her arched neck, his hands reaching up to her breasts. "I love the twins," he murmurs into her blouse. He feels himself growing stiff against her. He wants to fall to the floor with her, to loosen her buttons, spread those legs. He wants to take her the way he takes Ethena, with wild abandon, limbs locked in sexual acrobatics, but he will settle for a long heart-wrenching screw.

"Um," she says. "You love twins, period."

"That's what I said."

She tips her head but does move away from him. "What I meant was, I saw you leering," she says. "Earlier." She smiles and shakes her head.

"Leering?"

"At Alix," she says. She pauses and whispers, "I don't mind. She's a young woman. With a beautiful body."

"No way! I was not leering—I was looking."

"If you say so, dear."

He draws back. There is hurt in his voice when he says, "I didn't think I was leering. I was taking an interest in what she was talking about." But he was leering, he has to admit it. When Mark said *pounding* and she tugged his arm playfully, Michael was watching the jiggle of her breasts. Alix looks as if she enjoys pounding.

"I don't mind," Mary repeats. She steps back against him, curling her form into his, rubbing against him. "I don't, but she might."

Michael's hands fall to her waist, his fingers hooking into the bow she's tied to hold the apron tight. He sees himself standing off to Mark's side near the table before dinner, running his eyes up and down Alix's slim and muscular body. He feels sick to the stomach. "God," he whispers into Mary's neck, "I'm a pig. A lecherous old pig."

"She probably didn't notice."

Michael exhales dramatically. He says weakly, "I'm pathetic."

"You're not," Mary says. In the pause she leaves she takes his hands and lifts them back to her breasts and holds them there. "Anyway," she says, "the lecherous I can live with."

When she rocks back into him, revolving her face to his, he moves his hands in circles round her breasts, rubs himself into the crack of her buttocks. "It's you I want," he says.

"It's me you can have." She has been wearing pink rubber gloves to wash the glasses, and she draws them off and places them at the side of the sink.

With his hands on her shoulders, he turns her around. Her blue eyes, *cornflower blue* he called them years ago when they left their spouses for each other, have never seemed brighter, her mouth more eager. He tastes mint and chocolate. "You're beautiful," he whispers in her ear.

"You're horny."

"I am. But that doesn't mean I'm wrong about the other."

"No," she says, "and it doesn't mean I am when I say I was watching you all night."

"Leering, you mean?"

"No, forget that. Studying your arms and hands. Wanting you." Her fingers move to the buttons of his shirt, his to the waist of her skirt. "You look so good these days. So happy. Healthy."

Unlike Mark, he thinks. Meagan. So many people so sick. "God," he says. "I've never been this horny."

She laughs. "Me neither."

He places both his hands over the back of her skull and presses her mouth to his, drawing her tongue as far as possible into his throat. When they gasp to catch their breaths, he says, "I want you here, right on the floor. Now." He lifts his hands under the back of her skirt and cups her buttocks, rocking her into him.

"No. The bed." She has her hands on his bare chest, running her fingers in the curly black hairs. "Please."

"All right," he says. "Okay." He feels himself bent against his boxer shorts. The pain is excruciating but he doesn't want it to end.

"Then there's something I have to tell you. Something about me."

"I know," he says. The scent of her perfume is faint but when he buries his nose between her breasts he can smell what he thinks are yellow flowers.

She has her mouth over his ear and whispers, "Something about me and someone else."

"I know," he says. He slips one hand along his thigh and fumbles in his boxers until he frees himself. He is rigid, his heart is pounding. "I know," he repeats, "I know."

Mary is looking directly into Michael's eyes and has been for several minutes, though neither of them has spoken since he groaned and reached up to grip her bare shoulders with his hands. *Crab claw*, she thinks. *Pincher.* She is straddling him, her hands braced on the futon mattress below his armpits, her face only inches from his flushed cheeks. She had forgotten the rainbow in his irises. Brown, green, yellow, flecks of black. Hazel, they call it. She presses down with her pelvis, then relaxes, feeling him push up. She throws her head back. The gold chain around her neck, a chain he brought back from Japan a year ago and from which she has hung a tiny pierced medallion, bounces with each thrust of her torso off her breastbone and up to the tip of her nose. She swivels her head to dodge its arc. He reaches with one hand and encloses it in his palm. Mary listens to the boards of the futon frame beneath them groan with the weight of their bodies. Part of her fears they will break the slats, but part of her wants to break them. She pushes up with her palms, rearing above him for a moment, and then places her hands flat on his chest, straightening her back so she is riding directly above him. "God," she whispers. She closes her eyes and concentrates on the pressure she feels spreading through her pubis to the bottom of her spine. In a moment she looks down and sees Michael has closed his eyes too. His lower lip protrudes over the upper. After every stroke she hesitates, waiting for the counter thrust of his hips. They are getting closer. He has lifted his arms and taken her breasts in his hands, pinching the nipples between his thumbs and forefingers. She has her fingers in his mouth, now, spreading his lips, feeling the sharp edges of his teeth on her skin. Now they are really close. She is biting her lower lip and driving down on him, her mind going blank with the insistent cadence of her flesh. God, one more, she thinks, two. Oh God, one more.

When she opens her eyes he is stroking her hip.

"It's like you've been practicing," she says. "In training." She reaches out and touches his cheek, damp with perspiration.

He is looking into her eyes and he closes them for a moment. "Tell me," he says, "who it was."

Her mouth is dry. The first words she says squeak out. "It was Jilly." She clears her throat. "From the gym. Red hair?"

Michael smiles. "I thought it was a woman." He closes his eyes.

His breath is warm on her face. She smells alcohol. Orange. Was he drinking Grand Marnier after dinner? She saw him pouring Metaxis for Mark and Stephen. She asks, "You did?"

"You became, I don't know, more caring somehow. Dreamy."

Mary has been running her forefinger along his cheekbone, up into the hairs of his temple and back below his eye socket. "Dreamy?" she says. "Me? I never think of myself that way. Confused, maybe. Unfocused."

"Um."

"I thought maybe I had become louder. More brassy."

"More vocally assertive, maybe. But underneath, more gentle."

"I'll be."

"When you had that fling with Freddo years ago you were on edge all the time. More attentive to me, but on edge. Harder. You started drinking single-malt Scotch. This time you went the other way. White wine and herb teas. Definitely softer."

"You knew about that? About Freddo?"

"Um." He closes his eyes and in the silence Mary thinks she was a fool to suppose she had got away with it. No one ever gets away with anything, not really. Maybe you can dodge exposure and never be confronted with your betrayal. But the other person always knows, knows in their gut if not in their brain.

"Poor Freddo," she says. Eyes, hands, lips.

"Poor Mary. You liked him. I know."

"Stupid Mary." She sighs. Her knees are trembling still and something is wrong with her abdomen. Did she stretch a muscle? Or is she so tensed up with guilt that she has a cramp? She shifts on the mattress, hoping to relieve the pain spreading down into her groin. Doesn't. Makes it slightly worse. Thorn, she thinks. Hemlock.

Michael opens his eyes. "Were you seriously thinking of moving out?"

She blinks. "Moving? It's my house."

He sighs. "Of leaving, I meant. Leaving me."

"No. Of course not. Good grief."

Michael closes his eyes. "That's good."

"You would have come after me with lawyers? With writs?"

He laughs. "No. I would have been devastated. I don't think I could take the upset. As it is my stomach is churning around every morning. I take those pills but they don't seem to help, not all the time. I'm constantly burping up this bile. My body is giving up on me, I know it is. If you had left, I would have been a wreck, a basket case, dead in a year."

"I don't think so. You're tough. A survivor."

"Not this time. Lights out. Gonzo."

Mary grunts. "Anyway." She takes a deep breath. Wood smoke, goose fat, pumpkin.

"Anyway."

"Go see the doctor again." She says it more sharply than she intended, in the tone of voice that always makes Meagan wince.

"I will," he murmurs. But she knows by the way he says it that he will have to cough up blood before he's sufficiently scared to do it. Men.

Still she says, "Make an appointment next week. I'll do it if you want."

"No," he says. "I'll take care of it." He has opened his eyes again and he says, "So it's over now? This Jilly?"

"Yes." She hesitates, and in that hesitation, slight as it is, one heartbeat, no more, Mary realizes it really is over, she and Jilly have said what they had to say, words like fists that sent them to their separate corners. They have not spoken to each other for nearly a week and that week will stretch to a month before Mary will call her again. By then Jilly will have a new hairdo, she'll be eyeing someone else up at the club. Good for her. And Mary? She clears her throat and adds, "Except she tried to kill herself. Came after me with a field hockey stick. God."

"You weren't hurt or anything?"

"No, thankfully. But her therapist called me and said that breaking off completely might drive her over the edge. So we meet for coffee every week. Muffin Break kind of thing. Yakkity-yak." She pauses. "It's more painful than anything. I'd prefer to just nip it in the bud. But there you go."

Michael grunts. "But it's coming to an end."

"Definitely." Mary is silent for a moment, listening to the wind outside the cottage, to waves beating on the shore. November. Another season at Willow Island. A season of wonderful nights and glorious days. Well, not all glorious. Finally she says, "Everything's coming to an end." They have been lying naked, and she suddenly feels chilled. She reaches for the quilt they tossed aside earlier and pulls it up over her waist.

Michael has snuggled in close to her and mutters, "And Mary, there's something I want to tell you. I want to—"

But Mary is tugging at the quilt and, not hearing him, continues, "I'm thinking of shutting down the office."

After a moment Michael sighs and says, "I had a feeling you were leaning that way."

"I couldn't go in there now. You know?"

"Yeah." Michael is silent and then he adds, "So. Moving on? Quitting the business altogether?"

"I have some money. We had insurance—life insurance—

that will cover the condo losses. I could live on the interest from my GICs and stuff. The money my parents left me. A little stipend. A little pension kind of thing."

"They pay on suicide?"

"This one does. It's a special business insurance covering losses on the condo thing with fifty grand or so left over. Ironically, it was Freddo who insisted we get it years ago."

Michael grunts and rolls his head this way and that, repositioning his arms. "What will you do? If you pack it in?"

"No *if*." Mary cranes her neck to watch his face. "Oh, catch up on my reading. Garden." She watches while he blinks his eyes, taking it in. "You know what I'd really like to do?" She doesn't wait for him to answer. "I'd like to become your personal trainer."

He laughs. "Go on."

"No kidding."

"You mean—what?—fix carrot juice for me to drink at breakfast?"

"Give you daily massages—maybe two a day. Plan a diet for you. For us. Not some crazy weight-loss thing the bran and granola fascists preach, but a real diet. Alix was telling me about some. Food combining, for one. Shop for us at the markets, cook meals that actually nourished us. Exercise together. Nothing over-the-top. Walking. Cycling."

"You're serious."

"I'm deadly serious." Mary pauses. "Lifely serious. Taking possession of our health. Not control, control's out. Possession."

"It's a big change. Huge."

"It's time for a change." Mary hesitates, thinking of butterflies and other insects that mutate. "A transformation," she says. She fumbles for his hand and squeezes it once. "A sea change."

"A lake change," Michael says, laughing aloud. He sighs and breathes silently for a moment. "Massages," he says finally. He has lifted himself up on one elbow. "I'd love that. And they're supposed to boost your virility."

She laughs. "You don't seem to be suffering in that category."

"You neither." He laughs. She hasn't heard that laugh in months. Echo in the little room. Not relief so much as joy. A laugh that she used to laugh to hear, the way you smile seeing your child smile. Mary thinks, maybe he genuinely was afraid she would leave him. Maybe she would have.

"That would be nice," she says. "Wouldn't it? Just the two of us?"

"We'd drive each other crazy. We'll get cabin fever."

"You'd still go into work. Visit the grandkids. Retreat to the cottage and be dreamy in your way."

"Retire?" he says. "You really mean it? You'd just stay at home?" He has rolled back onto the mattress, looking at the ceiling.

"Stay home and look after you. In two years you would too. Once we saw the kids all settled."

"Fat chance of that."

"No," Mary says. "It will happen faster than you think. Meagan's gone. Things will work out for her now. Jane and Brad too. That business with the van and Randy scared the shit out of him—literally and otherwise. You watch. From here on he's going to be a model father and husband. He grew up in that driveway that night." She has raised herself on one elbow and is looking down into his face. Flushed cheeks. Beads of sweat beneath his nose. White of beard, red of lip. *My man*, she thinks.

"And Maurice?"

"We'll deal with that. He will. In two years—less—I guarantee it'll all be settled." He blinks and she repeats, "Guarantee."

"It's a crazy idea."

"It's a wonderful idea. And it will work."

"Just stay at home and be my personal trainer? Look after me?"

"Well," she says. "I'd go riding too." She smiles. "My one little treat. Out to the stables once or twice a week." She laughs. "Riding my pony there and riding the stallion here. You know."

He laughs, then closes his eyes again. Fumbles for her hand and, when he finds it, moves his fingers around until they interlock with hers. "All right," he says. "All righty."

"Every summer a trip to Europe. Nothing fancy."

"All right," he murmurs. "I'm game."

He squeezes her fingers. In a moment his breathing has become regular and Mary knows he is drifting off. Soon he will snore. One leg will jerk. His left arm will crook over his head and he will sigh. His mind, along with his body, will flatten into the space known as rest. But Mary's mind is racing. She lowers her head onto the pillows. Shopping at the markets for vegetables will be fun. She hasn't had time to do that in years. She'll grow her own herbs, of course, and plant tomatoes at the cottage near the shed. Buy bread at the shop in the neighborhood, if bread is allowed. Make her own pasta. Sauces. There are different kinds of flour you can buy at the bulk-foods store. Diets featuring vegetables and fruits. Books to read about nutrition. The Scoop and Weigh store sells brown free-range eggs and there are farmers on the outskirts of the city who advertise barnyard chickens already slaughtered and dressed. Maybe she could keep a little flock of hens and a red rooster in a run at the cottage. No. But she could plant garlic and ginger root, and learn where to find senega root and discover how to prepare dandelion so as to extract its maximum benefits. Dig in the dirt. Get in touch with natural rhythms. Swim on summer mornings as the sun comes over the horizon. Get one of those distilled-water dispensers. Learn about vitamins and supplements. Slippery elm bark. She won't need to pop Tylenol every day. Michael's stomach problems will vanish when he starts eating good food and exercises every day. She knows this. Yes. They shall grow healthy, transform. Yes, that is the word. They have transcended the bad time and now they can move on. They shall sleep the way they did twenty years ago and want to make love every night. Screw, fuck. There will be no more Jillys, no more anybodys. She can do the ironing and make jams and jellies in the fall. Red of pincherry, purple of chokecherry. Michael can fix things and build stuff out of wood. She will find out about meditation and inner peace. Go to the tai chi center. Buy those scented oils at the Body Shop and learn how to massage the muscles properly. Maybe take a course. Love Michael and be loved by him. Take care of him. Take care of both of them. Live to a fine old age practicing the silence of the goose and the wisdom of the frog.